THE MOUNTAIN VIEW MURDER

THE MOUNTAIN VIEW MURDER

A WINTERGREEN MYSTERY

PATRICK KELLY

Patrick Kelly

CHAPARRAL PRESS LLC

The Mountain View Murder. Copyright © 2021 by Chaparral Press LLC

All rights reserved. No part of this book may be used or reproduced in any manner whatsoever without written permission except in the case of brief quotations embodied in critical articles and reviews. For information contact Chaparral Press LLC, 2402 Sutherland St., Austin, TX 78746.

Published in print and ebook by Chaparral Press LLC.

Cover design by Sleepy Fox Studio.

This is a work of fiction. Some of the locations, restaurants, and other places referenced in the novel are real; however, the names, characters, and incidents either are products of the author's imagination or are used fictitiously. Any resemblance to actual events or events at a particular locale or to persons, living or dead, is entirely coincidental.

ISBN 978-1-7342392-2-5 (Print)

ONE

In the dead of the summer night, harsh winds blew from the north into the Shenandoah Valley. The cold front passed through Winchester and New Market and Harrisonburg, bringing relief from the steamy July heat that had gripped the valley for weeks. The chilling weather marched through the smaller cities of Staunton and Waynesboro. From Waynesboro, the front spread into a finger valley to the south and then through cornfields and chicken coops. Cows huddled together for warmth. Windows rattled on old farmhouses. The wind hit the east side of the small valley, sang through the forests of oak and hickory and maple, and rolled over the rounded tops of the Blue Ridge Mountains.

At fifteen minutes after three o'clock in the morning in the mountaintop resort community of Wintergreen, a seventy-four-year-old man woke in bed next to his slumbering wife. No more sleep for him that night. Insomnia. Wind whistled through an unlocked window in another room. He rose, stopped briefly in the bathroom, and dressed for his morning walk down to the Mountain Inn. The old man prided himself on maintaining his physical condition long after most of his contemporaries had given up. They were lazy and allowed wine and steaks and desserts to add to their figures year after year until they could no longer enjoy the greatest thrills life had to offer. Though the sun rose early that time of year—before six—he often returned from his exercise in time to make coffee and observe the day's dawning from his back deck.

The old man exited through the summer home's front door carrying a flashlight, but he kept it turned off. Even though clouds had rolled in, there was enough ambient light to distinguish the forest from the paved road. He lumbered a quarter mile up Hemlock Drive and crossed Devils Knob Loop into the Westwood Condos. At the end of the parking lot, he cut through the woods on an asphalt trail. Close-set trees snuffed out the remaining light, and he flicked on the flashlight to pick his way through wet spots on the path. He cursed the intermittent showers that had plagued Wintergreen for a week now—they mucked up the golf course roughs and made the greens slow.

He crossed Wintergreen Drive and soon came to the fitness center parking lot. Next to the mail hut on the left, two sports cars with weather covers waited for their owners to return to the mountain. On the right, a lone SUV sat parked under the branches of an oak tree. The shadows were dark, so he couldn't tell for sure, but the SUV's outline resembled that of a Honda Pilot.

At the far edge of the lot, the old man cut back onto Wintergreen Drive and began to make his way down the steep decline of that side of the mountain. At that early hour, he was more likely to see a raccoon or an opossum than a passing car; even so, he kept to the left side of the road. A gust of wind rustled leaves on the hardwood trees at his side. The exercise kept his core warm, but his neck and face and hands were exposed to the chill, so he zipped his windbreaker to his chin and tightened the Velcro straps at his wrists.

Back at the parking lot, the Honda Pilot engine turned over, and the headlights illuminated the mail hut. The driver engaged the transmission and pulled out. Then the Honda Pilot turned left on Wintergreen Drive, passed Devils Knob Loop on the right and Blue Ridge Drive on the left, and headed down the hill.

The old man heard a vehicle approaching from a distance. Who could be out this early other than another poor insomniac? Perhaps a worker with an early shift down in the valley? No. Few workers lived up here on the mountain. Maybe a Wintergreen patrol officer making the rounds? Yeah. That was more likely. Headlights appeared behind him, and though he stayed on the safe side of the road, the old man drew comfort from knowing he wore a bright reflective vest.

The engine came closer, disturbing the peaceful darkness of his routine. The old man would be glad when the car was gone. His heart beat faster, and he subconsciously touched his chest. No worries there. Not yet. Not like many of his buddies —high cholesterol, hypertension—who lugged with them everywhere a ticking disaster in waiting.

Headlights swerved into the trees on his left. Why? The vehicle's engine raced. It was insane to speed down this road, for the shoulders were narrow and the ditches deep. The old man turned to the uphill slope, and the headlights blinded him. He raised a hand to his eyes. The vehicle turned crazily to the other side of the street and then back toward the old man. His heartbeat thrashed in his ears. Signals rushed to his brain, and he clutched his chest. A terrifying noise of screeching tires pierced the air.

The grille of the Honda Pilot struck the old man, and he took flight. His body shot across the ditch toward the forest and hit the thick trunk of an old hickory. A sickening thwack echoed among the trees and down the nearby ski slope. The old man fell to the ground, and blood seeped from his skull onto dead leaves from the prior season.

The Honda rested three feet past where the old man had stood. The driver stepped from the SUV and shined a powerful flashlight into the ditch. Not seeing the old man, the driver stepped off the road and onto the muddy ground. The flashlight panned slowly across the area beyond the ditch until it found the reflective orange of the vest. There he was. A dark and shiny wet patch stained the ground beneath him.

Dead. Definitely dead.

The old man's face was turned up. His mustache and upper lip had been torn from his face, leaving his mouth open in a sickly grin.

Not so handsome now.

The driver searched the road in both directions. No cars approached, and the driver climbed back into the Honda and drove down the mountain.

TWO

After his morning walk, Bill O'Shea strung binoculars around his neck, grabbed a mug of freshly made coffee, and ambled onto his condo balcony dressed in running pants and a quick-dry T-shirt.

The crest of the hill across the wooded valley rolled softly down from the right. The curved line of the hill resembled a woman lying on her side, wider at the shoulders and the hips, narrower at the waist, beautiful and mysterious at the same time. The Mountain Inn lay at the top of the valley on the right. Idle chairlift towers and cables ran up the cleared ski slopes. Hidden ski runs cut sweeping lines through the forests. Silence hung heavy and comfortable, broken only by the intermittent chirping of small birds.

Stepping to the balcony rail, Bill leaned out and scanned the line of condo buildings along his side of the valley. To the right, more buildings climbed the ridge of the hill. The sides of the small gorge met farther down the mountain and leveled out into the Rockfish Valley. Off in the distance, a soft blue haze hovered over the rounded peaks of the Blue Ridge.

Sheesh. Would he ever tire of that view? Never. Hopefully

never. He had bought the condo a month earlier for two reasons: the vista and the low upkeep. Having lived his entire life in the city of Columbia, South Carolina—not a big city, but a city nonetheless—he relished residing in a sparsely populated part of the world, a place where beauty reigned over human conflict. Practically speaking, the ongoing costs of the twelve-hundred-square-foot condo fit well within his policeman's retirement budget. Even better, he had left behind the irksome and endless tasks associated with yard and house maintenance, the taste for which he had lost long ago.

Wait. There they were—Ricky Bobby and Cal—the American goldfinches Bill had nicknamed after observing them frolicking in roller-coaster patterns near his third-floor balcony. On first sighting, he had no clue as to their species, so he had given them names from a comedy about a race car driver. The crazy loops they flew in reminded him of the fast turns drivers made around the tracks. Ricky Bobby and Cal had inspired him to order the *Birds of Virginia Field Guide*, which is how he had learned their common name.

Ricky Bobby and Cal swooped from right to left and then returned to land on a branch at the forest's edge, half a football field away. Bill trained his binoculars on the tree limb and searched until he found one of the birds. The bird's yellow feathers puffed out and then settled. Ricky Bobby nervously searched the skies above him and then opened his beak to speak.

"Hello!"

Bill flinched and pulled back from the binoculars.

Lord. Did Ricky Bobby say that?

Bill's eyes returned to the binoculars and scanned the branch once more. Ricky Bobby had flown.

"Hello?"

A woman's voice hailed to someone from close by. Bill glanced at the building to the right. A hundred feet away, a woman waved at him from her third-floor balcony. Bill approached the railing and immediately felt self-conscious about his balcony's appearance, for hers was a lush airborne garden with hanging pots and colorful flowers and lots of other greenery. She was blond, medium height, and shapely. From that distance, he guessed her age at late fifties to early sixties.

"Hi," he called.

"Are you my new neighbor?" She waved at the condo buildings that lined the ridge. "Most of the owners come on weekends or rent their properties out to vacationers. Only a few of us live here full time."

Her voice was clear and confident and cheerful. She stood with her weight forward, her elbows pressing against the rail. One foot lifted playfully behind her, as a child's might when idly chatting with a friend. She wore jean shorts and a T-shirt. He couldn't see her face clearly at that distance, only that she smiled and had curly hair.

"Yes," Bill said. To his ears, his voice sounded hesitant, so he tried to speak more clearly. "I moved in two weeks ago and plan to live here year round."

The woman opened her arms and gestured toward the valley. "Welcome to heaven."

He laughed, for he found her exuberance contagious. "Thank you. By the way, I love your balcony garden."

She glanced at the overflowing pots around her and said, "It's a time-consuming hobby, but it keeps me happy. I try to have something blooming all the time, like these geraniums and begonias." Turning her gaze back his way, she said, "Yours needs work."

"Yes, I know." He examined his own balcony, barren save for two patio swivel chairs with a drinks table between them.

"Whatever you do, don't plant tomatoes," she said. "Last year, I grew two beautiful cherry tomato plants. They were laden with juicy red fruit, and then one night, a raccoon climbed up and ate them all. That bastard." Her full-throated laughter filled the air between them.

"Oh, no."

He stood taller and took a deep breath. In that instant, it appeared—to Bill at least—that the day grew brighter.

When her laughter subsided, she extended a hand toward him and said, "We should become properly acquainted."

Then his doorbell rang, and he shot a look inside his condo.

Darn. Who on earth could that be?

"I'm sorry," he said. "Someone's at the door."

"Well, aren't you popular?"

"I can't imagine who. I don't know a soul."

"Never mind. I've got to get ready for work anyway. We'll do it later. Bye."

His shoulders sagged slightly, and he frowned, thinking, perhaps irrationally, that the best part of his day had already come and gone.

He hurried inside, set his mug on the kitchen counter, and reached for the door handle.

This had better be good.

At the entrance to his condo stood Alex Sharp, acting chief of the Wintergreen Police Department.

"Morning, Bill. Sorry to barge in on you like this. We have a situation."

THREE

Wearing jeans, boots, a khaki work shirt, and a Wintergreen Police Department shield fastened to his belt, Acting Chief Alex Sharp stood a half a head taller than Bill. He had pale blue eyes overshadowed by dark eyebrows drawn tight with tension. Wrinkles crowded the corners of his eyes, and his lips were a flat line. He shifted his weight in the doorway.

"Come in, Alex. I'll get you coffee, freshly brewed."

"Thanks. But we don't have time for it."

When they first met, Alex had been all smiles and jokes and laughter, as you would expect from a real estate agent marketing a home. Alex owned the most prominent brokerage on the mountain and had sold Bill his condo. Mid-fifties in age, Alex had worked in the Wintergreen ecosystem for three decades as a house cleaner, waiter, carpenter, amateur appliance repairman, and volunteer for the fire department. Along the way, he'd picked up his real estate license, used his market knowledge and a lot of hustle to become the most successful agent on the mountain, and then opened his own brokerage. Several weeks earlier, Wintergreen's chief of police had resigned to take a lucrative position out west, and the board had asked Alex to step in on an interim basis.

Bill knew all of this because soon after moving into his condo, he'd stopped by the police department to introduce himself as a matter of professional courtesy. To his surprise, he had found Alex occupying the chief's office.

"What's going on?" asked Bill, and he motioned Alex inside.

In a few sentences, Alex gave Bill an overview. Lou Thorpe—a septuagenarian resident out for his early morning walk—had been struck and killed by a vehicle. The driver had fled the scene.

"Other law enforcement agencies will soon descend upon us," said Alex, "and I have no clue what I'm doing. Could you come along and give me some pointers?"

"What about Emily and Connor? They know the ropes."

The Wintergreen Police Department was small but staffed with competent personnel. Emily Powell and Connor Johnston—both seasoned law enforcement professionals—served as the deputy chief and the departmental investigator, respectively. The department also employed six patrolmen and an equal number of communications officers and administrators.

"Here's the thing," said Alex. "Emily's out on maternity leave—had the baby prematurely yesterday—and Connor's on a flight to South Africa for a two-week vacation. This couldn't have happened at a worse time."

"Okay. Sure. Let me throw on some jeans."

On the way to the scene, which was less than a mile away, Alex provided more details. An emergency call had come in at seven o'clock from a motorist who'd spotted the body off to the side of Wintergreen Drive. Law enforcement from Nelson County and the state police were now on the way.

"Unfortunately, by the time our patrolman arrived, several

other cars had stopped. I'm afraid a few people tromped around the crime scene in a futile effort to help. We've now moved those folks along."

"Did we get the names and contact information of those who stopped?"

"Yeah, I think so."

"What about the body?"

"Still there. Waiting on a state medical examiner."

Alex pulled his truck into the fitness center's lot. "We'll park here. There's no room on the street. Hey, the cavalry has arrived." He parked next to a squad car from the Nelson County Sheriff's Department. Three other law enforcement vehicles had parked in nearby spaces—one from Nelson County, one from the state police, and a Wintergreen cruiser. After parking, Bill and Alex made their way onto Wintergreen Drive and down the hill.

Two Wintergreen squad cars blocked the lane around the accident, and someone had taped off the scene. Officers with safety batons directed traffic onto the other lane. Across the ditch, a photographer stood over the body to take pictures. She moved to get a view from a different angle. A tall young man in a dark blue Wintergreen police uniform stood on the pavement, and Alex stopped to talk to him.

"Who's taking pictures?" said Alex.

"State forensics," said the patrolman.

"Wow. She got here fast."

"We were lucky. She lives in Staunton. The examiner from Roanoke should be here any time."

"Good. Have you met Bill O'Shea?" Alex gestured toward Bill, and the two men shook hands.

"Mitch Gentry," said the young patrolman. "I heard about you at the office. From Columbia, right?"

Bill nodded.

"Give me your thoughts while I play amateur forensics," said Mitch. He stepped a few paces over and directed both hands at the tire marks on the road. "I figure the victim was standing about here. The vehicle skids and then stops at the road's edge, thereby driving through the victim's body and launching him across the ditch."

Bill bobbed his head noncommittally and said, "Could be." He preferred leaving forensics to those trained in the science.

"So here's what's interesting," said Mitch. He strode to the edge of the pavement fifteen feet away and pointed at a square yard of ground that had been marked off with tape. In a muddy section of earth surrounded by wet grass lay a clear imprint of a running shoe.

"Huh," said Bill. He lowered one knee to the road and bent forward to inspect the impression. "Dang. That's a great shoeprint. You think that's the driver's?"

"Yeah," said Mitch. "Probably. Unless it's from one of the rubberneckers who stopped."

Bill gave Alex a tight grin.

"Mitch," said Alex, "here's your first assignment on this thing. We have to know exactly who got out of their car and what shoes they were wearing."

"Right, Chief. I'm on it. I think Hill has all the names."

Mitch walked over to talk with one of the officers directing traffic.

Bill rubbed his chin and said, "Won't make any difference if we can't find the car."

Alex's forehead furrowed, so Bill explained that hit-and-run crimes were challenging. The driver had fled the scene—not good—but there was a chance they would grow remorseful and turn themself in.

"That's your best-case scenario," said Bill. "You hand the

driver over to Nelson County to prosecute the crime, and your work is done."

But if the driver didn't report themself, you had to find the vehicle, which by now might be many miles away in any direction. Bill pointed at the shoeprint. "You can't send out an APB on a pair of shoes. We've got to find the car." He studied the tire marks on the pavement. "From those skid marks, I'd guess we're searching for a light truck or an SUV. Forensics will tell us for sure."

"What should I do?" said Alex.

"If you haven't already, I'd call in everyone on the team. They'll have to work overtime for a few days." Now Bill contemplated the mountain above them. There were over three thousand townhouses, condos, and single-family dwellings in the Wintergreen community, any of which could be home base for the guilty driver. "Wintergreen only has one entrance, right?"

"That's correct," said Alex. "There's an old logging trail that goes down to the Rockfish Valley, but it's never used and is closed to public access."

Bill pushed out his lips. "Good. Good. I suggest you send two patrol officers to establish a roadblock above the entrance to Wintergreen. They don't need to talk to drivers; just check the front ends of vehicles that come and go. The impact with the victim will have caused some damage to the front grille."

Alex waved Mitch back over, gave him instructions on the roadblock, and then called the office. Bill studied the corpse across the ditch. Out of habit, he felt the urge to hike over there and get a closer look, but he reminded himself it wasn't his case. He was retired.

Stay out of the way. Lend a hand if asked, but otherwise, let the pros do their job.

A little ways off, a state trooper was chatting casually

with two county deputies, talking about sports or their kids or anything else to pass the time. The group of three laughed at something one of them had said.

"What happens next?" said Alex.

"We only have foot soldiers here now," said Bill. "Soon, the county sheriff or undersheriff will arrive, as well as someone higher up on the state chain of command. They'll want to have a confab with you concerning who is going to do what. You might invite them down to the office so they can get a cup of coffee and hit the restroom."

Alex called the office back. Bill studied the cloud cover and then thought about the victim. Hell of an unlucky day for that guy. He goes for some early morning exercise, and a drunk or a sleeper or some other kind of wastrel comes along and knocks him out of life. At least he went fast.

"All right, what's going on here?" a new man said.

He was tall and broad-shouldered and wore a state uniform with the rank of lieutenant stamped across the top of his badge. A higher-up had arrived. Alex introduced himself and filled in the newcomer—whose name was Cameron Hughes—on what had transpired so far, including the shoeprint discovery and the plan to erect a roadblock.

"Where's Fletcher?" the man said, referring to Wintergreen's previous chief of police.

"He resigned for a position out west. I'm filling in on an interim basis."

Hughes turned to Bill and frowned at his jeans. "Who are you?" Clearly, he considered Bill a random citizen in the way.

Alex jumped in. "I asked Bill O'Shea to give me some advice. He recently retired from the Columbia police force after thirty-five years of service."

"Columbia, huh?" said Hughes as the two men shook

hands. Hughes's face visibly brightened. "Say, do you know a guy named Slater? Tall, big guy, funny as hell?"

"Sure, I know Wayne. We worked together for a while."

Hughes shook his head. "I met him at a conference. Damn, he was funny. He still on the force?"

"Yep. Still there. Made lieutenant last year."

"I'm not surprised. I don't know if he's a good cop or not, but he can sure work a crowd."

Another Nelson County vehicle parked on the road, and a short, thin man in khaki pants and a brown shirt got out on the driver's side.

"Okay," said Hughes. "There's Undersheriff Shields. Let's get organized. Alex, have you got a place we can meet?"

FOUR

Twenty minutes later, five men and one woman crammed themselves into an interview room: Hughes and a male state trooper, Undersheriff Shields and a female deputy from Nelson County, and Alex and Bill. The room was sparsely furnished, with a six-foot table and four chairs. Bill leaned against the wall in one corner, and the state patrolman took another corner. As the highest-ranking state representative, Hughes ran the meeting.

"As we all know," he said, "the vehicle could be a hundred or more miles from here and still moving. If so, we're probably screwed. The driver can hide the car for two weeks, clean it up real good, and take it to a body shop claiming they ran into a deer. But we might get lucky; you never know. We're all stretched for resources, so there's no way to mount a statewide or a countywide search, but we can give the mountain a thorough going over." At this point, Hughes turned to Alex. "What do you say? Can Wintergreen handle its own territory, or do you need help?"

Alex pressed his lips together, and his eyes slid from Hughes to Bill in the corner.

Hughes said, "Hey, Columbia. Alex wants your input."

Everyone looked at Bill. He folded his arms, and his neck grew tense. What the heck? This wasn't his deal, but then again, Alex hadn't asked for the acting chief headache either. When the owners' association board of directors had sought his assistance, Alex had stepped up. Maybe Bill should too. Yeah, okay.

"Wintergreen can search the community for the vehicle," said Bill. "And we can interview those passersby who stopped at the scene this morning. Also, we've got communications with the next of kin. If county has the resources, we could use help manning the roadblock for the next few days."

"Shields," said Hughes, "can you do that?"

"Yep. We'll provide half the staffing."

"Good," said Hughes. "Nelson County has criminal jurisdiction, so if we catch the driver, the county will take over. All good so far?"

Everyone nodded.

"State will handle forensics out of our Roanoke office," said Hughes, "and we'll coordinate with Augusta County, Waynesboro, and the National Park Service. Questions?"

The group discussed details of the coordination effort for the next twenty minutes. The possibility of video surveillance was raised, kicked around, and dismissed as the Wintergreen area had only a few cameras, all of which were focused on commercial buildings versus the road. When further discussion began to die down, Alex cleared his throat to get people's attention.

"A few of our patrol officers have put forth the hypothesis that a thru-hiker might be involved."

Every spring thousands of thru-hikers struck out from the southern tip of the Appalachian Trail with the aspiration of hiking the full 2,200 miles from Georgia to Maine. The trail passed close by Wintergreen, and at that time of year, perhaps a dozen or more hikers came through every day.

Hughes said, "So the hypothesis is that a backpacker came into the community, stole a car for a joy ride, and ran into our guy?"

Alex shrugged.

"Do you have a lot of trouble with thru-hikers?" said Hughes.

"No," said Alex.

"That strikes me as an unlikely scenario," said Hughes. "Nevertheless, we'll mention it to the Park Service folks."

They discussed the crime scene. Hughes said forensics would need it for another hour or so to do their thing. According to the state patrolman, the medical examiner was now on site and would calculate an estimated time of death as soon as possible. Hughes suggested they establish conference calls twice a day to share updates. Eventually, they ran out of official business to discuss, lapsed into idle banter for a few minutes, and then the state and county guys left.

"Who identified the body?" asked Bill, when only Alex and he remained in the room.

"I did. Even with the mangled face, I easily recognized Lou Thorpe. He had a distinctive appearance, tall and in great shape for a man in his seventies. I sold him his summer home twenty years ago. He and his wife, Jeanne, live in DC for the rest of the year. He was a retired lobbyist for the coal industry." Alex grimaced. "Hard to believe. I sent Kerry from admin and a patrol officer to inform Jeanne. Kerry is still there—she's good with people." Alex sagged in the chair and blew a long stream of air between his lips. "I saw the two of them—Lou and Jeanne—last Saturday night at the Devils Grill. Lou was a charmer, and he was holding court for a table of six. You could hear them laughing across the room—

they'd all had a few glasses of wine." Alex's eyes drifted off to the side as if he could recall the restaurant scene. "I need to go see Jeanne after we get things sorted here. She'll want to know what we're doing to find the driver."

"That'll be a tough conversation," said Bill.

Alex rubbed his chin. "Yes, it will." But then he came back to the matters at hand. "You were a big help in the meeting. Can you stick around awhile, maybe a few days? Help me run this thing?"

"Yep."

"I'll pay you. I have a budget."

"Don't worry about paying me. Put me down as a community volunteer."

"Awesome. Thank you. Maybe I should call an all-hands meeting to organize the search."

"Good idea."

Over the next thirty minutes, Alex escorted Bill around the office to introduce him to the team as a volunteer with a wealth of police experience. Near the end of the office tour, Alex received a text from Nelson County. The state medical examiner estimated a high-confidence range for time of death between two a.m. and five a.m.

"That's not a tight window," Alex said to Bill.

"It means his formula gives him an answer of three thirty, but time-of-death estimation is an inexact science, so he's only signing up for a range."

After the tour, the entire department assembled in the main room of the station. Alex stood at the wall next to a large road map of the Wintergreen community. The team sat in office chairs or stood as space allowed.

Bill leaned on a cubicle at one side of the group to observe the dynamics of the team.

The mood was somber—all eyes on Alex, no chitchat, no

joking. Alex brought everyone up to speed. He asked for reports of overnight activity to see if anything might relate to the hit-and-run. EMS had taken someone to the hospital. A patrol officer had responded to a bear sighting call. Nothing out of the ordinary.

The officer named Hill raised his hand and said, "I observed an SUV parked at the Devils Knob Overlook at twelve thirty. The cold front had not yet rolled in, and the star show was spectacular. I figured it was a young couple there to enjoy the view and perhaps grab some romantic time. I came back around thirty minutes later, and the SUV was gone."

"Okay," said Alex. "That sounds unrelated, but everyone keep it in mind. Now let's discuss the search."

They spent thirty minutes getting organized. The map of Wintergreen was divided into five sections. Five teams of two —a driver and a note-taker—would each take a section with the mission of observing every vehicle in their area for damage consistent with the hit-and-run accident. A skeleton crew would staff the office and the roadblock at the entrance to Wintergreen. Bill volunteered to work on a team and was paired with Mitch Gentry, the patrol officer he had met earlier.

It was a big task, and Alex urged the teams to move quickly. "Don't stop to chat with residents if you can avoid it. Inspect the cars and move on."

"Garages will slow us down," said Mitch Gentry. "Some people store cars in locked garages when they're gone."

"Shine a flashlight into the garage if possible," said Alex. "If you see a vehicle, knock on the front door and ask permission to go inside the garage. If no one is home, make a note, and we'll circle back later."

After the meeting, Alex pulled Bill, Mitch, and a communications officer named Krista Jackson into his office.

Krista appeared to be in her mid to late thirties. She had red hair pulled out of the way, soft green eyes, and a ready smile. Even the boxy police uniform could not disguise her attractive figure. She sat across the desk from Alex, as did Bill. Mitch stood next to a whiteboard off to the side.

"What do you think of the search strategy?" Alex asked Bill.

"It's a good plan. We might get lucky. If a drunk committed the hit-and-run, they might have driven home and still be sleeping it off."

"Let's hope so. Okay, Mitch and Krista, as you know, we're short-staffed with Emily and Connor out at the same time. Bill has agreed to help us out on this hit-and-run thing, and I want you to work with him. Take his direction on next steps. Mitch, you'll supply the wheels. Krista, you're here in the office to do whatever needs doing. Sound good?"

"Yes, Chief," said Krista.

Mitch nodded his agreement.

Alex's eyes turned to Krista. "Can you make Bill an official Wintergreen Police nametag with his photo and title?"

"Sure. What's the title?"

"Volunteer?" suggested Bill.

Alex frowned. "Nah. Residents don't always take volunteers seriously. Let's go with Police Advisor."

"Perfect," said Krista.

Alex opened his desk drawer. "I spotted an extra badge yesterday. Here it is." He slid the gold shield across the desk toward Bill.

"I don't think I'll need this," said Bill. "Seems over the top."

He was okay with assisting Alex at the crime scene and the inter-agency meeting. And he'd been happy to volunteer to help with the search because the department *was* short-staffed. But the nametag and shield took his involvement to a level he had not contemplated. Was he stepping onto a slippery slope?

"Put it in your pocket," said Alex. "Never know. It may come in handy."

"All right," Bill said with reluctance.

FIVE

Mitch and Bill's section included all of Blue Ridge Drive, which started near the fitness center, looped two miles down the southeast side of the mountain, and then came back up a mile to end at Fawn Ridge Drive. They were also responsible for all of the Blue Ridge Drive offshoot roads, including the mile-long Shamokin Springs Trail. Bill's own residence was part of their search area, as well as the other condo buildings lining the ridge.

They tackled the condo units first, one parking lot at a time. The buildings were nestled shoulder to shoulder to optimize the residents' view. To inspect the vehicles, Mitch rolled the squad car down the middle of each parking lot while Bill walked on the opposite side of the cars. They spotted a few bent fenders but nothing resembling the damage they expected to see on the hit-and-run vehicle. Working the parking lots was efficient, and they had canvassed three-quarters of the condo units by twelve thirty. Then Bill suggested they break for lunch.

They drove down to the Market, a convenience store near the Mountain Inn. Shopping was limited on the mountain, and Bill went to the Market if he needed a bag of pretzels or a half gallon of milk and didn't want to drive twenty minutes to the nearest town. With gas pumps and parking spots for a dozen cars, the Market resembled an old-fashioned general store with a pitched roof and wooden steps leading to a railed front porch. Besides a wide assortment of necessities, the store also stocked a good selection of local wines and had a deli that served pizza and sandwiches. Bill grabbed a pepperoni slice, an apple, and a soft drink. Being much younger and bigger, Mitch selected twice as much food, and they took their lunch out to the picnic table on the front porch.

Mitch ate with gusto. Bill guessed he was in his late twenties and single—no ring. About six feet tall and a bit over two hundred pounds, Mitch moved gracefully and quickly but thus far had little to say.

In an attempt to get some banter going, Bill asked, "Did you play ball in school?"

Mitch nodded, finished chewing his mouthful, swallowed, said, "Linebacker," and took another big bite of pizza.

Okay. Bill had sensed tension coming from Mitch as they worked the condo buildings that morning. Cops generally chattered a bit. It helped pass the time. But every time Bill had tried, Mitch had stuck to one-word answers. At first, he thought Mitch was shy, but the one-word "Linebacker" response bordered on rude. Mitch was either starving, an extreme introvert, or not inclined to warm up to his temporary partner. Bill decided to force the issue.

"Tell me about your life," he said.

Mitch blinked several times and swallowed. "You mean like my whole life?"

"Yeah. Start with the day you were born and work up to yesterday. I got today figured out."

Mitch licked his lower lip but didn't say anything.

"Do you have some sort of problem working with me?" asked Bill.

"Word at the office is you're out to get the chief slot on a permanent basis."

Bill shook his head. "No chance."

"Lot of us like Emily for the role, but with this being their third kid, she may not even want it."

"She'll get no competition from me."

"Why not? You certainly have enough experience."

"Two reasons. First, I never wanted supervisory roles. I made senior detective and stayed there. I always preferred fieldwork to paperwork—don't have the patience for the meetings and the BS. Second, I retired for a reason. I like this part of an investigation—searching for clues, trying to figure something out. But every job has a lot of overhead that comes with it, stuff you have to do, policy meetings, paperwork, and yeah, even target practice. At some point in life, time becomes more valuable than money. I've reached that point, so you don't have to worry about me wanting the chief slot."

Mitch studied Bill's face. Having spoken the truth, Bill had no trouble keeping his eyes steady.

"All right," said Mitch, "in that case, I was born on a Thursday."

And they both broke up laughing.

Turned out, Mitch was a local boy, having grown up in Waynesboro, the closest town with more than a few stoplights. Waynesboro was on the edge of the Shenandoah Valley, a thirty-minute drive from Wintergreen. Mitch went to community college for two years and then got a job with the police force in Richmond. But in Richmond, he had missed the mountains and his high school girlfriend, so he had taken a job in Wintergreen when he got the chance. He and the girlfriend—whom he had dated on and off for a decade—were now engaged. And so, as Mitch figured it, his life was pretty much set.

"Watch out for that part," said Bill. "Life has a way of biting you in the ass."

Mitch nodded as if that bit of sage wisdom was worth weighty consideration, but Bill could tell he was just another kid who would have to figure things out on his own.

A woman stopped by their table to ask about the hit-and-run. Mitch gave her the party line: Yes, there had been an accident. The police had begun an investigation, and regular updates would be provided to the Wintergreen community through online communications.

Grateful for the update, the woman left, and Bill said, "Let's get to work before anyone else stops by."

On the drive back up to the condos, they passed the crime scene on the right. Only one state patrol car remained. The forensics investigator Bill had seen earlier was now studying the shoeprint.

"What's your assessment of the thru-hiker theory?" said Mitch.

"Not sure. Give it to me play by play."

"You know where the Appalachian Trail abuts the property?"

"No. I haven't had a chance to do any hiking yet."

"It's right off Laurel Springs Drive. I'll show you later today."

According to the theory, Mitch explained, a hiker had come onto the property searching for food or alcohol or other mischief and found an unlocked car whose owner had absent-mindedly left their keys inside. Pressing their luck, the hiker took the vehicle for a spin and ran into the pedestrian. At that point, the hiker freaked out, ditched the car somewhere, and returned to the AT.

Bill squinted and said, "I don't know. Your basic drunk driver seems a more plausible scenario."

"We don't have a lot of drunk drivers up here. Most of the folks are well educated and mature. It's quiet at night. We get a few girls' weekend groups, that kind of stuff, but they keep to themselves."

Bill pointed out that if a hiker had stolen a car, the owner would soon report it missing. In the meantime, their best course was to do what they were already doing: search for the vehicle.

Back at the condos, they continued the process. After an hour, they had searched all the parked cars next to the buildings. Then they moved farther down Blue Ridge Drive to start on the freestanding residences. It was going to be an arduous task. Bill held a large map open on his lap so he and Mitch could study the three main roads that comprised their section.

Blue Ridge Drive took the approximate shape of a fishhook. It began at the T-intersection with Wintergreen Drive, ran along the condo ridge, and then looped west and came back up to end at Fawn Ridge Drive. Fawn Ridge was an approximately straight line that began at the hook's side midway down the condos, then ran a half-mile to end at Laurel Springs Drive on the western edge of the Wintergreen property. The third main road of their section—Shamokin Springs Trail—began at the hook's bottom, looped even farther down the mountain, and then came back up to end at the hook's other side. Many short streets connected to the three main roads like suckers on a tree's branches. Bill counted these finger streets and came up with twenty-four.

"Whoa," he said. "This is going to take a while."

"Yep."

"Let's do Blue Ridge Drive from beginning to end first, then we'll loop back for the others."

"Sounds like a plan."

They soon developed a system for inspecting freestanding residences that varied depending on whether there were visible vehicles or a garage. As Mitch had pointed out earlier at the office, homes with a garage took the most time. First, they checked for a window they could shine a flashlight through to search for a car. If the garage lacked windows or if a vehicle was parked inside, they knocked on the front door. If no one answered, Bill made a notation on the map and the iPad, and they moved on to the next house. If someone answered, they asked to see inside the garage.

This last scenario consumed time because invariably, the resident wanted to know why the police needed to inspect their garage. If they had heard of the hit-and-run, they soon guessed why and then wanted an update on the investigation. If they had not heard of the hit-and-run, Mitch gave a high-level overview.

The Wintergreen Police Department existed to serve and protect, and as such, they had a relationship to manage with residents. Bill let Mitch do the talking; as the uniformed officer, he commanded respect. When Mitch gave a talkative resident a subtle sign that time was of the essence, they generally clued in quickly. Even so, some residents followed them to the garage and then back to the squad car, asking questions the whole way. Bill guessed they were just hungry for human interaction. Mitch was loath to appear rude, and two times, Bill gave him the hook by pulling his elbow and saying to the resident, "Thanks for your help. We've got to get going."

It took Bill and Mitch four hours to inspect the homes located on Blue Ridge Drive and its finger streets. Bill had noted three residences with garages they couldn't access because no one was home. At one point, they received word that Alex wanted all search teams to return to the office at six thirty to compare notes and eat takeout barbecue. Before reporting to the office, Mitch took Bill to see the Appalachian Trail. They drove a mile down Laurel Springs Drive along the border of Wintergreen and parked in a small, unpaved lot on the left.

A path led into the forest, and they passed an elderly couple out for a stroll. The trail was marked frequently with yellow blazes painted on trees at eye level. High in a tree to the right, a woodpecker hammered the trunk in search of food. The sun had broken through the clouds earlier and now filtered through leaves to cast sparkles on the forest floor. The temperature had plateaued at sixty-five, and a light breeze ruffled the tops of the trees. A tenth of a mile from the parking lot, their path ended at another trail, and Mitch stopped.

"This is the AT," he said.

"Wow. That *is* close."

Mitch pointed right to where the AT headed up a gentle slope. "That way is Maine." Mitch turned. "And that way is Georgia."

To the left, the AT meandered down the hill. Not far below them, a car drove past on a paved road, its form an unclear image of movement through a patchwork of light.

"What's that road?" asked Bill.

"The Blue Ridge Parkway."

Bill was familiar with the scenic parkway. It began ten miles north at Afton and ran four hundred and seventy miles south through the Appalachian Mountains to Cherokee, North Carolina. Known for its beautiful overlooks and access to hiking trails, the parkway was used primarily for leisure day trips.

"I didn't realize the parkway came this close," said Bill.

"Yep. The AT crosses the parkway here and then crosses back onto our side again a few miles south." Mitch pointed to the uphill trail and swung his arm to the right. "The original route ran through forests where Wintergreen now stands, but when they developed the property, the AT was rerouted to its current location."

"What happened to the old trail?"

"Much of it is still there. It's shown on the map we have in the car."

"Do thru-hikers often veer into Wintergreen?"

"No, the trail is well marked."

"Where do hikers stay overnight?"

Mitch raised his eyebrows and gave his head a shake as if it were hard to fathom the mind of a thru-hiker. "Anywhere they want. My girlfriend and I like to hike stretches of the AT on weekends. There are a few shelters where hikers can stay out of the weather, but they often pitch a little tent on the side of the trail. We've met a few. They're quiet for the most part, determined, hungry—sitting there thirty feet off the path boiling water to make mac 'n' cheese. If you're not paying attention, you can walk right by without noticing them."

On the way back to the station, Bill pondered the determination of successful thru-hikers. They put their lives on hold for months and months to check a box. Depending on one's outlook on life, it was either a waste or an incredibly valuable use of time. If you desired a bigger house and more possessions badly enough to work fifty to sixty hours a week for three or four decades, you'd consider hiking the AT a ludicrous notion. But if you were smart enough in your twenties to suspect that the career grind you faced would produce little more in the end than a body that could no longer accomplish the task, you might shop for a good pair of hiking boots. And it was that sort of logic, Bill guessed, that had compelled him to accept the early retirement offer when it came along. At the age of sixty, he doubted his body could do the full AT even if he wanted to. Still, he retained sufficient energy and wit to take on a few new adventures.

Back at the station, the search teams reported their findings in between bites of pulled pork sandwiches. Each team had noted a few garages that needed follow-up inspections. These were consolidated for the communications team to pursue by phone. Like Bill and Mitch, three other teams had more homes to search, and they spent some time rebalancing the load so the work could be finished the next day. At the bottom of the mountain, the roadblock team had detained one car with suspicious grille damage. Upon inspection, they noticed tufts of fur stuck in the cracks, evidence supporting the driver's story that he had killed a deer.

Word of the hit-and-run had rattled Wintergreen residents, and many inquiring calls had come into the office. No one had reported a stolen or damaged car. Alex Sharp summarized the community update strategy. They had several available channels for electronic communications: the Fire & Rescue alert system, the Wintergreen Property Owners Association newsletter list, and various special interest email lists. A blast communication summarizing the incident and ongoing investigation had gone out to all channels that afternoon. They would withhold the victim's identity until the family had sufficient time to alert relatives and friends.

Alex asked everyone not on duty to get some rest and report back at eight the next morning to renew the search. When the meeting broke up, Alex waved at Bill to join him in his office.

"This is frustrating," said Alex. "I've had a dozen calls on my mobile today, angry friends of Lou Thorpe wanting to know what we're doing to find the driver. The directors want to know the same thing."

"How was the meeting with the victim's wife?"

Alex closed his eyes and rubbed the bridge of his nose. "Fine, I guess. Jeanne is in shock, sitting in a chair with a dazed look on her face. They were married for forty-three years. Her kids are on the way, and close friends will stay with her until they arrive." He bit his lower lip. "Is there something else I should be doing?"

Bill threw his hands to the side. "Not that I know of. We have to find the car."

Alex nodded. "Emily said the same thing. She's at home now, but the baby's still in the hospital. Connor called from South Africa to ask if he should fly back. What do you think?"

"He should stay there. Like Lieutenant Hughes said this morning, the vehicle could be hundreds of miles away by now. If so, there's not a lot for us to do."

Alex straightened his shoulders and took a deep breath. "Yeah. Okay. In any case, I appreciate you helping out."

"No problem."

Bill parked his Mazda CX-5 outside his condo building and rubbed the stubble on his cheek. Darn near a twelve-hour day. In the three short months of his retirement, he had grown used to a more relaxed routine. All he wanted now was to drink a beer, watch a little television, and go to bed. He climbed the wooden steps and trudged across the walkway to his building. Inside, he ascended eight more steps and observed that someone had taped an envelope to his door. The front of the envelope read *Neighbor* in clear cursive handwriting.

Inside, on a single piece of high-grade ivory stationary, a short statement in the same handwriting read: *If you're not too busy, stop by for a welcome drink. Text or call.* The message included a phone number and was signed: *Cindy, your neighbor from this morning.*

A printed tagline ran across the bottom of the card.

For special occasions – Quintrell's Catering – Wintergreen

Bill's eyes opened wider, and he read the card a second time. Then he fished his phone out of his pocket. When a woman answered—Cindy, he guessed—he apologized for calling so late. He'd been gone all day and just now returned to his condo.

"It's not *that* late," she said. "It's only five past eight o'clock. Do you want to come over?"

"Yes, I'd like to meet."

"What are you drinking, wine or tea?"

"Is that a trick question?"

"Nope."

"I'll take wine."

SIX

After washing his face, brushing his hair, and changing into a clean polo shirt, Bill hurried to the next building to knock on Cindy's door. Shoulder-length sandy blond curls framed her delightful face. She had merry brown eyes, and her smile carved dimples in her cheeks. A natural color gloss graced her lips, but she wore no other makeup he could detect. Their eyes were at the same level, and Bill guessed Cindy stood five foot nine. He estimated they were about the same age from the wrinkles around her eyes and on her neck. Her figure was decidedly feminine and fit, but not too fit. She wore a short-sleeved pale green shirt that showed off her strong arms, and she held her hand out for him to grasp. Firm handshake. Confident. Soft hands.

After quick introductions, she said, "Come in. I'll open the wine."

Two steps into her condo, he paused to observe the layout. It was a mirror image of his, with a large single living area in front of him. The kitchen and dining table were to his right, and the couch, fireplace, and television on his left. Two sets of sliding doors opened onto the balcony. He assumed the hall behind him led to a master bedroom suite, a guest bedroom, and a laundry closet. Yes, her condo matched his structurally, but the resemblance ended there. Cindy had done a masterful job of decorating her condo with contemporary furniture and lighting, an upgraded kitchen, and tastefully framed photographs on the walls. He was drawn to a trio of butterfly photos on the off-white wall near him. The photographer had captured the same butterfly species poised on the blooms of different flowers. The lighting varied as well, from soft early morning to the bright midday sun to the shadows of a dense forest. Bill guessed the images were from the Wintergreen property.

"Did you take these photos?" he asked.

"Uh-huh. It's a hobby."

"Do you sell them professionally?"

"Oh, no. There's no money in Monarch photos—too many available for next to nothing on the Internet." She lifted the freshly opened bottle. The sides were chilled from being in the refrigerator. "I hope you like Sauvignon Blanc."

"It's my favorite."

Cindy grinned. "Very tactful. Shall we sit on the balcony?"

Two planters filled with bright scarlet begonias hung from the left side of the balcony. Along the rest of the railing, a foot-wide shelf supported various potted plants: pansies, miniature roses, and herbs.

"That's impressive," he said. "You have a full garden out here."

"It takes some work, but I don't mind. I used to have a house with a big garden—guess I'm trying to compensate. I like to seduce the hummingbirds with flowers. If we're lucky, we'll see one, although it's getting late." Cindy leaned over the railing. "On the other hand, take a look down there."

Bill searched in the direction Cindy pointed. A furry gray creature eighteen inches tall stood at the edge of the lawn near the hillside brush.

"It's our resident groundhog," she said.

"Hey. How about that? Except for Punxsutawney Phil, I don't recall ever seeing a groundhog."

"No? We have tons of them up here. They're harmless."

The groundhog stood upright and serenely surveyed his immediate surroundings as if he were the master of his domain, an expert of some kind, perhaps a professor. Bill noticed a hole in the ground a short distance from the creature, wide enough to accommodate his girth. Bill guessed it was the entrance to the groundhog's home. Indeed, when a dog walker and her curious dog rounded the corner of the condo building, the groundhog hightailed it for safety and disappeared into the hole.

"What's his name?" said Bill.

"Name? Ha! We don't name groundhogs in Wintergreen."

"Hmm," said Bill. "That won't do; he definitely needs a name. I'll take that assignment."

Cindy smirked. "Be my guest."

They sat in bar-height chairs facing the valley. In addition to the wine, Cindy had placed a dessert plate filled with lemon bars on the small round table between them. The setting sun formed a shadow of the ridgeline on the mountainside across the gorge. The sky was a dark blue, and the air still and refreshingly cool. Crickets buzzed from the wild shrubs and bushes on the hillside below them.

"Mind if I ask you a couple of questions?" she said.

"Fire away."

"Are you divorced?"

"Yes."

"Children grown and gone?"

"Yes," he said. "What about you?"

"Same on both counts." Her eyes twinkled. "Now that we have the high-level summaries, should we spend the next hour wandering through the ups and downs of our mediocre lives, our failed marriages, et cetera, et cetera, et cetera?"

"No. Let's save that for another day. Tell me about your catering business."

"Okay. For starters, try one of my lemon squares."

"With pleasure." A burst of exuberant flavor took his taste buds on a thrill ride, a sensation induced by the combination of powdered sugar, creamy lemon filling, and fragile crust. "Wow. You *made* these?"

Cindy's smile conveyed both confirmation and appreciation for his reaction. She explained that she ran a business catering private events hosted by Wintergreen residents and visitors, everything from dinner parties to outdoor picnics for a hundred people. For small events, she prepared dishes at her condo and served them at the customer's residence with an assistant's help. For bigger to-dos, she used a shared kitchen facility in Nellysford and hired temporary staff for servers.

"The profit is not great," she said, "but it enhances my retirement income, and I like the work."

"You had me with the lemon square."

Switching subjects, Cindy said, "Hey, big news on the mountain today. Did you hear about the hit-and-run?"

"As a matter of fact, I know all about it."

"Do tell."

Bill related the timeline and activities of his day, the early observations from the scene, the interdepartmental coordination meeting, and the search for the missing vehicle.

"You're a retired police detective?" she said.

"Yes. I spent thirty-five years on the police force in Columbia, South Carolina."

Cindy's hands fidgeted in her lap, and she broke eye contact. He was used to the reaction. A lot of citizens didn't know any policemen. On first meeting one, they instinctively grew tense, as if they were speeding on a highway and had spotted a patrol car in the rearview mirror.

"I've never known a policeman," she said.

He couldn't tell whether she considered his chosen profession a good or bad one.

"Don't worry," he said. "I won't turn you in for smoking pot or anything."

"I don't smoke pot. I used to smoke pot, but that was forever ago, before kids."

"Yeah. I smoked pot too, back in high school. Most people have at one time or another."

She picked up the dessert plate and offered it to him again. "Have another lemon square . . . and thank you for your service."

Okay. Maybe the ex-cop thing won't be an issue.

"Do you want a top-up on the wine?" she asked.

"Yes, thank you."

She went inside for the bottle, and he stepped forward to gaze at the ridge to the right. The fast-setting sun colored the sky red over the crest of the mountain. Far off to the left, stars poked through the purple hue of the approaching night.

"You didn't mention the victim's name," Cindy said, after she'd returned and poured more wine.

"We're not supposed to. It's customary."

"But word has gotten out among the regulars on the mountain. I knew him—Lou Thorpe."

"Oh, did you? How?"

She took a rather large sip and then stared off the balcony. "I used to cater dinner parties for them, the Thorpes, did five or six last year, until . . ."

Bill watched Cindy collect her thoughts.

Finally, she said, "Lou Thorpe is, or was, what my daughter would call a player. You and I might use the terms philanderer, womanizer, or lech. Even in his seventies, he was a strikingly handsome man and quite charming. He told fascinating stories in a smooth tenor voice. His eyes were like magnets; he would lock them onto a woman until she returned his gaze, and then he would give her a promising smile, a smile that said, 'Come with me, and you'll have the time of your life.' I know this from experience. I've seen that gaze. I've listened to his stories and heard the promise of his smile." She paused to take a deep breath and then turned toward Bill and gave her head a little shake. Some events were better left in the past, best forgotten.

But the detective in Bill wanted to know more. "You said you stopped catering for the Thorpes. Why? What happened?"

"You're going to make me tell the story."

"Not if you don't want to."

Her eyes searched his, assessing him, judging him. Could she trust him? Was he the kind of man who would tell her story to someone else? Or would he keep it himself? How could she know? They had just met, and she had only instinct to guide her.

She said, "The dinner party was for eight, a friend's birthday celebration. I served beef tenderloin with scalloped potatoes and asparagus tips. Appetizers. Dessert. The whole bit. And it went off fabulously. The party began with cocktails followed by dinner and lots of red wine.

"Afterward, my assistant Chandler and I stayed to clean up. Jeanne, his wife, had a splitting headache and went to bed. Lou poured another glass of wine and hung around to keep us company, telling stories. Chandler had an early start the next day, so I let her go at eleven o'clock. I had only a few things left to do, dessert dishes and packing up.

"'Do you want some wine?' Lou said. 'The bottle's open, and this red is outstanding.'

"I'd had my eye on the wine—a 2014 Châteauneuf-du-Pape—so I asked for half a glass. I was standing at the sink, and after he poured the wine, he stood next to me, leaning against the counter within an arm's reach. He was close enough for me to feel him, his body heat, and as weird as it sounds, it was exciting to have him next to me like that. He didn't touch me, but he kept talking in his smooth voice. I don't remember what he said, only the tone and cadence of his voice. It was mesmerizing. After I had finished washing and drying the dessert plates, I stood at the counter to drink my wine, farther away from him, farther apart than we are now."

Cindy paused and spread her arms wide to indicate the distance between the two of them.

Bill held his breath, and his stomach churned. His mind focused exclusively on Cindy. She touched the side of her face.

"But then Lou placed his glass on the counter and moved to stand in front of me. His eyes grew needy, as if I was the only woman in the world, and he found me irresistible. It had been a long time since I had sensed a man's desire—such passion and heat. That we should move physically closer seemed inevitable. Then Lou reached out and ran one finger up my arm like this."

Cindy reached to touch Bill's bare elbow with her forefinger, and then she traced a line all the way up under his sleeve to his shoulder. A chill ran down Bill's spine.

Cindy continued with her story. "Then Lou said, 'We should go upstairs to see the view off the back balcony. The moon is beautiful tonight.'" Cindy put her hands in her lap and sat still. Her eyes closed but then opened abruptly, as if she didn't want to see the image in her mind. "I knew what he wanted, and I . . . I wanted to give it to him, anything, everything. He had seduced me with words and gestures. I could see myself putting the glass on the counter and taking his hand, letting him lead me up the stairs, not to the back balcony, but to a spare bedroom where we would lie down and make love. I . . . I almost did it, but something stopped me. I don't know what. I can't even recreate the thought pattern, but suddenly, I was blinking and then talking and then moving. I ignored his invitation altogether. 'Gosh, Lou. What a great event. I think it went off well. No, I don't need any help getting stuff to the van. It's fine.' And that was that. He told me I had done a great job, and he gave me a generous tip, as was his custom. He never touched me except for that one moment. He never again referenced his invitation. It was as if he knew exactly how far he could go without crossing into forbidden territory. In retrospect, the encounter seems surreal, as if perhaps I imagined it, and at times I've thought as much."

Bill said, "I'm quite sure every bit of your story is true."

Cindy ran her hands along the tops of her thighs. "I never catered for them again. I didn't make a big deal of it—whenever Jeanne called to ask, I pretended to be booked and referred her to a competitor, one run by a big man and his big wife. Eventually, she stopped calling." Cindy laughed nervously. "I'm probably making something out of nothing. Lou was just flirting. He wanted to look at the stars."

"No, he propositioned you. And in any case, you made the right decision."

She shook her hands as if to fling away the memory and then asked Bill if he believed the police would catch the driver. He told her it all came down to finding the car. They would search for it again the next day.

Cindy grew quiet, perhaps still reflecting on that night. Bill had not wanted the evening to take such a turn. Seeking to change the subject, he gestured toward the Mountain Inn and said, "I understand Wintergreen hosts a music festival every year."

They were the magic words, for Cindy blinked several times, and her mood changed instantly. "Oh, it's brilliant this year but nearly finished. The musicians performed in that white tent below the Edge restaurant." She pointed. "You can see the corner of the tent from here. Different groups played everything from bluegrass to classical quartets to gospel."

"I'm sorry I missed it."

"There's more to come," she said. "In August, a traveling musical theater group will perform *Mary Poppins* on a temporary outdoor stage at the bottom of the main ski lift. Wintergreen hosted *The Sound of Music* a few years ago. From my balcony, I could hear the actors rehearsing. And the production was fantastic."

The bright mood of their earlier conversation returned, and they chatted easily as the sky grew dark and the crickets' chirping rose to a noisy, constant chorus. When their wine glasses were nearly empty, Bill said he must take his leave, for he had an early start the following day.

Cindy held her condo door open, and Bill stood on the landing a few feet away with his heart racing. Never one to mince words, he said, "I enjoyed our visit tonight, and I would like to see you again."

"Yes." She grinned, and her eyes sparkled. "It felt something like a first date, didn't it?"

"Very much so."

She shook a finger at him. "No kiss, though. As my daughter says, 'First date kisses are awkward.'"

"She's wise beyond her years."

Cindy threw her free hand to the side. "Well, you have my number. I made the first move. It's your turn."

"So it is. You'll hear from me soon."

Back at his condo, Bill filled a glass of water and stepped onto his own balcony. He glanced at Cindy's building across the way. The lights were off in the main room. Farther along the wall of her unit, rectangular lines of light framed the drawn shades of two vertical windows. That would be her master bedroom.

A million stars filled the sky. The air of Wintergreen smelled clean and pure. But of course, life here was no different than anywhere else, some good, some bad, and the occasional bit of evil. One soul fewer breathed in Wintergreen tonight than did the previous night. What sort of man was Lou Thorpe? A player? A philanderer? Whatever sins he had committed, they were all now in the past.

SEVEN

The next morning, Bill rendezvoused with Mitch Gentry to continue their search. By noon, the teams had inspected all of the mountain residences with no new results. Alex asked Bill to join him for lunch at a café near Bill's condo.

Several people had recommended the café to Bill, but this was his first time to try it. Café Devine occupied a small building on Blue Ridge Drive near the intersection with Wintergreen Drive. The entrance was guarded by the statue of a giant black bear standing on its hind legs. After crossing the sidewalk behind the bear, Bill opened the café door, and a bell jingled loudly. Inside, prepared salads and casseroles tempted him from a display case on the right, and he paused to consider them.

"Welcome," a woman said brightly. "We have some great salads today."

Behind the cash register stood a small energetic woman in her forties with a gloriously full head of frizzy brown hair. After wiping her hands on an apron, she pointed to the display salads and described them briefly. Farther behind the counter, a young man prepared food in a back kitchen. Bill selected the curried chunk tuna salad, a side of kettle chips, and a flavored seltzer.

At the cash register, she asked if he was vacationing. No, he told her, he'd moved into the Vistas Condos two weeks ago. Apparently, given that he was now a full-time resident, she believed they should meet, for she introduced herself as Kim Wiley, proprietor of Café Devine for over twenty years. She lived down in Waynesboro, and her nephew Nathan, who waved from the kitchen when she pointed, helped her run the café.

The bell at the door jingled, and Alex Sharp strolled in.

Kim stared at him. "Oh my goodness," she said. "It's Alex Sharp in the flesh. You scoundrel. You haven't come to see me in months."

"Uh, I believe it was last week."

"Pants on fire," she said.

Alex nodded at Bill.

"Bill, you know this guy?" she said. "Give me that plate. I'd have served you less if I'd known you were with Alex."

Bill held the plate tight to his chest, and Alex laughed.

"I see you've met Kim," Alex said. "She's difficult, but we love her all the same."

Kim looked askance at Alex, but her lips turned up in a smile.

Alex ordered a sandwich, and Bill perused the wine racks for Châteauneuf-du-Pape. He found bottles from four vineyards priced from forty to seventy dollars. Hmm. He'd keep that in mind for a special occasion.

He and Alex stepped outside to the patio and sat in the shade of a table umbrella. Alex's sandwich had not yet arrived, but he told Bill to go ahead. Hungry, but not wishing to finish before Alex had even started, Bill picked at his food, and they discussed the investigation. No one had confessed to the hit-and-run, and the guys on the roadblock had discovered nothing new. Neither had the follow-up calls for the homes with inaccessible garages. Alex had asked Krista Jackson to call auto body shops within a fifty-mile radius. Several had reported deer strike damage but nothing to match what they sought. Apparently, the state police had sent a similar query to body shops via a blast email, which gave Alex comfort that the hit-and-run was still on their radar. Oh, and forensics had determined the shoeprint's brand and size: Nike, size eleven.

"Do we know it is the driver's shoeprint?" said Bill.

Alex grimaced. "Not one hundred percent. Officer Hill collected names from bystanders, but several men had already left the scene. Krista tracked down those we know and found no match with the Nike shoeprint. We sent a blast email to the community asking the missing men to come forward. So far, nothing came of that."

Kim brought Alex's sandwich and stood next to the table with a hand on her hip. "What's going on with the hit-and-run? Everyone's freaked out."

"The investigation is ongoing," said Alex. "I can't say more than that, but I assume you already know the identity of the victim."

"It's a terrible thing. Apparently, the Thorpe children arrived last night, the son and daughter, not the in-laws or the grandchildren. They're still in DC and Norfolk. Jeanne has decided on two memorial services. Locally, they'll have a service at the Baptist church in Beech Grove. You know the one on the left past the gas station?"

"Yep," said Alex, and then he bit into his roast beef sandwich.

"Later on, they'll have a bigger do up in McLean."

Alex chewed a few times and then said around his food, "Any other whispers in the wind?"

Kim blinked several times, and then her eyes looked up to the right and then the left as if searching her mind for other gems of information. "No, that's all I know."

Alex swallowed. "Well, keep your ears open. Call me if you hear anything interesting."

"Of course I will."

"By the way, this sandwich is awesome."

"Not too much horseradish?"

"It's perfect."

"Thanks. I'll tell Nathan."

Kim gave Alex's shoulder a squeeze and then turned to go back inside.

Alex reported that residents continued to call his personal cell. It was the downside of having sold many of the homes on the mountain—all the former clients had his number, a small price to pay, he said, for the living he'd earned from the commissions.

"We may be nearing the end of the road," said Bill. "I don't know what else you can do."

"That's frustrating. When selling a home, I work until I make the sale. None of this lingering doubt."

Bill said, "Yeah, on the television series, the cops always solve the crime. In reality, the cold case file is thick and covered with dust. Without the car or a confession, we'll never know who killed Mr. Thorpe."

Alex shook his head.

"If it's okay with you," said Bill. "I'm going back to my condo to work on personal stuff."

"Sure."

"Let me know if anything comes up."

After finishing his sandwich, Alex took off, and Bill

pulled his chair into the sun, closed his eyes, and soaked up the warmth. He thought about Cindy Quintrell. Then he pulled out his phone and composed a text message.

Would you like to have dinner with me at the Edge tonight?

Her reply came a minute later.

I can't. Working. Tomorrow?

Bill was quick to respond.

It's a date.

Back at his condo, he toured each of the rooms with a notepad in hand. To prepare the unit for sale, the previous owners had painted the walls and removed the clutter. Everything else—the furniture, the flooring, and the fixtures—came from the 1980s, the decade of the building's initial construction. Even the beds and the washer/dryer were original stock. As the first order of business, Bill had purchased mattresses and a television in Charlottesville, but his visit to Cindy's condo had underscored how much remained to be done. He made a list: Artwork. Fireplace tools and screen. Flooring. (carpet or wood?) Paint kitchen cabinets. New door handles. Ceiling lights. Dining room chandelier. Kitchen knives. Drapes. Paint natural wood doors and trim. Replace living room furniture. New master bath vanity? Plants on the balcony.

Whew. It was a long and incomplete list. He washed his face, took a short nap, and drove to Lowe's in Waynesboro to buy some plants. Back at the condo, he arranged his new planters on the balcony railing and filled them with zinnias, marigolds, and pansies. Satisfied with his work, he made a quick supper, watched some television, and fell asleep reading a *Sites of Virginia* tour book.

In the morning, he went for a walk on a forested path that took him behind the tennis courts and alongside a golf course fairway. When he had nearly returned to his condo, his cell phone rang.

"Morning," said Alex. "I have something."

"What's up?" Bill stopped to catch his breath. He stood at the top of a hill across Blue Ridge Drive from his condo.

"The police in Waynesboro picked up a thru-hiker at a restaurant. He was blind drunk and kept mumbling something about an old man. They brought him in to sleep it off."

"Interesting."

"Mitch talked to them. Apparently, the hiker spent the night before last a bit north of Afton, about ten miles from here. Then yesterday, he decided to spend a night in a hotel and hitchhiked into Waynesboro. The kid's still sleeping, and the chief has asked if we want to talk with him. Otherwise, they'll cut him loose."

"Yes, I'd like to talk to him."

"Can Mitch pick you up in thirty minutes?"

"I'll be ready."

EIGHT

They had put Andre Lewis—the thru-hiker—inside a white interview room. Bill glanced at him through the small square window. A thin, light-skinned black man, Andre sat slumped in a metal chair with his arms crossed. He had bags under his sullen eyes and long hair that needed grooming.

"Have you charged him?" said Bill. Bill wore dark khakis, a white shirt, and the lanyard with the nametag around his neck. He had fastened the gold Wintergreen shield onto his belt.

"No," said the policeman, who was a big and muscular white man. "The chief wants to cut him loose—avoid the paperwork—unless you guys want him."

"What's his story?"

"He's hung over and contrite. Doesn't remember much. Apparently, he picked up a pint at the ABC and drank most of it on his way to Buffalo Wild Wings. He ordered food and beer, tried to flirt with the waitress, and then fell asleep."

"You get prints?"

"Yes."

"Search his stuff?"

"He has a backpack with some camping gear. I gave him his phone."

"Any running shoes?"

"No. He's wearing hiking boots. Oh, and he stinks."

"Thanks."

Bill steeled himself for the odor and walked into the room with Mitch behind him. The stench of crusted sweat was overwhelming, and Bill's eyes smarted. He swallowed hard and sat across from Andre, determined to minimize his reaction.

Mitch cleared his throat, and his eyes widened.

"Sorry I smell," said Andre. "I haven't bathed in two weeks. It would be nice if you guys offered me a shower."

"We're not Waynesboro police," said Bill. "We're with the Wintergreen police department."

Andre lifted his head, and his eyes narrowed. "Wintergreen? What do you want with me?"

"Do you know Wintergreen?"

"No." His eyes rolled from Bill to Mitch, trying to read them. "I camped near there three nights ago. Why? What happened?"

"Did you by any chance wander onto the property?"

"No."

Andre answered calmly. His eyes were tinged pink from his hangover, but they maintained solid contact with Bill. He was telling the truth or an excellent liar.

"The waitress at Buffalo Wild Wings said when you rambled on last night, you referred to an old man. What was that about?"

"I don't remember."

"Guess. Surely you can do that."

Mitch leaned forward and put his arms on the table.

Andre rubbed his hands together. He had large hands and fingers. Inanely, Bill wondered if he had ever played football. Any wide receiver would love to have those hands.

"Had to be my father," said Andre. "He called me recently. He's a jerk." Andre lowered his voice to mimic his father. "Do something big with your life. Do something big." Andre then resumed his natural pitch, but his words grew rushed. "When I set a big goal—hiking the AT from Georgia to Maine—two thousand long miles—he gives me endless crap. Won't underwrite me even though he has truckloads of cash. Then when I'm desperate, he banks me a few thousand and gloats. My father's a certified jerk."

Mitch looked at Bill and raised his eyebrows. Lots of history here.

The kid's story sounded plausible, but Bill should ask another question or two in the interest of tying off loose ends.

"Anyone camp with you that night next to Wintergreen?" he said.

Andre closed his eyes and rubbed his forehead. "Yes, a couple. Janette and Derrick. I hiked with them for a few days, but we split up two days ago."

"Do you have a number for Janette or Derrick?" asked Bill.

"Uh-huh. I have Janette's." Andre pulled out his phone and hit a few buttons. He showed Bill the number, and Bill typed it into his own phone.

Then Bill stepped outside and called the number. Janette answered after four rings. He explained the situation and asked where she was at the moment. She and Derrick were farther north on the AT. With a few more questions, Bill ascertained they were not far from Skyline Drive. He asked if they could meet for a few minutes. Janette said yes, but would he please bring fast food? Lots of calories.

Bill went to look for the chief of police.

"You've got nothing," said the chief from behind his desk. "I'm not holding him."

"Just give us an hour or two," said Bill. "I'm sure he's fine. Let us talk to the couple to double-check the story. We can at least tell the Wintergreen residents we're chasing down every lead."

The chief had a gut and a big head covered in curly gray hair. He frowned and put his hand out in supplication. "You know how it is with kids. Don't tell me you never got drunk off your ass. I can't arrest him because he smells."

"I get it. Don't charge him. Just keep him around for a while."

The chief nodded. "I guess we could buy him some breakfast."

"What he really wants is a shower."

"Yeah. We could do that. Might even have Jeffries take him to the laundromat to wash his clothes."

"Now you're talking."

NINE

Mitch and Bill drove four miles east on US 250 and then jumped onto Skyline Drive. Thick green forests lined the sides of the curvy three-lane road. Occasionally, spectacular views of the Shenandoah Valley opened on the left. Bill tried to imagine the landscape in autumn with all the reds and oranges and yellows. He'd have to come back.

"Don't you find it a bit suspicious?" said Mitch. "Andre camping next to Wintergreen on the night in question?"

"Coincidental? Yes. Suspicious? No."

"But it plays right into the thru-hiker theory."

Bill pinched the bridge of his nose. "Run the theory by me again."

"Andre comes into Wintergreen searching for something interesting. He finds a car, takes it for a joy ride, and runs into Lou Thorpe."

Bill sat forward and rubbed his lower back. He needed to start doing yoga.

"It's conceivable," he said. "But it strains credibility. What did Andre do with the car? And why hasn't anyone reported that car stolen?"

"I don't know. Maybe he did a great job stashing the car. Maybe the owner is out of town."

"Maybe," said Bill. "But we're going to need proof. Talking with Janette and Derrick is the next step. For all we know, *they* went into Wintergreen looking for a joy ride."

Mitch had the kind of temperament Bill liked in a cop. Steady. Slow to anger. Skeptical.

Mitch narrowed his eyes and said, "If you don't subscribe to the thru-hiker theory, why are we up on Skyline Drive?"

"Because it's an anomaly—three thru-hikers camping outside Wintergreen on the same night as our hit-and-run. We'll check anything that seems out of place from the everyday routine. Like the SUV Hill saw parked in the overlook that same night. At the time, Hill thought nothing of it, just a couple out for a late-night car canoodle. But knowing what we know now, if we had the license number, we'd check it out."

Mitch bobbed his head thoughtfully, eyes on the road, one hand on the wheel and the other resting on his leg.

Janette was standing next to Skyline Drive, close to milepost 86. Derrick sat on the grass in the shade of an oak tree a short ways away.

Mitch parked the squad car on the shoulder. Bill had bought thirty dollars' worth of Egg McMuffins, Apple Fritters, and coffee with lots of cream and sugar. He gave Janette and Derrick a few minutes to eat. They had encountered a big rattlesnake on the trail that morning and kept talking over each other as they related the story. They were young, healthy, and attractive in an outdoorsy kind of way. Like Andre, they bore the odor of warmed-over sweat, but Bill managed to stand upwind. He couldn't tell if they were romantically involved or just friends.

Yes, they had camped three nights with Andre.

"He was a lot to handle," said Derrick. "So we split with him two days ago."

"I thought he was okay," said Janette.

"Did any of you wander into Wintergreen that last night you camped with Andre?" asked Bill.

"This is about the hit-and-run, isn't it?" said Janette.

"What hit-and-run?" said Derrick.

"It was on my local news app," she said. "A man was killed, and the driver left the scene."

Derrick, who had wolfed down two Egg McMuffins in twice as many minutes, sat straight and stared at Mitch. Mitch nodded back.

"Did any of you leave the campsite that night?" asked Bill.

"No," said Derrick. "At the end of a day's hiking, I want food and rest. It had rained off and on for a few days, so we felt safe building a small fire to warm up. But by ten o'clock, I was in my tent sleeping like death. You too, right, Janette?"

"Yes, but not Andre. He stayed up awhile tinkering with the fire." Janette had gone quite still. Her face drained of color. She stared at Derrick and lowered her voice. "And he left the campsite that night."

The two kids sat on the ground, but Bill had remained standing, not wanting to soil his khakis. Mitch stood too. Now Bill squatted so his eyes were on the same level as Janette's.

"Okay," he said. "Tell me."

Janette had freckles and straight brown hair that needed washing. Still seated, she crossed her legs and leaned forward. "Derrick and I went to bed at the same time, and I fell asleep right away, but a few hours later, I woke up and needed to go to the bathroom. Firelight flickered against the side of the tent, and I thought it was weird for Andre to stay up so late. I went to pee and came back to the fire, but he wasn't there. It was irresponsible for him to leave a fire burning in the open like that."

"Told you he was a lot to handle," said Derrick.

She bobbed her head as if to acknowledge that Derrick had a point. "Anyway, I waited ten minutes in case Andre was nearby. When he didn't show, I doused the fire and went back to bed, but I couldn't sleep for wondering where he was. We had spotted a mountain lion a few days earlier, and I started thinking maybe he was in trouble. Should I wake Derrick? What could we do? Nothing. Not in the middle of the night. I lay there worrying for over an hour, and then he came back. I heard him open his tent and climb inside."

"Do you have any idea what time that was?" said Bill.

"Uh-huh. I checked my phone. It was three thirty-seven."

"What happened then?" said Bill.

"Nothing. I went to sleep. We got up early. Derrick likes to get up early and hit the trail."

"Not Andre," said Derrick. "He sleeps in. Janette and I had already decided it was time to split with him. I gave him until seven thirty, then woke him by calling through the tent wall. Told him we were taking off."

"Did he get up?"

Janette and Derrick both shook their heads.

Derrick said, "He mumbled something like, 'I'll see you on the trail.' Then we left."

"Did he ever wear running shoes?" said Mitch.

"No," said Janette. "Boots and flip-flops. We don't carry extra stuff."

Mitch asked a few more questions, but they didn't learn anything new. Bill thought through the timeline. The estimated range for death was two to five a.m. Hard to fathom that Andre could run into Lou Thorpe, stash the car, and hike back to the campsite by three thirty. Still, it was theoretically possible. But how did he get a car? And why had no one reported that car stolen? It didn't add up.

"Do you believe Andre had something to do with the hit-and-run?" asked Janette.

Concern drew her dark eyebrows together. Derrick's tongue slid across his lip.

"No," said Bill. He always tried to keep rumors to a minimum. "I'm sure he just went for a late-night stroll."

"You guys have a good trip," said Mitch. "Steer clear of mountain lions and rattlesnakes."

On the way back to Waynesboro, Bill waited for Mitch to bring up the thru-hiker theory again. To his credit, Mitch resisted the temptation until they had reached US 250 and were headed back into town.

"The timeframe is tight," said Mitch.

"Very tight," said Bill. "And he doesn't have running shoes."

"True. But we're not sure the shoeprint is the driver's. Andre could have done it. And he lied to us."

"No, he said he didn't go into Wintergreen. I didn't ask him if he'd stayed at the campsite. Probably should have."

"You think he went for a midnight walk? To do what? Check out the moonlight?"

"We'll ask him."

TEN

Bill and Mitch stopped at the police station and were redirected to the laundry at Broad Street and Poplar Avenue. In the parking lot outside the laundry, Patrolman Jeffries sat in a squad car with the window rolled down. The chief had told him to let the kid do his laundry and then drive him back to the AT.

"We'll do that," said Mitch. "You can take off."

"Sounds good to me."

Inside the laundry, buttons and zippers clanged against the walls of dryers. Rows of ceiling fixtures bathed the room in artificial light. A middle-aged man sat in a plastic chair watching a wall-mounted television while the woman with him folded clothes. The room was warm and smelled of detergent. Two white women worked on their laundry together, and when Bill and Mitch walked past—Mitch in full uniform—they stared.

"How y'all doing?" Mitch said in a friendly voice.

Andre slouched in a plastic chair near the back and studied his phone. He wore a bathing suit, a T-shirt, and flip-flops. His backpack leaned against the wall.

Bill guessed the rest of his clothes were in the wash.

Andre saw them and pointed at his phone. "You guys are looking into this hit-and-run, aren't you? I searched for Wintergreen. It's all over the web. Why didn't you mention that before?" His eyes were clearer than earlier, and his hair was clean and combed.

Two machines over, a dark-skinned, young black woman dressed in jeans and a short-sleeved top stopped what she was doing to listen.

"How's your laundry coming?" Bill asked Andre.

"Ten minutes to go in the dryer. I don't know anything about that hit-and-run."

"Let's talk outside for a minute," said Mitch.

Andre scanned the laundromat. The two white women were staring too.

"All right," he said.

Outside, the day had grown hot, and Bill was glad the overhang of the strip mall provided shade. Even so, a bead of perspiration slid down his side. Andre was taller than Mitch but thinner and looked underdressed in his bathing suit and flip-flops. He couldn't figure out what to do with his hands. He held them together at his front, then behind his butt, then back to his front.

They might as well get to it.

"We talked to Derrick and Janette," said Bill.

"Okay, good. They told you we camped together, right?"

"Yes, they did," said Bill. "But they also said you left the campsite for a while, came back late. Where did you go?"

Andre frowned as if Bill's words didn't match his recollection of the evening, but then he nodded. "That's right. I went for a walk."

"Uh-huh," said Bill. "Think carefully now. Did you

happen to venture into Wintergreen? Maybe you saw something that could help us with the hit-and-run."

Andre sucked on his lips, and his eyes cut from Mitch to Bill. He was taking too long to formulate an answer, like he was calculating. Or maybe he was afraid because he was a black kid talking to two white cops. Bill had seen that reaction many times in Columbia.

"No," Andre said. "I headed in the other direction. There's an overlook not far from where we camped. I had learned of it on the thru-hiker chat room. Someone said it was an awesome view at night, so I went up there to check it out."

"You went up there late at night?" said Mitch, skepticism in his voice. "By yourself?"

"Yes," said Andre with no hesitation.

"Why didn't you ask the other two to come along?" said Bill.

"The idea didn't occur to me until late. They were already asleep."

"What did you see?" said Mitch.

Andre gazed past the overhang to the cloudless azure sky. The laundry was on the corner of a busy intersection, and someone honked a car horn at the stoplight.

"No stars at all," said Andre. "Clouds had come in to cover the sky, and the wind had picked up. Down in the valley, the lights from a small city shone—Waynesboro, I guess."

"How long were you there?" said Mitch.

Andre's forehead wrinkled. "Longer than an hour, maybe two hours or more. I fell asleep for a while. I put on my hood, zipped my windbreaker all the way up, and lay back to stare at the sky. It was incredibly dark, a dark gray, like a void. I remember thinking I was in a void. I tried meditating but fell asleep instead. When I woke up, I went back to camp."

"Anything else?"

"No."

Bill glanced at Mitch to see if he had any more questions. Mitch gave him a slight shrug in return.

"Okay," said Bill. "Thank you. Finish your laundry. We'll get you some lunch and take you up to the trail."

Back in the squad car, Mitch fired up the AC, and they stared at the laundry.

"You ever try meditating?" said Bill.

"No."

"I have. Puts me to sleep every time."

"What do you make of our buddy Andre?" said Mitch.

"Not sure. All that stuff about the gray void? He might have gone up there to smoke a joint and fallen asleep."

"I have my doubts," said Mitch. "Once he got going, his story rolled out too smoothly. His sentences were like lines he had rehearsed for a play."

"Yeah, I noticed that too. On the other hand, did you see his feet? He's no size eleven. That's for sure. He's at least a thirteen."

They collected Andre, took him to get lunch at a Burger King drive-through, and drove him to where the AT crossed US 250. Mitch took the Blue Ridge Parkway route back to Wintergreen. On the way, he shook his head one too many times for Bill.

"What is it?" said Bill.

"He's lying about something."

"We had to let him go. We have nothing that connects him to the hit-and-run."

Which, of course, was true. But Bill had to admit he believed Andre was lying too.

ELEVEN

Mitch dropped Bill off at his condo and returned to work. Inside, Bill ate lunch and studied a Wintergreen trail map he had unfolded on the dining table. He had it in mind to take a hike that afternoon and sought to find one of medium difficulty that covered compelling terrain.

The map was white with black lines for the road system and brightly colored lines for trails. Light gray contour lines indicated elevation. Wintergreen Drive began midway up the mountain where they had constructed the roadblock. From there, the winding road rose a thousand feet in elevation before it came to a stop at a T-intersection. At the T, Laurel Springs Drive proceeded north and down the mountain on the property's western border. To the left of the T, Devils Knob Loop ran south and then east to the summit. On the way, it passed the overlook where Officer Hill had seen the SUV parked late at night.

Bill traced his finger up Laurel Springs Drive to the little parking lot where he and Mitch had stopped near the Appalachian Trail. A trail began at that spot, paralleled Laurel Springs Drive south for more than a mile, and ventured into the forest before ending at an offshoot street from Devils Knob Loop. According to the map, there were several good views from that trail. The trail was called the Old Appalachian Trail (the OAT), and Bill decided it was as good a place as any to begin exploring the mountain.

Fifteen minutes later, in shorts and a T-shirt with binoculars in hand, Bill hiked through the forest behind homes on Laurel Springs Drive. Soon, the houses petered out, giving way to densely packed hardwood trees. The narrow path came to a T-intersection with an unused dirt road wide enough for a passenger vehicle. A wooden marker indicated Bill should turn right. To the left, the track headed farther down the mountain, and it occurred to Bill that someone could stash a car on such a trail. How many old roads crisscrossed the mountain?

Water flowed in a stream out of sight on his left. The voices of small children bounced against trees ahead of him, and he soon passed a family of five. Sloping upward gently, the trail came within sight of the stream. Water splashed around rocks and lingered in small pools before continuing down the hill. A fit couple about his age hurried past him without speaking. After twenty minutes, the trail cut across Laurel Springs Drive and then angled away from the road. Huge boulders covered with lichens lay like litter on the side of the trail, castoffs from the receding glaciers of long ago. In those rare places where sunlight managed to break through the forest canopy, yellow and white wildflowers took advantage and flourished. The mountain sloped downward on the right, and eventually, Bill came to one of the overlooks he had seen on the map.

The trees gave way to a short and narrow section of barren rock that jutted toward a small valley. The sky was a soft blue. Bill had never been a fan of heights, and he got down on hands and knees before venturing the last four feet to the edge. The cliff dropped a hundred feet or more to the treetops below him. From there, the mountain descended steeply until it met its counterpart at a small valley. In the middle of the valley, a two-lane road headed northeast toward the giant Shenandoah Valley. Some of the land bordering the road had been cleared for agriculture.

Through his binoculars, Bill followed a large bird in flight. Was that a hawk or a vulture or some other kind of bird? He must study the descriptions in his new book. Next to the two-lane road, a red barn covered with a tin roof was set back a ways from an old white house. A light breeze blew up the side of the mountain and whisked the sweat from his neck.

Bill eyed both sides of the trail to make sure no one was watching him. Then he shouted, "Hey," to the valley before him. "Hey!"

Not given to public displays of his emotions, the view's sheer beauty had ripped the exclamations from Bill. He had lived and made his living in a world of concrete and buildings and traffic and people. Now he lived in a world of trees and mountains and far fewer people. He filled his lungs with clean air and looked to the heavens. Bill was not a particularly religious man, but moments like these brought him as close as he ever came. He understood why Andre Lewis would hike a mile at night to sit alone at the world's edge and stare at the gray void. People did many ugly things to each other as a result of their struggles to survive and find love and appreciation. On occasion, people must escape those struggles, or they would surely go mad.

TWELVE

Bill sat across from Cindy Quintrell in a booth at the Edge. A long bar was on the right inside the entrance, and a right-angle of picture windows and booth seating closed off the large square room. The décor was ski lodge, with varnished wooden tables and chairs, ancient skis and poles mounted high on the walls, and chandeliers.

Cindy wore a casual short-sleeved shirt with a scoop neck in a light blue color that complemented her blond curls. Their conversation was light with lots of laughter, and Bill felt at ease, which was seldom the case for him around women he considered attractive. They discussed the project he had undertaken to redecorate his condo. She suggested he first make his flooring decision, as that would narrow the choices for furniture and rugs and so forth. She had placed wooden flooring throughout her condo, but in retrospect, she might have kept carpeting in the bedrooms—winter was cold on the mountain. Bill grew distracted thinking of Cindy walking around her condo in bare feet.

Then, inevitably, she asked about his divorce.

"It was cliché cop," he said. "I got wrapped up with the

job, and Wanda got wrapped up with someone else. But honestly, the marriage was tired before that happened. She's an attorney. With both of us working and the juggling act of raising kids, we never focused on the marriage. When Brandon, our youngest, graduated from college, neither of us acknowledged the weakness of our relationship. That's when she had an affair."

"I'm sorry."

Bill glanced outside at the rolling mountains and the bright green grass of the main ski run. He tried not to think about what he had lost. Even five years later, the painful hollow in his chest remained, but by staying busy, he could nearly ignore it.

"It was a good marriage," he said. "Even the divorce was amicable, and I made out fine. We're still friends, nothing to fight over now, but we don't talk often."

"She's remarried?"

"No. Wanda's affair fizzled out quickly. It was a symptom of the disease. But tell me about your situation. Give me the sordid details."

Cindy laughed naturally, and the sound of her laughter filled the hollow in Bill's chest. She sipped her wine and told her story, which resembled Bill's in many ways minus the infidelity and with different timing. She and her husband had called it quits after the last child graduated from high school and left for college. They had lived in Northern Virginia for many years, and their home's value had appreciated a ton. After the divorce, she had sufficient capital to quit her job and buy the condo in Wintergreen.

Her career had been in restaurant management, a grueling profession, and the prospect of chucking that to do her own catering thing proved irresistible. The biggest challenge of the catering business, she discovered, was managing labor. The workload was volatile, an unattractive characteristic for people who required a steady paycheck. She often found that as soon as she trained a new person, they landed another job.

"Next time you get in a jam, call me," said Bill. "I can hardly boil an egg, but I look great in a cocktail dress."

He chuckled, but she pointed at him. "Don't laugh. I might take you up on that offer."

She went on to describe her kids. Her daughter had a low-level but good job working for a congresswoman and was now considering law school. On the other hand, Cindy worried about her son, Justin, who had a BA in English and worked as a bartender in Virginia Beach.

"He wants to write a novel," she said, "but I'm afraid he's distracted by the after-party scene. Every time we speak, he seems tired. It's the classic problem for English majors. If they don't want to teach, they have to find another career."

"Has he considered joining up?" Bill said, but he regretted the words as soon as they left his mouth. Not that it was a bad idea for a young man working in a bar, but for those who had lived their whole lives in the white-collar world, a stint in the armed forces seldom made the list of good career moves. If he had given it a moment's thought, he could have predicted Cindy's reaction.

She squinted at him and said, "You mean like in the army or something?"

No point in trying to weasel out of it; heck, he honestly considered it a good idea.

"I was in the army," he said, "but if I had to do it over again, I'd try for the coast guard. Those guys do some gnarly stuff on boats."

"Uh . . . I . . . I don't know."

"If he needs structure, the military will give it to him. Boot camp, for starters, is no picnic. After that, you always have a place to be and something to do. Orders to follow." A new thought occurred to Bill. "How are Justin's grades?"

"Straight As, both high school and college. He's a good student."

Bill put his hand out. "He could even apply for Officer Candidate School. It's tough to get in right away, but after a stint as an enlisted man, he'd have a good shot."

During his pitch relating the upside of military service, Cindy's arms had drawn close to her body. Darn. He might have doomed his chances with her already, which would suck, but at the same time, if they viewed the world in vastly different ways, it served them both to sort that now. Or maybe not. He had dated a fair number of women in the past five years, but none lasted for more than a few dates. Perhaps he came on a bit strong.

Fortunately, before he could do any more damage, the waitress appeared to take their dinner orders. The Edge offered uncomplicated dishes ranging from salads to grilled salmon. She ordered the fish and chips, and he opted for the veggie burger.

"I wouldn't have taken you as a veggie-burger guy," she said.

He shrugged. "I'm trying to be good, mostly for health reasons. I eat red meat twice a month. The rest of the time, it's fish, poultry, or vegetarian."

Cynthia's eyes met his, but she appeared deep in thought. She tilted her head, and he guessed she was still processing his earlier comments.

"How long would that take?" she said. "If Justin were to join the military."

"Varies. Anywhere from four years to forty years. I guarantee you one thing: It would give Justin something to write about."

Cindy shook her head. "I couldn't bear it if he had to go to war."

"I get that. It's a valid concern. Most servicemen and women never fire a weapon in combat. I never did, but it's always a possibility. Now let's discuss something else before I totally bomb this date."

That at least earned a smile, and Cindy lifted her glass for another sip.

"I heard something interesting about the hit-and-run today," she said. Her eyes grew alive, and she leaned forward until her abdomen touched the table.

"Yeah?"

"There's a rumor that the driver was a thru-hiker. That they stole a car for a joy ride, accidentally hit Lou Thorpe, and then stashed the car in the woods somewhere."

"Who told you that?" Bill asked.

"Kim Wiley at Café Devine. She heard it from several people in the shop today. It even has a name—the thru-hiker theory."

"Word flies on the mountain."

Cindy rushed her next words. "So that's a real thing? The theory? And the police are working on it?"

Sheesh. Bill had never worked in a community like Wintergreen, where residents talked to the same people every day. The closed system fostered a rapid exchange of ideas. If a person heard the same theory from several others, then the theory, no matter how preposterous, was soon accepted as fact.

"I can't discuss the underlying investigation, but I have doubts about this theory."

"Why?"

"It's natural for residents to want the driver to be from outside the community. To believe someone here got drunk off their ass or played with their phone too long and ran over Lou Thorpe is abhorrent. So, on its face, the thru-hiker theory has emotional appeal. But the truth is thru-hikers are laser-focused on getting to Maine—not coming into Wintergreen to steal a car."

"Huh. You really think this stuff through, don't you?"

"I try."

Bill sipped his Vienna Lager and gazed at the sky. The sun had slid behind the mountain. He had a rather odd question to ask and wasn't sure how to proceed.

"Say, did you hear there's a memorial service for Lou Thorpe tomorrow?"

Cindy nodded.

"Were you planning to attend?" he said.

"No. I don't know Jeanne that well and only knew Lou through the catering stuff."

"Here's the thing. Alex asked me to go. I think he wants to use me for cover because some of Lou's friends have been after him about the investigation."

Cindy wrinkled her nose, not sure where Bill was headed.

"Would you like to come with me?" he said. "You could give me some background on the friends, and then afterward, we could go to Devils Backbone for a beer."

She sat straight with her eyes wide. "Are you asking me to help with the investigation?"

"Don't feel like you have to."

"Are you kidding? I'd love to. This is exciting."

"It's in a church, so it's probably not going to be *that* exciting. But you might know some of the people."

"I'm sure I will."

After dinner, they drove back to the ridge in Bill's Mazda and then stood on the sidewalk under an oak tree. The night was fast approaching, and Bill could scarcely discern her face. Though the dinner had gone well, he regretted the suggestions he'd made concerning her son's career.

"Listen," he said, "sorry if I stepped over the line on the stuff about Justin joining up. The military is not for everyone."

She stepped closer, within arm's reach, and the details of her face became more apparent. Her eyes were a dark blue in the twilight.

"I'm not sorry," she said. "Truthfully, the idea had already occurred to Justin. He mentioned it to me last week, but we don't know anyone in the armed forces. He doesn't know what to expect."

"It's not brain surgery, at least not for an enlisted man. Listen carefully. Follow orders. Don't screw up."

"Maybe you could talk to him."

"Oh. Sure. I'd be happy to."

"Thank you."

Cindy stepped even closer, and his heart raced forward. If they were so inclined, they could lean a little and kiss. Was she so inclined? Was that why she had moved closer? Moments like these were difficult to navigate. He had screwed them up in the past, misread signals, and embarrassed himself.

"This is our second date," she said.

"Yes, I suppose it is."

"In case you're wondering, I'm standing this close so that we could kiss if you want to. Do you want to kiss me?"

"Yes."

"Okay."

He took the final step, and their lips met nervously. She put an open-palmed hand on his chest. He tentatively touched her side. Her lips parted, and the kiss grew passionate. Excitement swirled through his mind. And then Cindy stepped back. She glanced at her condo building and turned to him.

"I think we should leave it at that," she said.

"Fine."

"We should proceed with caution. We're neighbors, and if we screw things up, we'll have to look at each other awkwardly for a long time."

"Makes perfect sense."

They parted and returned to their respective buildings. Bill poured a glass of water and sat on his balcony to watch the moon and the stars. A passenger jet descended northeast toward the airport in Charlottesville.

Cindy was right; they should take it slow. He really didn't want to screw things up.

THIRTEEN

With spaces for a dozen cars, the Beech Grove Baptist Church had the smallest parking lot of any place of worship Bill had ever seen. The sign out front read *Established in 1932*. Perhaps at that time, fewer members owned vehicles. Behind the church on the left was a cemetery with several dozen headstones. The church building was white with a pitched roof and modest steeple. The eight rows of pews could accommodate a hundred people; half that number had chosen to attend Lou Thorpe's memorial service. At the front, a gray-haired woman played a hymn on a piano.

Bill and Cindy sat in the back row on the far right. She had heard from Kim Wiley that a second, much larger service would be held in DC at a later date. This memorial was for Wintergreen friends.

Alex Sharp arrived in a dark suit and white shirt with a tie and stopped by their pew to have a word with Bill. They shook hands.

"I see you two have met," he said. "Nice to see you, Cindy."

"Same here, Alex," she said.

"Oh, that's right. You're in the Vistas also. Same building?"

"Next one over."

Alex crouched behind them and spoke in a lower voice. He pointed with a finger toward the front left of the room. "The fellows I mentioned are in the second row on the left. Three men. They're Lou Thorpe's golfing buddies. Two of them are married, and their wives are with them. Cindy, you probably recognize all of them."

"Who's that man on the left?" she said.

"Cyrus Hunt. He's not married. Cyrus is relatively new to Wintergreen." Alex closed his eyes and tapped his forehead as if trying to search his mind. "He got a place up here last summer, maybe the previous year." Alex placed his hands on the rounded back of the pew and eyed Bill. "I appreciate you talking with these folks. They've been after me because they know I'm not a real police chief. Meeting you might settle them down."

"I'm happy to talk with them, but there's not much to say."

"These guys are corporate types. They feel a need to do something even when there's nothing to do. Hang around the parking lot after the service. I'll send them over."

"All right. Sure."

Alex left, and Cindy shared with Bill what she knew about the two couples. The tall man in the middle was Marty Capaldi, and he sat next to his wife, Barbara. He was a retired corporate executive with a coal company headquartered in West Virginia. The other man, Victor Bishop, had worked for the same company as general counsel. He and his wife, Marilyn, had a second home in DC. Lou Thorpe knew the two men from his work as a lobbyist for the industry, and the three couples often socialized together. Cindy had catered dinner parties for the Capaldis as well as the Thorpes.

The two coal industry men must have known Lou Thorpe well, for the presiding clergyman called them up one at a time to give remarks. Capaldi went first and kept it light—a joke at his own expense and a few stories reminding everyone of Lou's charms. Bishop, the attorney, articulately spoke of the deceased man's contributions to an industry that had provided heating and lighting for much of America over the last century. Neither of the men shed tears.

After the brief service, the clergyman asked those in attendance to allow the family to leave first so they could arrange a reception line outside. The family consisted of the widow and her grown son and daughter. Bill guessed the extended family would attend the DC service.

The early afternoon sun beat down on the blacktop parking lot. Bill was uncomfortably hot in his shirt, tie, and jacket. He marveled once again at how much warmer the valley was than the mountain, reliably ten to twelve degrees different.

Bill had planned to skip the receiving line, but once outside, he realized that was impractical. With such a small crowd, everyone would notice. Cindy saved the day by leading them through. The widow, Jeanne Thorpe, recognized Cindy and thanked her for coming. Cindy introduced Bill as a friend. He shook Jeanne's hand and was a little surprised at the warmth and strength of her grip. She was an attractive woman in her seventies, the same age bracket as most of those in attendance. A few inches shorter than Bill, she stood erect and had strong shoulders and arms. Her face was framed by a stylish haircut, brown tinged with gray. Bill and Cindy passed through the line quickly and then stood next to his Mazda.

A few minutes later, the golfing buddies strolled over. The two wives stayed behind to chat with Jeanne and her grown children. Alex was nowhere in sight—he must have ducked out already. After quick introductions, the lawyer, Victor Bishop, led the charge.

"I understand you're running the hit-and-run investigation," he said.

Victor was a thin man and quite a bit shorter than his two companions. He spoke sharply, as if addressing a junior member of his former legal team.

"Um, no, that's not accurate," said Bill. "There's a coordinated interagency effort underway that involves the state police, Nelson County, the National Park Service, and Wintergreen. Wintergreen is handling the mountain search for the vehicle. Alex is short-staffed right now, so I helped a little with that."

"I'm glad to hear the park rangers are involved," said Victor. "With all the hikers coming through every day, it seems highly probably one of them did the deed."

Jeez. The thru-hiker theory. Would it never die?

"What I want to know," said Victor, his face growing red, "is why you would choose to let a suspect thru-hiker go when you had him in custody. Apparently, the guy admits leaving his campsite in the middle of the night."

Surprised but calm, Bill glanced at Victor's buddies. Cyrus Hunt raised his eyebrows but didn't say anything, and Marty Capaldi looked at the ground. How in the world did Victor know all this? Mitch Gentry? No. Mitch was well trained and reliable. It had to be Alex, feeding scraps to Victor to keep him from barking so much. Bill raised his hands to lower the temperature of the conversation.

"Let me make a couple of points," he said in a measured tone. "First, I don't have authority to hold anyone in custody.

Second, saying that a thru-hiker left a nearby campsite is comparable to saying that a Wintergreen resident took their dog out to mark a bush. It doesn't mean anything unless we can link it to the crime. Right now our biggest challenge is that we don't have the vehicle."

With his hands on his hips, Victor scowled. "You don't know what you're talking about. I have a home on Laurel Springs Drive. When hikers come through, I can smell them from my back deck."

Marty Capaldi was a big man with rounded shoulders and thinning gray hair. Probably a few years older than Victor, his hands trembled slightly. He reached to touch Victor's elbow and said, "Come on. Hyperbole won't get us anywhere. Let the police do their job."

Victor grunted angrily and pulled his arm away from Marty.

The third golfing buddy, Cyrus Hunt, now stepped forward. He had enough wrinkles on his face and hands to suggest he had reached his early seventies, but he was in great shape. He moved with the confidence and coordination of a man in his fifties.

"It's tough," Cyrus said in a clear, calm voice, "for Victor and Marty and me to have Lou taken away like this. We knew him well. Heck, these guys knew him for twenty-five years, even longer. We just want to know what we can do to help."

"It's simple," said Bill. "Find the car."

FOURTEEN

After the service, Bill and Cindy drove a mile into the Rockfish Valley to the Devils Backbone Brewpub at Highway 151. The brewery had outdoor seating filled near to capacity with a boisterous young crowd dressed in summer clothes. As they wore heavier clothing, Bill and Cindy went inside the air-conditioned restaurant, where a hostess seated them in a wooden booth. Mounted above them was the stuffed head of a large buck with an impressive set of antlers. The hostess left them with full menus that included everything from appetizers to sandwiches to steak.

"I think it's too early for dinner, don't you?" said Bill.

"Yes, definitely."

"But it might be nice to have something to go with a beer."

"We should order the pretzel," she said. "I've had them. They're enormous and warm and come with delightful spicy mustard."

"Perfect."

Bill relaxed his shoulders and watched Cindy read the descriptions of the available craft beers. The conversation with the golf buddies had rankled him a little. Sitting across the table from a pretty woman certainly helped. She had a cute nose, and a wisp of sandy hair hung lazily across her forehead. Perhaps she sensed his eyes on her, for she glanced up and smiled.

He asked about her catering business. She had three events in the next week, two dinner parties and an anniversary reception. Each client had chosen a different selection of dishes from her three-page catering menu, which annoyed her because it meant she had to buy a greater variety of ingredients. He suggested that perhaps she should reduce the number of choices she offered. She said she had tried that earlier, but clients seemed to like having that third page of options.

The waiter came to take their orders. After he left, they discussed their children. His son Matt, a freelance graphic artist living in Savannah, had reported that he now had a two-month backlog of orders, which was tremendous progress over the hand-to-mouth existence he had to endure his first two years in business. She had spoken with her son Justin, and he would like to talk with Bill about joining the armed forces. Was he still willing to have the conversation? Yes, of course. Then their conversation veered back to the memorial service.

"I noticed something odd at the service today," she said.

"You mean other than the awkward conversation in the parking lot?"

"By the way, you handled that well. Candid but tactful, and most importantly, you didn't lose your cool."

"Thank you."

And thank goodness age had mellowed him. He would not have wanted Cindy to witness a younger version of himself. He had lost his temper often, which partly explained why promotions had proven slow to come.

"But it struck me as strange," she said, "that no one showed much in the way of emotion. Jeanne Thorpe was a rock. Here's a woman who lost her husband of forty-plus years in a horrific tragedy, and her eyes were as clear as a cloudless sky. Maybe that's understandable, with her kids nearby, which always cheers a mother up, but even they were tearless. Same thing with the buddies. Victor Bishop's little show was mostly about power and influence, not grief. The friends were somber but not particularly shaken. Am I making any sense?"

"People show their emotions in different ways."

"You're right, of course, but I couldn't help thinking back to that moment I had with Lou Thorpe at his house. You remember?"

"Of course."

"That was a physical thing, a sexual overture. It had nothing to do with emotion."

"Maybe a guy like that doesn't deserve tears at his funeral. Is that what you're thinking?"

"Yes, but it sounds awful when you say it like that, so bluntly. I'm reaching." She heaved a sigh. "Gosh, how depressing. Let's talk about something else."

The pretzel and beers came. The salty pretzel and tangy mustard complemented the hearty flavor of the amber beer Bill had ordered. Each bite of pretzel made him want to drink beer, and each pull on the beer made him want to hit the pretzel again. With great restraint, he strung the beer out for twenty minutes.

Another one would taste good, but the glasses were full pints, and the beer was strong. After a second drink, he might grow tired on the curvy road up the mountain. Better have a glass of water.

"Know what might be fun?" Cindy said.

"What's that?"

"First, we grab a six-pack here and have another beer on my balcony. When the sun begins to set, we'll make dinner."

"Everything about that sounds fun."

∽

"Do you know how to peel and clean shrimp?" Cindy asked, holding a deveiner in the air.

"Yes, I can do that."

She now wore jean shorts and a sleeveless top. Her eyes crinkled. After a second beer on her balcony, he had begun to feel a bit tipsy, and she had giggled several times during the conversation. Then she had suggested they cook and eat dinner, for if she had another beer first, she might be inclined to make a poor decision. Of course, he chose to agree.

He leaned over the sink to clean the pound of shrimp. While he worked, she put water on the stove for pasta, chopped garlic, and made a spinach salad with strawberries, chopped walnuts, and feta cheese. As the linguini cooked, she sautéed garlic in olive oil with sliced cherry tomatoes and then added the shrimp. The aroma of cooking garlic made Bill's stomach rumble; fortunately, the stovetop fan covered the noise. Magically, the shrimp and pasta were done at the same time. Cindy gave him instructions on finding things to set the table; then she folded the pasta and shrimp together and sprinkled Parmesan cheese on top.

With a full plate of savory food before him, he hesitated over the decision of where to start, finally settling on a forkful of linguini followed quickly with a shrimp. If they could sing, his taste buds would have serenaded the heavens.

"That's excellent," he said, "and you made it look easy."

"Actually, deveining the shrimp is the hardest part." But she appeared pleased with his compliment.

After dinner, they sat on her couch to talk and gradually moved closer, until he put his hand on her neck, and then she leaned in to him for a kiss. They kissed for a while and then grew more excited. Soon they came to a point where they would stop or take it to the next level. Cindy pulled away and sighed.

"That was nice. You're a good kisser, but maybe we should slow the train before it runs off the track."

He caressed her arm. "Sure. Whatever works."

"I hope you don't consider me prudish. I haven't been with many men since my divorce."

"Not at all. We've only known each other for a few days. And I haven't been with many women since my divorce."

He put his arm around her, and she leaned against him.

Bill knew he was lucky to meet Cindy. He had been alone for several years, and on occasion, the unsettling notion had come to him that he might be alone for the rest of his life. When he had kissed her, she had definitely kissed him back. The scent of fresh air came through the sliding balcony doors. The fireplace was decorated for the summer with an array of unlit candles. Come winter, it would snow on the mountain, and the ski resort would open. The temperature would drop below freezing, and the wind would blow. If his luck held, and he didn't screw things up, he might wind up sitting here with Cindy before a crackling fire.

Wouldn't that be something?

FIFTEEN

Bill felt lazy the next morning, so instead of exercising, he drove to the Mountain Inn for a latte and a pastry. Unable to decide between the almond croissant and the blueberry muffin, he settled on both and returned to his condo building. The lot was nearly full, and he was forced to park at the end near the dumpster.

After retrieving his coffee and the pastries, Bill pulled out his phone to check for messages. He turned to walk toward his unit, stared at his phone, and began deleting junk mail. After six paces, he sensed something out of place and lifted his eyes. There before him, not twenty feet distant, stood a large, black, furry animal.

Hell's bells!

What was that? A massive dog?

No.

It's a bear!

His heart pounded in his chest, and his knees wobbled.

He dropped his coffee cup, and hot liquid splashed on the pavement. The bear advanced at an excited pace. Bill scurried backward, then tripped and fell on his butt. Not ten feet away, the bear slurped at the spilled latte with enthusiasm. But after a few seconds, the bear grew impatient and gazed hungrily at Bill.

Bill's jaw clenched. Terror gripped him, and he cast his bag of pastries aside and ran across the lot toward the condo building. He bounded up the nearest walkway's steps and had nearly reached the entrance when a tall woman with white hair exited the doorway. Bill paused, heaving, and glanced over his shoulder. The bear had ripped the white paper bag apart and was now happily consuming its contents.

"It's . . . it's a bear," he gasped.

The woman laughed. "I see you've met Ms. Betsy."

Clearly not fearful of the several-hundred-pound omnivore feasting on Bill's breakfast, the woman's eyes sparkled as she observed the black bear. She offered Bill a bemused smile, and he began to believe he might survive the morning.

"Are we in danger?" he said.

She shrugged. "Not unless you try to take your breakfast back. Otherwise, Ms. Betsy's not interested in us. She's busy foraging food for the winter. Watch for a minute. She'll wander off soon."

Once he grew calm, Bill enjoyed the spectacle of the bear, and he decided the ten dollars' worth of food was a small price to pay for such a show. Ms. Betsy had small eyes, rounded ears, and a long brown snout. Her body was covered with thick black fur. Standing on all fours, her shoulders were about three feet high. As predicted by Bill's neighbor—a year-round resident named Mrs. Spooner—Betsy soon licked the paper bag clean of crumbs and then ambled into the woods across the lot.

Mrs. Spooner returned to her building, and Bill settled for a breakfast of cereal and home-brewed coffee. Shortly after eleven in the morning, long after Bill's heart rate had settled from the earlier excitement, he sat bent over his laptop perusing the Lowe's website when his cell phone rang.

"The Park Service found the car," said Alex Sharp.

"Oh." Bill bolted upright, the website forgotten. "That's fantastic."

"It's an SUV. Mitch is on the way to pick you up."

"I'll be waiting outside."

Mitch picked Bill up in the parking lot, and they began to drive down the mountain.

"Where is it?" said Bill.

"Just off the parkway. Not far. Remember the spot off Laurel Springs Drive where the AT comes through? It's a mile north of there at a picnic area."

Why the heck didn't the rangers find it sooner?

But Bill didn't say anything. It was best to not point the finger at a fellow agency until you had all the facts. The location couldn't be more than four miles from Bill's condo, but it took them nearly twenty minutes to get there. First, they had to wind their way halfway down the mountain on Wintergreen Drive, and then they had to climb back up on 664 to get to the Blue Ridge Parkway. Once there, they turned north and drove five miles to a place on the right called the Humpback Rocks Picnic Area.

A single-lane road formed a loop with picnic sites along its outer edge and a restroom building at its center. Except for two families who had set up for lunch and games at picnic tables, the facility was deserted. When Mitch and Bill were three-quarters of the way around the loop, they approached an offshoot lane whose entrance was blocked by an orange cone and a park ranger. The ranger explained that the road led nowhere and was typically closed to public access with a lock and chain.

"The vehicle is two hundred yards down on the left," he said. "The ranger who found it is there."

"Thanks," said Mitch, and he pulled the squad car forward.

"Wait," said Bill. "Stop."

Bill got out of the car and hiked back to the ranger. He stood on the other side of the cone, studied the posts that supported the chain, and scratched his head.

The ranger said, "You're asking yourself, 'How did the driver get past the lock and chain?'"

"Did they break it?"

Mitch arrived to observe the conversation.

"No," said the ranger. He pointed to the left post. "The poplar tree there is only three feet from the post, but on the other side, there's more room." He crossed the lane to the right post and stretched his arms wide. "We think he, or she, drove around the post."

Bill walked to where the ranger stood. Two feet of clearance existed between the ranger's outstretched hand and a large boulder. "There's not a lot of room."

"You're right," said the ranger, "but take a look at this sapling. See these lower branches? Something pulled them back until they snapped."

"Huh," said Mitch. "Pretty clever driver to figure out on the fly they could fit around that post."

"Yeah," said Bill. "Pretty darn clever."

A couple of hundred yards farther along, they came upon a female ranger and a Park Service squad car on the right shoulder. A thick forest interspersed with boulders lined both sides of the road. Mitch pulled behind the ranger's car, and they got out and introduced themselves.

Bill examined the road ahead of them and behind them. He scratched his head again. "Where's the SUV?"

"Exactly," she said. "I figure we've been up and down this road five or six times searching for the hit-and-run vehicle. I drove by here twice myself without spotting it. But then today I thought, 'If I were trying to hide a car here, what would I do?' Then I started searching the roadside differently. I checked for tire tracks. See that boulder? Look at the leaves."

At the edge of the forest stood a boulder the size of a small house. The forest climbed a gentle slope behind the boulder, and dead leaves covered the ground beneath the trees. Only after studying the scene did Bill notice something odd. Dead leaves littered the surface around the left side of the boulder and into the grass.

"No," he said.

"Yep," said the ranger. "Let me walk you around this way."

She led them twenty feet laterally on the road, across a thin strip of grass, and into the forest. From there, they trudged along the edge of the hill until they could see a gold-colored SUV tucked behind the boulder.

"It's a Honda Pilot," she said. "The front grille and bumper are damaged. I didn't want to mess up the scene, but I put gloves on to try the door. It's locked. We called the state guys. They're sending forensics and a locksmith."

"How long until they get here?" said Mitch.

"Who knows? A half hour maybe?"

"Nice work," said Bill. The SUV had Virginia license plates, and he typed the number into a note on his phone.

Back at their squad cars, the ranger got inside of hers to talk on the radio.

"What do you think?" said Mitch, leaning on the front bumper of their car.

"I don't know. It could be a few hours before we learn anything."

"Let me check something," said Mitch, and he pulled out his phone.

Bill was hungry because he'd missed his usual mid-morning snack.

Staring at his phone, Mitch stood and turned slowly until he faced forward and to the right. He pointed in that direction. "The Appalachian Trail is two hundred yards that way."

"You're kidding. Can we get there from here?"

"Probably. We could go cross country, but there might be an access trail back at the picnic area."

"How far are we from Wintergreen?"

"About a mile on the trail."

"Let's hike it," said Bill. "See if we learn anything."

Someone had driven the Honda Pilot into Lou Thorpe and then ditched the car here not far from the Appalachian Trail. The fact pattern fit the thru-hiker theory well, which was one of the reasons Bill chose to hike the trail back to Wintergreen. He wanted to see the overlook that Andre Lewis claimed to have visited in the middle of the night. But also, if Bill asked Krista Jackson nicely, she might buy sandwiches and meet them at the dirt parking lot on Laurel Springs Drive. He needed to talk to her anyway about running down the plates.

The seldom-level trail wound through a dense forest of tall trees. They climbed a hundred feet in elevation, then descended a hundred feet, and then the process repeated itself. Rocks lay on the path, and roots crept in from nearby trees. To avoid tripping, Bill kept his eyes on the trail. Mitch led the way and seemed quite comfortable hiking in the woods. He was a big man with strong legs and broad shoulders.

"What did Krista say when you asked her to bring sandwiches?" said Mitch.

"Nothing. She asked what we wanted."

Mitch swiveled his shoulders and cocked an eyebrow at Bill. "You must have a magical voice. I can't get her to bring me a cup of coffee when I'm in a hurry."

"It's not her job to bring you coffee. You can do that yourself."

"It's not her job to bring us lunch either."

In fact, Krista had sounded cheerful when he reached her at the office. Sure, she'd be happy to stop by the Market and get sandwiches. Did he mind if she joined them for lunch? Not at all. Yes, she'd be sure to run the license plate down first. Maybe Mitch didn't know how to ask nicely.

Bill asked Mitch whether he had previously hiked this section. Mitch had not; however, he said the terrain and flora here resembled other trails in the area. For a while, Mitch called out different species of trees along the way: birch, American beech, and chestnut oak. The track came to a steep incline, and Bill grew winded. It was like climbing an endless set of stairs. Finally, they reached the top of the hill and came upon a rocky overlook. Below them, the mountain leveled out into the Shenandoah Valley. Waynesboro lay to the north.

Bill pointed to a flat spot in the rock. "Andre Lewis might have lain right there and gazed up at the gray void."

"Maybe," said Mitch. "Or he might have never come here that night."

SIXTEEN

The trail led them around the right side of the overlook and then down a steep hill. Beyond a thick curtain of leaves, cars drove past on the parkway. They passed a family of five moseying in the opposite direction, and the three small children stared at Mitch's uniform. He gave them a bright greeting and kept going.

They had been hiking twenty minutes and reached a level section of trail when Mitch stopped and pointed to the right. The ground appeared no different from any other patch—dead leaves, the trunks of fallen trees, and sunlight freckles that had broken through the forest canopy. Mitch tromped into the brush, and Bill followed.

"Here," said Mitch, and he pointed to a small cleared area with charred wood in the middle. "They camped here."

"How did you notice that from the path?"

"See the flattened leaves here and over here? They pitched their tents in these spots. And the bark on that log has been disturbed. Someone sat on that log and watched the fire."

"Sheesh. I wouldn't want you tracking me in the woods. Are we close to Wintergreen?"

"Yes."

When they reached the little parking lot off of Laurel Springs Drive, Krista was waiting for them. The back door of her Toyota Sienna was open, and she had taken out two folding camp chairs. Krista and Bill took the two chairs, and Mitch sat on the back bumper of the SUV. They began to eat lunch, and Mitch and Bill told Krista about the Honda Pilot at the picnic area.

As a communications officer, Krista spent much of her time on a computer or a phone. In the camp chair, she sat with her knees together and her back straight. Her red hair was pulled back in a ponytail. Her facial appearance had changed slightly from when Bill met her a few days earlier. Her cheeks were rosier, and she wore a touch of eyeliner.

"Oh, I have to tell you," she said, growing excited. "I got a hit on the plates. The car is registered to Mr. Joel Turner. You'll never guess the address: 197 Fawn Ridge Drive."

Mitch turned suddenly to look southwest on Laurel Springs Drive. "Why, that's only a mile from here."

Krista lifted her chin, and her eyes sparkled. "I drove by on the way over to check it out. It's a nice two-story house with a detached garage. They have a wooden porch with shrubbery in the front and a small grass yard."

"I know that place," said Mitch, turning to Bill. "We stopped there the second day of the search. They had no cars out front or in the garage, so we checked it off the list."

Bill's heart fluttered. His eyes darted from Mitch to Krista, and he leaned forward in his chair. "Okay, here's the plan. We wolf down these sandwiches and then go to the house. See what's up."

Mitch took a huge bite and chewed like a madman.

THE MOUNTAIN VIEW MURDER

The concrete driveway sloped down from Fawn Ridge Drive and onward a hundred feet to the house. On the front porch, Mitch rang the bell, and Bill peered through the picture window. To Bill's right, Krista leaned to look through the next window over. The room had a wooden dining table with eight chairs. Beyond the dining room, the natural wood flooring continued into what appeared to be a larger living area. Bill detected no movement inside the house. Although the interior seemed to be tidy and well maintained, the table's varnished surface did not gleam in the natural light, as if a fine layer of dust had dulled the finish. Mitch tried the door, but it was locked.

"What do you think?" said Bill.

"No one's been here for a while," said Krista.

"Let's check the garage."

The double-bay garage had a side door with window panes. The door was open, and they ventured inside. One of the bays was cluttered with a few objects, a golf bag, a hand-push lawn mower, and an old armchair. The second bay was empty and cleared as if to make room for a vehicle. The rest of the garage contained nothing noteworthy: some fishing gear, yard tools, and a workbench.

On the way from the parking lot, Bill had sat up front, but for the ride to the parkway, he sat in the back to give Mitch room for his long legs. Someone had left two candy wrappers on the seat and an open soda can in the drink holder. An apple core lay on the floor.

"Sorry it's a mess back there," said Krista. "I have two boys."

"No problem. I have grown sons myself, so I've been there. How old are your kids?"

"Twelve and fourteen." Krista laughed nervously. "I'm a single mom; it's nonstop action."

As they retraced the route Mitch and Bill had taken earlier, Krista chatted about her kids' activities—sports, fishing, video games, but no girlfriends yet, thank goodness. At one point, she complained about a lack of support from her ex-husband.

Mitch shook his head, then gazed out the passenger side window.

"What?" said Krista.

"Nothing," said Mitch.

"Mitch knows what a disappointment Tyler turned out to be. They're third cousins or something."

"Leave me out of this," said Mitch.

After she turned onto the parkway, Krista caught Bill's eye in the rearview mirror and said, "Word has it you're skeptical of the thru-hiker theory."

Bill cleared his throat. "A bit, yes."

Mitch turned around in his seat to look at Bill. "You must agree that all arrows are pointing in the direction of Andre Lewis."

"Is that so? Draw the map for me."

"Andre camped out with the other couple, but they went to sleep early, and he got bored. He knew Wintergreen was a few hundred yards away, and he moseyed over to see what was up. He came upon the open garage door at Turner's house and found the keys in the car. Then he figured he'd go for a ride—maybe find a convenience store and buy some beer."

"Why were the keys in the car?"

"It's reasonable to assume that the Turners are elderly. Elderly people are sometimes forgetful."

"What time of night was this?" said Bill. "Two a.m.? Stores don't sell beer that late."

"Candy, snacks, whatever. Stay with me. Andre got on the road, and the unthinkable happened when he ran into Lou Thorpe. He was scared. He panicked, ditched the car at the picnic area, and hoofed it back to the campsite."

"How did he know about the picnic area?" said Bill.

"He found it on his GPS."

"Don't forget his feet. Andre's shoe size is too big to fit the print."

"We still don't know if the shoeprint is from the driver," said Mitch. "Two of the bystanders have yet to be identified."

"Hmm," said Bill, as if he were mulling over Mitch's scenario. He didn't want to get into the details of why he considered it implausible. Mitch had concluded Andre was guilty and then arranged the facts to fit that conclusion. The notion that Andre had stumbled across the open garage door and found keys inside the SUV struck Bill as extremely unlikely. And the driver had so cleverly gotten around the post and hidden the Honda behind the boulder. Could Andre have cleared those hurdles so cleanly in the middle of the night? Possibly. But again, unlikely. For the first time, Bill entertained the notion that the hit-and-run might not have been an accident at all. If so, now that they had the car, they would surely find the driver soon.

"I agree with Mitch," said Krista. "I haven't met Andre, of course, but Wintergreen is a quiet place. I can't imagine anyone up here driving like a maniac in the early hours of the morning."

Still twisted in his seat, Mitch smiled wryly at Bill. "You don't believe the thru-hiker theory."

"Let's get more facts."

"Tell me the truth," said Mitch. "What would you say is the probability that the driver was a thru-hiker?"

"Less than ten percent," said Bill.

"Okay. Let's make a bet. You give me ten to one odds."

"I don't want to take your money, Mitch."

"We'll make it low stakes, at least for me. I'll bet five dollars. If the driver turns out to be a thru-hiker, you owe me fifty bucks."

Krista bounced in her seat. "Oh, I want some of that. Put me down for five too."

Bill took a deep breath. It was only ten dollars. They could afford that easily, and perhaps the loss would teach them a lesson on the importance of using logic to solve a crime.

"Okay. You're on."

SEVENTEEN

Krista and Bill discussed her next steps on the short drive along the parkway to the Humpback Rocks Picnic Area. Wintergreen maintained a directory of all owners on the mountain. Krista would consult the directory, call the house owner, and report her findings back to Bill and Mitch. At the picnic area, Mitch and Bill got out, and Krista gave them a cheerful wave before driving off.

"Krista seems excited to be working on the investigation," said Bill. "I guess it's a big deal compared to the daily grind."

"She's excited about *something*," said Mitch. One side of his mouth turned up.

"What that's smirk about?"

"Let's put it this way: she didn't apologize for her kids' trash when *I* sat in the back seat."

"What do you mean by that?"

"You're the detective. Figure it out."

Mitch lumbered ahead of Bill.

Bill reflected on the smile Krista had flashed a moment earlier. She had smiled at both of them, right? Yes. Certainly. Krista was a woman in her prime with a pretty face and an enticing figure. What would she need with an old guy like him? No, Mitch had misread her.

∽

The locksmith had already opened the SUV and gone, and the same state police forensics analyst who had worked the original crime scene was now examining the vehicle. She stood hunched under the open hatch to take photos of the cargo area. When she heard Bill and Mitch tromping through the leaves, she came over to introduce herself. Her last name was Stowers, and she was a small woman, thin, and not much over five feet tall. She spoke in a low booming voice that surprised Bill.

"Anything you can tell us so far?" said Mitch.

"Yeah, a few things. First, it's a 2015 Honda Pilot, gold, EX model. The front end is dented, obviously. There is a trace of mud on the floor liner that appears similar to that of the accident scene. No visual shoeprints in the car or the ground between here and the road. Two other things of note: remote controls for two different garage door openers are mounted on the passenger side visor. Also, I found three pairs of men's casual shoes in the cargo area, two pairs of loafers, and one pair of lace-up suede shoes. Two pairs of the shoes appear to be the same size, but the third pair is clearly larger."

"Can you tell if any of the shoe sizes match that of the crime scene shoeprint?" said Bill.

Stowers shook her head. "No, that will take some time. I can let you look in through the doors, but don't touch anything. I still need to do the fingerprint work."

Bill and Mitch inspected the interior from the outside but noticed nothing new. Back in the squad car, neither spoke until Mitch had driven back through the picnic area to the parkway. Then Mitch said, "A lot of residents up here have another home somewhere, so the second remote control makes sense. What do you think about the casual shoes in the cargo area?"

"I don't know. I can see one pair of shoes, perhaps, but three? That's odd."

"And they're not all the same size."

Bill's cell phone rang. It was Krista, and he put her on speaker so Mitch could listen.

"Okay," she said. "I called the local number for the Turners and got an answering machine—no surprise there. But the directory listed a second address and phone number for a residence in Florida. I called that number and reached Lindsey Turner, Joel's wife."

"She's in Florida?" said Bill.

"Yes. Ponte Vedra, near Jacksonville. She was in a hurry, and we only spoke for a minute. But here's the thing. According to Lindsey, they haven't been up here in nearly two years."

Bill and Mitch regarded each other. Mitch's eyebrows squished together.

"Apparently, Joel has Alzheimer's disease," said Krista. "They've known it was coming for years, but it got much worse last year. He's in a memory unit now. That's why Lindsey was in such a rush; she had an appointment at his facility."

Bill stared at the parkway ahead of them.

"What should I do next?" said Krista.

"Just a minute," said Bill.

The Turners had left their Honda in Wintergreen, probably intending to come back, but then Joel got worse. Assuming Lindsey Turner had told Krista the truth, someone else had run into Lou Thorpe with the Honda, someone who had access to the vehicle, perhaps their grown children or a friend.

"Call her back," said Bill. "Keep calling until you get her and then set an appointment, hopefully today, when she has more time to talk. We have questions."

EIGHTEEN

Bill, Mitch, and Krista sat around the table in the small white conference room at the police station and planned for the follow-up call with Lindsey Turner. Krista's laptop was open and ready on the table. Mitch had his smartphone. Bill would lead the discussion, and the others would take notes. Toward the end of the call, they would put Lindsey on hold to discuss whether they had missed anything.

Bill fidgeted with a half-full Diet Coke can on the table. After three days of near-zero progress, things would happen quickly now that they had the car. Forensics data would tell them more about what happened that night. Lindsey Turner would tell them something that led to someone else. They would interview that person, and he or she would give them more information. They would keep following the trail until the mystery unraveled, and they found the driver. Or maybe not. Sometimes a new piece of evidence breathed life into an investigation only for the team to see forward progress fall off again, until the case lingered on life support and eventually entered a coma in the cold-case file.

At one minute past the hour, Bill nodded at Krista to dial

the call from the conference phone. Lindsey Turner answered immediately and spoke in a clear, crisp voice. Bill thanked her for taking time to talk with them, made quick introductions, and explained they were investigating a hit-and-run accident. Lindsey knew of the accident and that Lou Thorpe had been killed—she had heard about it from a friend. How horrible.

"Do you own a 2015 Honda Pilot with a Virginia license plate number of DS7-439?" asked Bill.

"I . . . I can't remember the number," she said with hesitation creeping into her voice, "but we do own a Honda Pilot. We keep it at our home in Wintergreen."

Krista sat straight with her eyes glued to the conference phone. Mitch leaned back in his chair and stared at a corner of the ceiling.

"Unfortunately," said Bill, "I must tell you we believe your Honda is the vehicle that struck and killed Mr. Thorpe."

Lindsey Turner gasped and then said, "For heaven's sake, that can't be! Our Honda is locked in the garage."

Bill gave her some time to process the information.

"Are you saying someone stole our car and ran over Lou Thorpe?"

Bill rolled his neck. His stomach felt tight. "We don't know what happened, Mrs. Turner. Maybe you can help us sort it out. First, let me confirm that you and your husband have not visited Wintergreen in some time."

"That's right. I told Krista earlier. Our last trip up was in November of two years ago."

"Do you know if someone may have visited your home and used the Honda? Friends? Family?"

"No. My daughter and her family came to ski last winter. They usually visit in the summer as well but haven't been able to get there this year."

"What about renters? Have you listed your home in the Wintergreen resort program or Airbnb? Anything like that?"

"No. No. We never wanted to do that. I don't like the idea of strangers using my home."

Darn. Just as Mitch and Krista clung to the thru-hiker theory, Bill had his own hunch—that a renter had gotten drunk and taken the SUV for a ride.

Mitch typed on the keys of his phone. He showed what he had written to Bill and Krista.

Did they keep a spare key in the garage or somewhere else on the property?

Bill dipped his head to Mitch.

"Mrs. Turner," Bill said. "Could anyone else have gotten access to the car? Maybe you left a spare key somewhere on the property that someone found. Or perhaps you gave a key to someone you know up here in Wintergreen."

"I don't think so. No, my daughter doesn't have a key. They use their own car when they come up. But wait . . ."

Bill's hands tingled, and his heartbeat raced ahead. They were close to finding the driver. In a moment, Mrs. Turner would give them a vital clue. He wiped his palms on his khakis. Mitch licked his lips. Krista's fingers tapped lightly on the table.

"Joel was concerned about the car sitting idle for so long. He said long-term storage had its own set of problems—mice would nest in the engine and chew the wiring. The battery would run down, tires go flat, that kind of thing. So he gave a spare key to someone, but I can't for the life of me remember who."

Krista clenched her fist. Mitch's eyes bulged, and he covered them with his hand.

"Did you have any particular friends in Wintergreen?" said Bill. "Perhaps he left a key with one of them."

"But we have gobs of friends in Wintergreen. We've had the home for thirty years, and we were active in the community. We have a resort membership, and during the summer, we ate at the club two or three nights a week. I played tennis. Joel played golf. We both loved to hike, and we volunteered at the Nature Foundation."

Mrs. Turner paused and then named another activity. Her voice grew strained.

"Okay," said Bill. "We'll sort it out. Let me ask you a different question. Were you close friends with Lou Thorpe?"

The phone was silent, as if Mrs. Turner was considering the question, but then the silence grew longer. Had they lost the connection?

"Mrs. Turner?" said Bill.

"Yes, I'm here. In all honesty, I would say that *we* were not particularly good friends with Lou Thorpe. Joel played golf in a foursome with Lou for years; they were definitely friends. But we were never social friends with the Thorpes."

Bill detected a trace of distaste in Mrs. Turner's voice.

"Was there any particular reason you didn't socialize with them?" asked Bill.

"Frankly, I never much cared for Lou. Jeanne was nice. I played tennis with her regularly, but Lou made me uncomfortable. He always stood too close, invading my personal space. And he would touch me on the arm all the time. I didn't like it, and whenever he came around, I stood close to Joel."

Krista scowled and instinctively drew away from the speaker.

Bill wasn't sure where to take the conversation next, so he put Mrs. Turner on hold.

"Eww," said Krista, "Lou Thorpe sounds like a creep."

"Noted," said Bill. "What else should we ask Lindsey Turner?"

Neither Mitch nor Krista had additional questions. Krista came up with the idea of going through the Wintergreen directory with Mrs. Turner. Perhaps seeing the names would help her remember the person that her husband had given the spare key.

"That's a great idea," said Bill. "Make a list of anyone she considers a candidate, and we'll follow up."

They brought Mrs. Turner back on the phone to go through the directory search plan. She looked forward to working on that puzzle with Krista. Bill thanked her again for her time, and they ended the call.

"Krista," said Bill, "can you find an image of a similar Honda Pilot on the Internet?"

"Yes, I've done that already. Here, check it out." She turned her laptop around.

"That's the one," said Mitch.

Krista said, "I'll send it to both of you, so you have it on your phones. Also, I can print high-resolution copies."

They discussed sending an email with the image of the Honda out to the Wintergreen online distribution channels. The email would ask anyone who had seen the vehicle on the mountain in the last few weeks to contact Krista. They would undoubtedly get some false leads but might learn something useful.

"I'm on it," said Krista.

Mitch shook his head. "That was a frustrating call. I believed for a minute that she was going to give us the name of the driver."

"Yeah," said Bill. "So did I. But consider how far we've come in a single day. We have a lot to follow up on."

They broke up their meeting, and the three of them went

to give Alex Sharp an update. Bill said that as a next step, he wanted to meet with Mrs. Thorpe.

"Why do you want to speak with Jeanne?" said Alex from behind his desk.

Bill and Mitch sat in the two chairs in front of Alex's desk. Krista leaned against the doorjamb.

Bill made a steeple with his hands and said, "We now know the owner of the vehicle knew Lou Thorpe. There is a connection, and that puts the investigation in an entirely different light."

Alex wore a plaid shirt with a buttoned-down collar. His brow slowly furrowed. "You don't mean—you think this is murder?"

"We don't know for sure, but if the owner of the vehicle knew Thorpe, there's a distinct possibility that the driver knew Thorpe." Bill pointed the steeple at Alex. "*And* that he or she meant to kill Thorpe."

Alex lowered his head, and his shoulders slumped. "I like the thru-hiker theory a lot better."

Mitch chimed in. "Me, too, Chief. And I still think that's where we'll end up. But Bill's right. We have to check out all the possibilities. If we don't do it, Nelson County surely will."

This reality slowly dawned on Alex, and he gave them a quick nod. "Bill, you have to go easy on her. No rough talk."

"Of course."

"The police up here have a good working relationship with the residents. We can't do anything to upset that balance."

"I understand. Kid gloves all the way."

Alex grimaced. "Can you imagine losing your spouse like that? Marilyn Bishop called me this morning. You met her husband Victor at the memorial service."

Bill remembered the angry man in the parking lot—he had pressed Bill about why they hadn't kept Andre Lewis in custody.

Alex said, "Apparently, Jeanne's kids have gone back home, so some of her friends have set up a rotation to make sure she spends as little time alone as possible. One of them will likely be there when you visit."

"That's fine," said Bill.

"I'll call Jeanne to warn her you're coming," said Alex. "When do you want to see her?"

"Right now, if we can."

NINETEEN

At the bottom of Hemlock Drive, Mitch parked in the spacious driveway of a two-story house. Hemlock Drive stemmed off from Devils Knob Loop, which ran a three-quarter circle around the mountain's summit. Standing next to the squad car, it occurred to Bill that the overlook he had hiked to a few days earlier was through the woods behind the house.

Barbara Capaldi greeted them at the door. She was a tall, statuesque woman with stylish gray hair. Bill had met her husband, Marty, at the memorial service. Dressed in dark pants and a red sweater, Barbara's age—which Bill guessed at early seventies—had done little to taint her physical beauty. She led them into a large living room covered on one side with windows, and he paused a moment to take in the stunning view of neighboring mountains and the Shenandoah Valley.

This was the house—Bill reminded himself—where Cindy had catered dinner parties until Lou Thorpe made his inappropriate physical overture. Bill glanced over his shoulder at the kitchen area with its marble counters and white cabinets. Cindy had rebuffed Thorpe there.

Jeanne Thorpe stood in front of an armchair dressed in jeans and a long-sleeved navy shirt. She stepped forward spritely to shake Bill's and Mitch's hands, asked them to take the sectional, and then returned to sit in the chair. Barbara sat in a matching chair that faced the sectional.

Bill extended their condolences for her loss, and Jeanne showed her appreciation with a half smile.

"I miss Lou terribly," she said, "but more so in the evenings. He played golf constantly, so I've been a daytime widow for years."

Jeanne chuckled. Barbara laughed lightly, and Bill realized this was Jeanne's attempt at humor. Visibly, Jeanne displayed no signs of grief. In fact, she seemed rested and relaxed, as if she had recently returned from a stay at a spa. The observation struck Bill as odd, and he recalled that Cindy had formed a similar impression at the memorial service.

"Alex tells me the investigation has reached a point where you'd like to speak with me," she said. "How can I help?"

From her accent, Bill knew Jeanne had spent her formative years in the Carolinas, probably North Carolina, perhaps the state's eastern region. She had a tendency to drop *r* sounds when they came after vowels. Charlotte became Chalotte.

"We've located the vehicle involved in the accident," said Bill. From a manila folder he carried, Bill pulled two copies of the large prints Krista had made and gave one to each of the women. "This is not the actual vehicle, but it is the same color and model, a gold Honda Pilot. Do you recognize the vehicle? Perhaps you've seen it here on the mountain."

Jeanne frowned with concentration. "It seems familiar

somehow, but I can't place it. Honda Pilots are a common model, aren't they? Maybe I've just seen them on the road."

Barbara Capaldi pointed at her copy. "You know, Jeanne, I think this is the car the Turners drove when they were here. I remember seeing Lindsey get out of the car at the tennis courts. Of course, they haven't come to Wintergreen for two or three years. Joel has Alzheimer's."

Jeanne shook her head to convey she did not share Barbara's recollection.

Barbara's finger tapped the print. "Yes, they owned a Honda Pilot. I remember because Marty and I rode down the mountain with them to go to dinner at Basic Necessities. I was scared for my life. Joel was a frightful driver."

"As a matter of fact," said Bill, "it was the Turners' Honda that struck your husband, Mrs. Thorpe."

Jeanne gasped, and her hand flew to her chest. "Good Lord. The Turners' Honda?"

"Yes, ma'am."

Barbara's brow wrinkled, and her eyes darted from Bill to Jeanne.

"But how can that be?" said Jeanne in a shaky voice. "As Barbara mentioned, the Turners aren't here this summer. They weren't here last summer either."

"That's right," said Bill. "We spoke with Lindsey Turner. She mentioned that her husband Joel left a spare key to the Honda with someone. Do either of you know who that might be?"

Both women shook their heads.

"They had a lot of friends," said Barbara. "It could be any of many men. Marty played golf with Joel. So did Lou, for that matter."

Bill assured the women that he had not expected them to know who possessed the spare key. From here on, the interview would take a different tack. Now that the prospect of murder had surfaced, he had to consider motive. But he'd like to get more background information before Jeanne and Barbara realized his true purpose for the meeting.

"Your husbands worked together, didn't they?" he said in as innocent a voice as he could manage. "That's how you know each other, isn't it?"

Jeanne relaxed her shoulders at the change in subject. "Yes, Lou worked as a coal industry lobbyist for many years. Marty was COO for Appalachian Energy. We lived in Northern Virginia, and Marty came to DC often." Jeanne looked at Barbara. "When did *we* first meet? I can't even remember."

"It was at a dinner party you threw at your home in McLean. Gosh, that was a long time ago. But we didn't become friends until we all bought homes here in Wintergreen."

Bill cleared his throat. "This next question may sound a little strange, but we have to consider all of the possibilities. The owner of the vehicle, Mr. Turner, knew your husband, so it's possible that whoever has the spare key also knows your husband."

Jeanne's eyebrows drew together, and she pulled on her ear. "What's the question?"

"Did your husband have an argument with anyone recently?"

"Argument?" said Jeanne.

Barbara's eyes widened.

"Can you think of anyone who might have wished him harm?" said Bill.

Jeanne drew back in the chair. "You believe Lou was murdered?"

Bill leaned closer and put up a hand. "We don't know anything yet. But we have to consider the possibility."

Barbara sat still with her hands in her lap. Her lips formed a flat line. Did she know something? Was she aware of a conflict? Bill made a mental note to interview her separately.

Jeanne's posture stiffened, and her expression turned sour. "Years ago, I would say Lou definitely had enemies. When he was still working, environmental protestors would gather outside our house on special occasions. Earth Day. That kind of thing. Lou used to say, 'Yeah, they'll carry a sign now, but when they get home, they won't complain that the light goes on at the flip of a switch.'"

"Did he hear from any environmentalists recently?" said Bill.

"No. He's been out of it for a while now."

Barbara shifted her weight in the chair. Bill definitely needed to talk to her.

"If it was murder," said Bill, "it's unlikely to have been an environmental activist. I'm thinking closer to home. Did he ever argue with someone here in Wintergreen?"

"No," said Jeanne with emphasis. "Lou was the life of the party. Everyone loved Lou."

Bill nodded to show his understanding. Time to switch angles, explore the field of opportunity.

"The medical examiner estimates the driver struck your husband between two and five o'clock in the morning. Did he often leave the house at that time?"

"*I* can answer that question," said Barbara. "Lou took the same route every morning, three miles down to the Mountain Inn and back." She lowered her voice. "He bragged about his exercise routine to everyone. I heard the story a dozen times, at least. He walked very early because he suffered from insomnia. Right, Jeanne?"

"Terrible insomnia. I told him to cut back on animal protein. Not that he listened to my advice."

Jeanne's last sentence indicated frustration at her husband's lack of deference to her counsel. Bill made another mental note.

He asked more questions around motive and opportunity but didn't learn anything new, so he turned it over to Mitch. Mitch asked Jeanne if she'd heard her husband leave the morning he was killed. No, she was a sound sleeper and had rarely noticed when Lou left the bed.

Outside, Bill paused at the squad car. Hemlock Drive dead-ended in a cul-de-sac, and the Thorpe home was the next to the last on the downhill side of the street. A trail marker with yellow letters stood at the opposite end of the cul-de-sac.

"Where does that trail go?" said Bill.

"Down to the Old Appalachian Trail. We talked about it the first day. Remember?"

"Yeah." Bill rubbed his chin. "So, if someone wanted to, they could hike all the way from where the Honda was stashed to here without ever leaving the forest."

Mitch turned his gaze northeast. "Uh-huh. They'd have to cross Laurel Springs Drive twice, but otherwise, they'd be in the woods the whole time."

"How far is that?"

"Let's see—four miles or so. You're not thinking Mrs. Thorpe did it? Killed her husband that way?"

"No, I'm gathering facts, but for the sake of discussion, could she manage that hike?"

Mitch's brow wrinkled. "I doubt it. In the daytime, maybe, but in the middle of the night? With the rocks and the ups and downs? That's not easy."

Bill disagreed with Mitch's assessment, but he kept quiet.

In his time as a detective, he had seen people accomplish incredible feats under stress. Jeanne and Barbara were both in good shape for septuagenarians. He had no doubt they could hike that distance and longer in the middle of the night.

According to Cindy, Lou Thorpe was a lecher. He may have cheated on Jeanne many times. Perhaps she'd finally had enough. Maybe Joel Turner had given Lou the spare key. If so, Jeanne might have known about it and used the Pilot to run her husband over.

It was late in the day. Mitch dropped Bill at his condo, and they agreed to meet the following day. Cindy Quintrell had told Bill that she had another catering event to work. With nothing exciting on the calendar, Bill made himself a simple dinner, read a book for an hour, and went to bed early. But he lay awake awhile pondering his conversation with Jeanne Thorpe and Barbara Capaldi. There was definitely more to their stories.

TWENTY

At eight o'clock the next morning, Mitch collected Bill at his condo, and they drove directly to the police station. Another patrol officer, John Hill, had been working the crime scene bystander list to determine whether the shoeprint belonged to the hit-and-run driver. Hill wanted Mitch to go over his work and brainstorm next steps. At the same time, Krista Jackson had received some tips from the blast email asking for Honda Pilot sightings. Bill and Mitch split up, Mitch working with Hill and Bill working with Krista.

Bill approached Krista's cubicle. With her red hair pulled back in a bun that revealed her long neck, Krista concentrated on her monitor. Bill stood to one side and watched her work. She clicked through email screens at a rapid pace, unaware of his presence.

"Morning, Krista," he said.

Startled, she jumped up, turned to face him, and spoke in a rushed voice. "Hi, Bill. I was just going through the tips that came through. Nothing too exciting. Can I get you coffee?"

She wore a trace of makeup that enhanced her beauty. Standing a few feet away, Bill noticed that something about her face reminded him of his ex-wife. It was her strong chin and full lips. This realization distracted him for an instant. He used to tell his wife she had irresistibly kissable lips.

"Uh, no," he said. "I'll get the coffee. You want some?"

"No, thanks. I've had plenty."

A few minutes later, Bill rolled an office chair next to Krista's desk and examined her monitor.

She pointed at the screen. "So this woman says a gold Honda Pilot cut her off in traffic a month ago, but that was in Lynchburg."

"Next," said Bill.

Krista chuckled. "You'll love this one. The dude says a blue Pilot almost ran over his dog last week on Shamokin Springs Trail."

"Blue? Next."

Krista's eyes twinkled. "Gosh, you're hard to please." She cocked an eyebrow. "Wait, this one is special." She searched her list of emails. "This man lives in the Ledges and says the renters in the next unit threw a big party last weekend that kept him up all night."

"Okay, how is that relevant?"

"The group was on leave from Langley Air Force Base. Get this—they were a bunch of pilots."

Bill snorted. "A bunch of pilots?"

Krista's shoulders shook as she laughed. "Some days, this job is the best."

Once Bill caught his breath, he said, "Are they all like this?"

She turned more serious. "There is one that seems relevant but not necessarily helpful. A woman saw a gold SUV on

Wintergreen Drive last Friday, but she's unsure whether it was a Honda Pilot. She was driving down from Devils Knob, and the vehicle turned from Blue Ridge Drive onto Wintergreen a little ahead of her. She then followed the SUV down to the yield sign below the Mountain Inn. At that point, the SUV turned left toward the Market, and she continued down the mountain."

"That's it?"

"Yep. She didn't see it again after that point."

Bill sat back and rubbed his chin. The route from the Turners' house down the mountain went via Blue Ridge Drive to Wintergreen Drive. Krista was right—while intriguing, the tip on its own gave them no next steps. Bill noticed Krista had framed photos of two children on her desk. They were middle-school-aged boys dressed in soiled football uniforms.

"Are those your kids?" he asked.

"Yes." She turned and touched the frame of the nearest boy. "They're a mess in these photos, but I like the images anyway. They're not staged."

"My boys played football too," said Bill.

For a moment, both of them smiled quietly at each other. Bill fondly recalled the days of rushing from the job to catch a practice or a game. He and Wanda were still going strong. His boys' middle-school years might have been the best years of his life.

"Any good tips?" said Mitch, walking up behind them.

Bill's head turned quickly, and his brain shifted gears. "Not really. One sighting seems legit but nothing for us to look into. What about the shoeprint follow-up?"

Mitch shook his head. "We're at a dead stop. Hunt has tracked down the bystanders who were men; none of them wore Nike running shoes at the crime scene. However, several of them recall another man at the scene we cannot identify. And we have no way of tracking him down."

"That's not perfect," said Bill. "But it's not a total loss. We have a fifty-fifty chance it is our guy's shoeprint. That could still prove to be useful."

"What's our next move?" said Mitch.

"I'm not sure. Let's think for a minute."

Bill recalled the feeling he'd had about Barbara Capaldi the previous day. She'd reacted strangely when he asked Jeanne Thorpe if anyone had wished her husband harm. He wanted to talk with Barbara but needed to discuss it with Alex first.

"Wait. Hold on," said Krista. "Here's a new email. The subject line reads: I've seen the gold Honda Pilot."

She clicked on the email, and the three of them read it in silence.

Dear *Wintergreen Police,*
A gold Honda Pilot drives up to my neighbor's house three times every week.

The tipster's name was Robert Fields, and he left his contact information.

"Where's that address?" said Bill.

Mitch said, "It's a small development off Blackrock Drive behind the Market."

"Let's go see him," said Bill.

TWENTY-ONE

Mitch drove the cruiser up the mountain and took a right past the Market on Blackrock Drive. Down a side street on the left were a dozen cottages tucked into the woods. The homes had grand views of a ski run and a ridgeline to the north.

Krista had called Robert Fields to let him know they were coming. Mitch parked in the short driveway, and they approached the entrance, but as Bill reached to ring the bell, Fields opened the door.

"You boys didn't waste any time," he said.

Fields was in his late eighties, his face covered with wrinkles. He wore a short-sleeved shirt, and his skinny arms were browned by the sun and dotted with age spots. Though he walked with a cane and his shoulders were permanently hunched, the eyes behind his glasses were keen with energy.

After quick introductions, Fields said, "Come on in, y'all." He turned and shuffled toward the living room. On the way, he gestured to the small kitchen on the left. "There's still coffee in the thermos if you want some. I'll meet you on the balcony and tell you all about your Honda Pilot."

Mitch and Bill both got cups of coffee and joined Fields outside. He sat at a round wooden table shaded by a massive umbrella. Bill strolled to the edge of the balcony. The forested hillside fell steeply away and then leveled out to become a cleared ski run. The hillside to the left angled out so that Bill could see the driveway and right side of the next home.

"Look at that," said Fields, pointing to the air above the ski run. He grabbed a set of binoculars from the table. "It's a red-tailed hawk."

A broad-winged bird floated high in the air, and Bill wondered how Fields had known it was a hawk. He must spend more time with his *Birds of Virginia Field Guide*.

"I sit out here all day," said Robert, "unless there's a game on worth watching. I see all kinds of wildlife. At dusk, the deer come out of the woods to nibble grass on the ski run. I've counted a dozen at a time. And occasionally, a black bear comes out of those woods and climbs the mountain searching for food."

"No kidding," said Mitch.

"Sure enough. They sniff around the dumpsters, you know, to see if anyone's been stupid enough to leave one unlocked."

Still self-conscious about his own encounter with a black bear, Bill didn't mention it to the others.

"Do you live here by yourself, Mr. Fields?" said Mitch.

"Uh-huh. Yeah. My wife died twelve years ago. I sold the home in Richmond to move up here. I like it in the mountains, but my kids give me a hard time. They want me to move back. 'It's too cold in the winter,' they say. They're probably right."

Like other people who lived on their own, Robert Fields tended to give long answers to short questions. Generally speaking, Bill welcomed long answers that provided lots of information, but they needed to move the conversation into relevant territory.

"Mr. Fields," he said, "you mentioned in your email that you've seen a gold Honda Pilot."

Fields nodded fiercely. "Yep." He leaned forward and turned toward the small house to the left. "Every Monday, Wednesday, and Friday, a gold Honda Pilot drives into the garage over there. I never see the driver. They enter the driveway, the garage door opens, and the Pilot cruises in. Then the door comes down. Two to three hours later, the door goes up, and the Pilot leaves."

Bill rubbed his eyebrow, not sure he understood Robert Fields. "Are you saying the owner drives a Honda Pilot?"

"No, she drives a BMW. You can see it from the corner of my balcony."

Bill strode to where Fields pointed and looked back. Sure enough, a white BMW was parked in a side space off the main the driveway.

"And you never see the driver?" said Mitch.

Fields shook his head. "No. It's not like I'm a Peeping Tom or anything, but most of the time, she keeps the shades on her big side window open. I could see into her living room if I wanted to. See? They're open now. But every Monday, Wednesday, and Friday morning, she closes those shades."

The picture window Fields referenced afforded a clear view into the neighbor's home. Bill saw a sitting area with a couch and a side table.

"What time of day does the Honda come?" said Bill.

"It comes about eleven and then leaves between one o'clock and one thirty."

"Every Monday, Wednesday, and Friday?" said Mitch.

"Uh-huh."

"How long has this been going on?" said Bill.

"All summer," said Fields. "Last summer too. I first noticed it in the middle of May last year. But in October, the Honda stopped coming. Which makes sense, I guess, because the woman that lives there leaves for the winter. I don't know where she goes, but she doesn't stay here. About the middle of May this year, the woman came back, and the Honda started visiting again."

"Have you met your neighbor?" said Bill.

"No, she keeps to herself. I've seen her walk to her car." Robert's face brightened, and his hands rubbed together. "She's an attractive woman. I can tell you that."

They asked a few more questions, but Robert had already told them what he knew. Bill thanked him for his time, and they left.

The woman's house was less than a hundred feet away, so they didn't bother moving the car. Bill and Mitch stepped quickly through the fallen leaves that separated the two lots. Bill's heart rate picked up speed. This had to be Turner's Honda. Didn't it? The woman would tell them who came to visit, and they would have their hit-and-run driver.

Standing at the door after ringing the bell, Mitch cracked his knuckles. Bill shifted his weight from one foot to the other. After an interminably long wait, a tall woman opened the door. In black yoga pants and a white workout shirt, she breathed heavily, as if she'd been exercising. Fields had called her a young woman, but with no makeup and crow's feet around her eyes, Bill guessed her age at mid-forties. At a distance, she might have appeared younger, for she had a trim and strong body.

"Sorry to keep you waiting," she said, pointing a thumb over her shoulder. "I was doing some poses."

"No problem," said Mitch. "I'm Officer Gentry from the

Wintergreen Police, and this is Bill O'Shea. Could we get a few minutes of your time?"

"Sure. I guessed you might come sooner or later. You're investigating Lou Thorpe's death, aren't you?"

"How did you know to expect us?" said Bill.

"Simple. I've been Lou's mistress for over twenty years."

TWENTY-TWO

Her name was Rachel Dunn.

Two or three inches taller than Bill, she led them into the kitchen. The leggings she wore hid little of her figure; with perfect posture and strong hips, thighs, and arms, she matched Bill's mental image of a yoga instructor. Her straight blond hair hung below her shoulders, and she moved with confidence and ease.

"I was just going to make myself a soda and lime. Do you care to join me?"

They both declined. Over the next minute, she made sparkling water using a kitchen appliance, poured the fizzing drink over ice, and squeezed a freshly cut quarter lime into the glass. The resulting drink looked so refreshing that Bill wished he had accepted her invitation. He took a mental note to search for the appliance online.

Ms. Dunn offered them seats on her couch, and she sat in a facing chair with her legs comfortably crossed. She was barefoot, and her toenails were painted a bright red. She regarded each of them in turn and said, "How can I assist your investigation?"

Mitch shifted his weight on the couch.

Bill cleared his throat. "Yes, I guess you can start by describing your relationship with Mr. Thorpe."

"You want all the details?"

"Give us the highlights," said Bill. He glanced over and noticed Mitch's face had turned a light shade of pink.

"We met in Washington when he was still working. I found him charming and attractive. One thing led to another, and at some point, I became his mistress. When he retired ten years ago, he and his wife began spending their summers up here, and I only saw him in the winter. But he missed me, and I missed him, and two years ago, I got this place up here for the summer."

A mistress. It struck Bill as an antiquated term reserved for celebrities and wealthy Europeans. Of course, many people, both men and women, had affairs outside of marriage, but in his many years of policing, he could not recall interviewing a self-proclaimed mistress. He wasn't sure how to begin.

"Um, did you see Mr. Thorpe often here at Wintergreen?"

"Every Wednesday at midday for certain. Then whenever he could get away for a few hours, which was not often. Maybe once a week for an hour or so."

"What about Mondays and Fridays?" asked Bill. "Did Mr. Thorpe visit you on Mondays and Fridays?"

"No. Not often. Only if he could get away."

Bill scratched the back of his neck. Rachel Dunn's statement was out of sync with what Fields had told them. Perhaps Bill had misunderstood. He had brought the folder with copies of the Honda Pilot image, and he showed one to Rachel Dunn.

"Is this the vehicle Mr. Thorpe used when he came to visit?"

"I don't remember seeing that SUV." She said the words with no hesitation. Her eyes were steady.

"You've never seen this SUV?" said Bill, his voice tainted with skepticism.

She gave him a half shrug, never breaking eye contact. "I'm sure I've seen one on the road sometime, but I don't recall a specific instance."

"Ms. Dunn—"

"Please, call me Rachel."

Bill breathed deeply.

Stay calm. There's a simple explanation. Surely.

"All right," he said. "Rachel, we have an eyewitness who saw a vehicle fitting this description drive into your garage at midday on Mondays, Wednesdays, and Fridays."

"Oh," Rachel said. She turned her gaze to the picture window that faced Mr. Fields's home. "The old man next door with the binoculars." She shrugged again. "He keeps tabs on me, but he's harmless. I give him a show sometimes. Put on short shorts and a bikini top. Did he mention that part?"

Mitch pulled on his neck collar. He was no help at all.

"Let's get back to Mr. Thorpe," said Bill. "What time of day did he come on Wednesdays?"

"About eleven in the morning. And he would stay until one o'clock or so."

"But he didn't come in the SUV?"

"Honestly," she said. "I don't know what vehicle Lou drove, or the other two for that matter. Lou asked me to keep my BMW parked in the driveway and to give him my spare garage door opener. He would park in the garage and come in through the door to the hallway. I always kept that door unlocked."

"And you never checked to see what vehicle he drove?"

"No. Why should I? I would wait for him here in the living room or sometimes on the balcony if it was a nice day."

Or in the bedroom, Bill thought. But he wouldn't go there. Not yet. Not unless it somehow pertained to the hit-and-run.

Bill said, "Is it possible that Lou came to visit in the Honda Pilot?"

"Yes."

Bill leaned forward and put his hands on his knees. "You mentioned 'the other two.' I take it that other men came to visit on Mondays and Fridays. As far as you know, they might have come in the same vehicle. Is that correct?"

"I suppose so." For the first time, Rachel Dunn appeared uncomfortable. She placed her drink on a side table, uncrossed her legs, and clamped her knees together. "You want to know the identity of the other two men."

"Very much so," said Bill.

Rachel's brow furrowed as if she were struggling with a difficult decision. Her eyes fell to the image of the SUV she held in her hand, and she said, "This is the vehicle that ran into Lou Thorpe?"

"Yes," said Bill. "Have you not seen the image we emailed to the Wintergreen community?"

"I don't read those emails." She nervously tapped the photo with her index finger. "That's how you found me, through the SUV?"

"Uh-huh," said Bill. "Now about those two other men . . ."

Rachel handed him the image and squared her shoulders. "Very well. Lou came on Wednesdays. Marty Capaldi came on Mondays. Victor Bishop came on Fridays. No one has come since the hit-and-run accident."

Marty Capaldi and Victor Bishop. Bill had met them both at the memorial service when Bishop had given him a hard time. Apparently, by some means, they both had access to Turner's Honda Pilot. Once again, he was not exactly sure how to proceed.

"So these three men are coming to see you every week—Thorpe, Capaldi, and Bishop. I don't suppose you are, ah, mistress to them all."

"No," she snapped, "of course not. The others are just friends. I was only intimate with Lou Thorpe."

Sure, thought Bill. *The others only came for the sparkling water with lime.*

Rachel must have read the skepticism on his face, for she added more explanation. "I suppose Marty and Victor came to visit because I'm a woman, but they didn't come for sex. I gave them something they couldn't get in their married life, a flash of excitement. I'd make them lunch, and we'd sit on the balcony and have a glass of wine. If the sun was out, I might take off my shirt, but what's the harm in that?"

"Without sharing the intimate details," said Bill, "what else can you tell us about the two men and their visits?"

She pushed out her lips as if trying to recollect something of interest, and then her face brightened. "For one thing, they wore similar outfits: khakis and casual shirts. On hot days, they might wear short pants. And they always wore the same pairs of shoes—loafers for Lou and Victor, and lace-up suede shoes for Marty."

Bing. We're rolling now.

Rachel's description matched that of the casual shoes they'd found in the Honda Pilot.

"How long have you known the other two men?" Bill asked.

"I've known Marty a long time, twenty years or so. Back

in DC, he came to dinner parties Lou hosted at high-end restaurants. I met him at one of those parties. I only met Victor last summer. Lou introduced us here in Wintergreen."

"Did any of the men mention conflicts they might be having with one of the other two men?" asked Bill.

She narrowed her eyes. Rachel struck him as intelligent, always trying to sort out the rationale for his questions. She had probably guessed he was now searching for a motive.

"No. Nothing comes to mind."

"You sure?" he asked.

"Yes. I'm sure."

Bill leaned back with his shoulders slumped and his hands on his stomach. He studied Rachel's face. Her story was a lot to take in, and he needed time to process it. She waited patiently for him to ask another question. Several came to mind, but perhaps he should confer with Alex first.

"Okay. Mitch, what did I miss?"

Mitch asked her if she knew of Lou Thorpe's exercise routine. She didn't. Then he asked for her contact information in case they had follow-up questions or needed a formal statement.

Back in the cruiser, Mitch started the engine but left the gear in park. "What was really going on with these men and Rachel Dunn?"

But Bill was distracted by his thoughts. She was definitely lying, certainly about the SUV. No way the men drove a Honda Pilot into her garage for two summers without her seeing it. Why lie about that unless she had a reason? Maybe she not only knew of the Pilot but also had a spare key and a reason to run Lou Thorpe down. Bill finally noticed Mitch was staring at him.

"What?"

Mitch repeated his question.

"I don't know," said Bill. "What do you think was going on?"

"Sex. She was having sex with those men."

"So?"

"Isn't that illegal?"

Bill frowned. Mitch was young and had more to learn about his job. Even so, this question struck Bill as naïve, and as such, deserved a little lecture. "I don't know Virginia law, but I'm sure prostitution is illegal. Nevertheless, we have no evidence that Rachel Dunn is a prostitute. For one thing, according to her, she wasn't having sex with two of the men. Also, prostitutes sell sex for money. We have no evidence that money changed hands. We can also look at it this way: assume Rachel Dunn *was* having sex with all three men. Lou Thorpe was married and had sexual relations with Rachel and perhaps other women. Did that make him a prostitute? No, just a jerk."

Mitch scratched his cheek and studied Bill. "You're right. It was a stupid question."

"Forget it. It's definitely a weird arrangement, and it might tell us something about motive if we can figure it out."

"What do we do now?"

Bill stared through the windshield and then pointed forward with his hand. "Back to the station. I need to talk to Alex."

When Mitch turned onto Wintergreen Drive, his radio came alive. It was Krista.

"Alex wants you to come to the station now. He has new information."

TWENTY-THREE

After having them rush back to the station, Alex kept Bill and Mitch waiting outside his office with the door closed while he finished a phone call. Alex spent most of the call listening, offering a comment now and again in a measured voice. Not being able to hear Alex clearly, Bill reflected on what he'd learned from Rachel Dunn.

Didn't it stand to reason that either Marty Capaldi or Victor Bishop had run over Lou Thorpe? They each had access to the vehicle. Joel Turner must have asked one of them to watch over the Pilot in his absence. As a next step, Bill would move on to motive and opportunity. He must interview the men and their wives, separately if possible. But first, he'd return to Jeanne Thorpe and see how she reacted to her husband having a mistress on the mountain.

The door to Alex's office flung open, and he stepped out. "Good. You're here. Come in."

Alex closed the door behind them and let the drama build as he settled into his desk chair. His eyes locked on Bill. "Forensics came back on the SUV. We've found our driver. It's Andre Lewis."

Bill thrust his head forward, and his eyes widened. Andre Lewis? The thru-hiker kid? He glanced at Mitch.

Mitch observed him through the corner of his eye with a bit of a smirk on his face.

"Don't say it," said Bill.

Alex chuckled. "They found prints all over the car from five or six different people. Of course, some of those are likely old, probably from the Turners. Andre's prints were on the passenger side door and leather seat."

"Wait," said Bill. "The passenger side?"

"Yeah. The way I figure it, Andre came into the garage and approached the parked SUV from the passenger side. He found the door unlocked and the keys lying on the seat or the console. Then he took the Pilot out for a ride and ran into Lou Thorpe."

Bill shook his head. It sounded so improbable.

"Andre has a cool head," said Alex. "I have to give him that. He had the presence of mind to drive the car around and ditch it in the picnic area. Forensics found no prints on the steering wheel, which means Andre remembered to wipe it clean. But in his haste, he neglected to wipe down the passenger side door."

"Where is he now?" said Mitch.

"Nobody knows," said Alex. "Still up on the AT, presumably. They tried his cell phone—no answer."

"I'm not surprised," said Mitch. "He turned it off so no one could trace it."

"Or maybe his battery ran down," said Bill.

"State is working with his mobile service provider to get records," said Alex. "That should tell us where he went and who he called before his phone went dead. In the meantime, the National Park Service is organizing a search on the AT. Mitch, I volunteered you for the search team."

Mitch squared his shoulders. "I'm ready, Chief. I've hiked that section of the AT twice. It's not difficult."

"How far do you think he's gone?" asked Alex.

"Let's see," said Mitch. He turned to Bill. "We dropped him at the Afton Mountain trailhead three days ago. If he's covering ten to fifteen miles a day, that will put him thirty to forty-five miles north of Afton."

"That's a lot of territory," said Alex.

Mitch drummed his fingers against his leg. "We'll find him."

"You better get going," said Alex. "I'll forward the contact info for the team leader."

Mitch left the office, but Bill stayed in his seat.

Alex smoothed his shirtfront and gave Bill a thumbs-up sign. "Thanks a lot for your help. Looks like we're at the end of the chase."

"I want to keep working the investigation here."

Alex narrowed his eyes and pulled his head back. "What for? We got the guy."

"I'm not sure. Let me tell you what we learned this morning."

Bill went through the interviews with Robert Fields and Rachel Dunn. As he listened, Alex pulled a pen from a holder on his desk and clicked it several times. Then he fished a packet of gum from his pocket, unwrapped a piece, and began chewing it violently. Finally, he shook his head.

"No, Bill. A mistress? Clandestine meetings with three men? We don't need that kind of press up here."

"We shouldn't drop the ball on this. Two of Lou's buddies had access to the car that ran him down. We can't ignore that."

Alex sighed heavily. "For heaven's sake, Bill. We've got the guy. Case closed."

"Maybe. Maybe not. There are holes in that scenario. We're a long ways from proving anything. Let me meet with a few more people."

With his jaw set in a hard line, Alex fidgeted in his chair. "This is a community police department. We work for the residents. You know that."

"I'll go easy."

"I have a business to run. If people's feelings get hurt, I lose listings."

"I've done this before, Alex. Down in Columbia, they called me the diplomat."

Alex snorted and said sarcastically, "The diplomat. All right, but proceed with care, please."

"Count on it."

Bill hurried from the chief's office to search for Mitch. Krista told him that Mitch had left a minute ago, and Bill ran to the parking lot. Mitch's squad car was pulling out, and Bill flagged him down.

Mitch lowered his window and said, "What's up?"

Bill breathed deeply to calm his racing heart. "Be careful."

"No sweat. I'll be fine."

Bill squeezed the window frame. "I'm more worried about the kid than you. With a big search like this, everyone gets excited, and it's easy for something to go wrong. Remember, we met this kid. We watched him do his laundry. Andre might be afraid, but he's not armed or dangerous."

Mitch studied Bill. With his mouth closed, he ran his tongue around the outside of his teeth. "Yeah. That's good advice. I'll be careful."

Back in the office, Bill asked Krista to conduct Internet research on Marty Capaldi and Victor Bishop. He wanted to know of anything she found that connected them to Lou Thorpe.

"They've been retired awhile," he said, "so you might not find much."

"I'm on it."

"Oh, one other thing. Could you give me a ride up the mountain? I came in with Mitch today."

"Sure."

On the five-minute ride to Bill's condo, they discussed Krista's kids and the family dogs.

"My ex is a real clown," she said. "Eight years ago, he got us this tiny dog—a Chihuahua—and my ex named him Goliath."

Krista was a born storyteller, but she liked to look her audience in the eye, even while driving, which made Bill nervous. He clung to the door handle and watched the road ahead of them as if he could do the job for her.

"Then two years ago, I got the boys a puppy, a Great Dane. At six weeks, he was twice as big as Goliath. I'm sure you can guess what the boys named him."

"Ah, let's see. David?"

Krista laughed so hard Bill had to join in. With shaking shoulders, she leaned forward and grabbed the steering wheel with both hands. Thank goodness.

"It's hysterical what happens at our place with these dogs. Of course, you know who's the alpha dog, right? The Chihuahua! David is terrified of Goliath! It cracks me up."

Bill burst out laughing, guffaws that filled Krista's SUV. He wiped tears from his eyes.

"The other day, Goliath has a little accident on the kitchen floor. And he's tiny, right? So it's a tiny accident. But Goliath pretends that David caused the accident, as if *I* couldn't tell the difference. David weighs a hundred and sixty pounds, so when he has an accident, it's like a *big* accident."

Bill covered his eyes with a hand.

"Goliath starts barking at David. He glares at the poop and barks some more. David doesn't know what the heck is going on. He's standing there with a blank stare on his face. Then Goliath barks again and starts chasing David around the living room. It's mayhem. David's so big, he's knocking stuff off the coffee table, and Goliath is barking like crazy. Then the boys start yelling, and I don't know what the hell to do."

Krista pulled into Bill's complex with both of them still laughing and parked in the lot next to his building. An image of Krista and her boys and the dogs running around the living room formed in Bill's mind. For some reason, Krista wore athletic tights and a sports top in his imagining. She looked good in the outfit.

"That's funny," he said. Still chuckling, he got out of the car. "Thanks for the ride, Krista."

"Anytime."

Bill took a few steps toward his building and noticed Cindy Quintrell standing under a nearby tree.

"Oh, hey, Cindy. How're you doing?"

Cindy watched Krista's SUV leave the lot with a neutral expression on her face.

Bill gestured toward the SUV. "You know Krista Jackson? She's a communications officer."

"I know her."

"She gave me a ride from the station. Krista was telling me about her kids and their dogs. She's funny."

"I'll bet she is."

"What are you up to?" he said.

Cindy stood with her legs planted wide apart. She seemed a little tense.

"Not much," she said. "Just picked up some groceries. I saw you coming in with Krista and thought I'd say hi."

"Great! I'm glad you did. I'm going to have lunch. Can I make you a sandwich?"

"No, thanks. I've got to work. Just wanted to say hi."

"Okay. Thanks. Maybe I'll see you later?"

"Maybe. It depends on how the afternoon plays out."

Cindy turned and marched toward her building.

What is up with her?

Up until that point, every interaction he'd had with Cindy had gone better than he could have imagined. Now, all of a sudden, the air had turned frosty. Did that have something to do with Krista giving him a ride? At times, women were incomprehensible. He shook his head and walked into his building.

Over a sandwich, his thoughts returned to Andre Lewis hiking on the Appalachian Trail. If the other team members could read a forest like Mitch, they would soon find Andre. Without incident, Bill hoped. Never mind. That part was out of his hands. He must conduct a different kind of search—follow all the leads until he found the truth.

First step: return to the home of Jeanne Thorpe.

TWENTY-FOUR

Standing on the porch of Jeanne Thorpe's home, Bill rang the bell. A moment later, someone moved inside the house, perhaps in the living room. He leaned to peer through the side window but saw no one. Turning his shoulders, he examined the driveway. A Lexus had sat parked outside the garage the previous day. Now that spot was empty. Was the Lexus Barbara Capaldi's car? A full minute later, Jeanne opened the door. She wore white slacks and a royal blue long-sleeved shirt.

"Oh, hello." She read the name card that hung around Bill's neck. "Mr. O'Shea."

"Yes, Mrs. Thorpe."

"You're alone."

"Yes, Officer Gentry was called away. We've discovered some new information. Could I ask you a few more questions?"

"Certainly. Come in."

She offered him a glass of ice water, which he accepted to give them a way to interact before beginning what would likely become an awkward conversation. He complimented her beautiful home and the stunning view from the living room windows.

"Tell me," she said, after they were seated on the same sectional and chair as before. "What is your new information?"

"I'm sorry to say we have learned your husband was having an affair with a woman here in Wintergreen. Apparently, he met her weekly, and they have known each other for a long time."

Jeanne Thorpe sat straight and pulled her hands together in her lap. Her face adopted a stern expression.

"Were you aware that your husband was having this affair?"

"No," she said simply. "But I'm not surprised. Lou was not a faithful man. He had affairs with many women over the years." At this admission, Mrs. Thorpe's composure faltered. Her shoulders sagged, and her chin quivered.

"I'm sorry," said Bill.

A box of tissues sat on the side table. Mrs. Thorpe reached for one and wiped her nose. "It's certainly not your fault." She cleared her throat. "Lord knows why I stayed with him all this time. For the children, I suppose, at least in the early years. And then, I guess I just grew used to it. It was easier to ignore his infidelity than to try living on my own."

Bill tried to imagine Jeanne Thorpe crashing the Pilot into her husband on a dark street. His gut found the notion improbable.

"Do you want to know the one thing that b-bothered me the most?" she said. "Despite his endless cheating, Lou insisted on having sex with me regularly." She shook her head in disbelief. "Why am I telling you this? Might as well tell someone, I suppose. What does it matter anyway? Absurd. His conjugal right, he would say. Every Saturday night, without fail. He called it making love." She looked away from Bill and stared at nothing in particular. "Now I'm left to wonder if he ever loved me at all."

Bill shifted his weight. He pulled the Honda photo from the folder and showed it to Mrs. Thorpe again. "We now know that your husband actually had access to the vehicle that struck and killed him. Do you have any idea how he would have access to Mr. Turner's SUV?"

"No."

Jeanne Thorpe seemed quite confident with her answer. Bill wanted to believe her, but he had known murderers who tolerated infidelity for years. Until the day they snapped.

"As we discussed with Barbara Capaldi yesterday," she said, "it's possible that Joel Turner gave Lou a spare key, but if he did, I never knew of it."

"Okay," said Bill. "I want to discuss something else. It turns out that Marty Capaldi and Victor Bishop also had access to the Honda Pilot."

Jeanne tilted her head. "Marty and Victor?"

"Yes."

Bill gave her a moment to process this new information.

She stared at Bill and said, "Do you believe Marty or Victor killed Lou?"

Bill kneaded the palm of his left hand with his right thumb. "We don't know anything for certain. I'm checking boxes at this point, standard procedure. Did Lou quarrel with one of the other men recently?"

"Not that I know of. They were friends for a long time."

"Nothing unusual going on? Anything your husband might have mentioned?"

"No. Lou didn't say anything to me. It was all good times for him. But . . ."

Bill leaned closer. "Yes?"

"It probably doesn't mean a thing. I'm a little concerned about money. My husband managed all the finances, and he enjoyed spending more than he made. He has a good pension, but it's not enough to cover the parties and the trips and the two houses. Lou always told me not to worry because he had a lot of bonus money saved up. Anyway, I asked my daughter Phoebe to look into it. She's an engineer, so she's good with numbers."

"Okay."

Jeanne clenched her hands into fists. "Phoebe gave me some bad news last night. I'm going to have to sell one of the houses. That's not interesting from your perspective, but Phoebe mentioned two other things I didn't know. First, Lou had a million-dollar life insurance policy. He took it out three years ago, never said a word. Second, he owed Marty Capaldi a great deal of money, five hundred and fifty thousand dollars."

Whoa. What?

Bill always tried to keep a straight face during interviews, but his expression clearly gave away his surprise.

"Yeah," said Jeanne. "That was my reaction. Apparently, Lou borrowed the money from Marty to cover second mortgages. The bank had run out of patience. The insurance policy was collateral for the loan from Marty. Phoebe says I'll get the money from the policy, eventually, but then have to pay more than half of it to Marty."

Bill tried to recall Marty Capaldi's physical appearance. He had met the man at Thorpe's memorial service—tall and big but stooped with age. His hands had trembled.

Jeanne's finger tugged on the corner of her lower lip. "I've never heard Lou and Marty arguing over money, and I'm quite sure it had nothing to do with Lou's death. They were friends."

"You're probably right, but I appreciate you telling me about it. Can you recall anything else out of the ordinary?"

She could not, and Bill took his leave. Outside, he walked a hundred feet to the end of the cul-de-sac and examined the trail marker he'd seen the previous day.

The marker read *OAT 0.1 miles* and was accompanied by a yellow arrow pointing down the hill.

Hmm.

The rocky trail dropped sharply from where he stood and soon disappeared into the woods. Was it reasonable to assume Jeanne Thorpe could hike home from the picnic area in the dark? He had already covered two-thirds of the distance on two different hikes: from the parking lot to the overlook by himself three days earlier and from the picnic area to the little parking lot with Mitch. Bill now resolved to explore the last leg early the next morning.

Jeanne Thorpe had two possible motives for killing her husband. First, rage over his infidelity. She had tolerated his affairs for many years—had Rachel Dunn's presence on the mountain pushed Jeanne too far? The second motive was money. Had she truly known so little about their financial situation? Perhaps she had worried Lou would run through their money and leave her destitute. By killing him now, she could stop the bleeding, pay off Marty, and bank four hundred and fifty thousand dollars from the life insurance. She knew Lou's morning exercise routine. Maybe she knew about the Pilot as well. Or perhaps she had schemed with someone else, her own lover.

Hmm. Jeanne didn't strike Bill as the type.

No, he clearly needed to keep digging. He thought of Mitch hiking on the AT. Maybe the search team would find Andre Lewis soon. Maybe Lewis would confess.

Maybe. Maybe. Maybe.

He definitely wanted to talk with Marty Capaldi. Victor Bishop too, the guy who had given him a hard time at the memorial service. Bill looked forward to asking Victor about his afternoon dalliances with Rachel Dunn. Uh-huh. Detective work had its moments.

But before interviewing either of those two, he'd revisit Ms. Dunn. Without Mitch at his side, they could have a more candid conversation concerning those harmless dates with the married men.

TWENTY-FIVE

Rachel Dunn had bathed and changed. She wore tight jeans and a loose-fitting white shirt that buttoned up the front.

"Back so soon?" she said after opening her front door.

"I have a few more questions. Do you have some time?"

"Where's Deputy Dogood?"

"Very funny. Officer Gentry got called away."

"Sure. Come on in."

She turned on her heel and strode toward the main room, leaving Bill to close the door. He found her already seated with her legs crossed. She didn't offer him a drink this time.

"How can I help?" she asked, snapping out the words as if she wished to move on to more pressing matters.

Bill pulled out the photo of the gold Honda Pilot. "I wanted to ask you about the vehicle again. Are you sure you didn't see Mr. Thorpe or one of the other men driving it into your garage?"

"I already told you I didn't."

"I thought with all of those visits, at some point, you would have noticed the SUV coming into your driveway. Or perhaps you accompanied one of the men into your garage. Maybe to give him a good-bye kiss?"

"I said no." But Rachel Dunn shifted in her chair. Her face appeared flustered. "I didn't see it."

Bill returned the image to the folder and gently set it beside him on the couch. He gritted his teeth. "Listen, Ms. Dunn. I don't want to give you a hard time. I'm not even an official member of the police department. I'm just helping them out. But there's a kid on the Appalachian Trail who's in trouble, and I need to figure out what happened to Lou Thorpe."

As Bill delivered this speech, Rachel's hand raised so she could nibble on a fingernail. But then she hurriedly dropped her hand again.

Bill continued. "Now we both know that money changed hands up here. The word is going to get out. These two men that you gave massages to, or whatever, are well known in Wintergreen. Things could get uncomfortable for you. To be honest, I don't care about any of that, but you need to tell me the truth."

Rachel's elbows pressed against her body. "I was afraid. You're right. I've seen the Honda, you know, here, when the guys came over. But I also got the email the police sent around." Her eyes opened wide. "When I read the email and saw the Honda, I thought, 'Holy crap. One of those guys killed Lou.'"

"Why didn't you call the police?"

"I didn't know what to do. I considered packing a suitcase and driving the hell out of here."

"Did Mr. Capaldi or Mr. Bishop call you?" asked Bill.

"No. Nothing. I've heard nothing from them."

Bill studied her face. Scared but telling the truth now. He put his hands out in an attempt to calm her. "Take a few deep breaths. Let's go through this one step at a time. We don't know who killed Mr. Thorpe. I want you to reflect on the conversations you've had with the men. Did you pick up on any tensions between them?"

Rachel did as Bill asked and began to settle down. She pursed her lips, and her eyes turned upward as if she were trying to recall past conversations.

"Now that I think about it," she said, "I haven't seen Lou together with either of them in a long time. I knew Marty from ages ago. He reached out to me on his own. Lou introduced me to Victor Bishop at a winery, but that was last summer."

"Tell me about the sex," said Bill. "What was going on? Maybe one of the men became jealous at some point?"

She shrugged. "Not much to tell. Marty's getting older. Once a month or so, he'd come in all randy and give it a try. Maybe it would work. Maybe it wouldn't. And Victor Bishop? Nothing with him. I mean nothing. Back rubs and a peep show—that's as far as I ever got with Victor. Those guys weren't in it for the sex. I was telling the truth about that—more than anything, they wanted to enjoy a glass of wine with a younger woman."

"And Lou Thorpe?"

"Oh, no, he was Mr. Eveready. Never missed a week. Lou always wanted sex."

A weird setup, for sure. Bill had never come across anything quite like it. But that's what made detective work interesting—the people side. Humans could find so many ways to get tangled up with lies and deceit.

"Um, can I go off the record on something?" said Rachel. "Something you might find interesting."

"I'm not a journalist. Just tell me."

"Okay. You mentioned the money side of things earlier.

And there was some money. Not a lot, but Lou covered this lease and paid me an allowance. Here's the thing, though. Marty made it clear to me on several occasions that *he,* and not Lou, was underwriting the arrangement."

"But Lou paid you the allowance."

"That's right. Marty led me to believe he was floating Lou for that money and more."

"I see," said Bill.

Marty Capaldi had become the banker for Lou Thorpe's lavish lifestyle, the mistress, the real estate, and the parties. Maybe Marty had grown weary of that role but known Lou would never have the discipline to pay him back. The only way for Marty to get his money was from the life insurance policy. Five hundred and fifty thousand dollars might represent a sizable chunk of Marty's overall net worth. With Lou out of the way, Marty could assume the lead role with Rachel Dunn if he wished. But how did Victor Bishop fit into the picture?

"What should I do?" asked Rachel innocently. "Am I in danger? Should I pack a bag?"

For the first time, Bill fully understood the attraction the older men had felt toward Rachel Dunn. With a perfectly symmetrical face, soft eyes, and a thin nose, she could easily pass for a makeup model, and her body would draw the attention of men half her age. When she wanted to, as she did right now, Rachel could appeal to a man's baser instincts. She was a damsel in distress. He was a big strong man. If he helped her, she would feel an unstated obligation to repay his kindness.

So wandered his cynical mind. On the other hand, she had a point. If Marty had killed Lou to get his money back—an admittedly drastic action, but not unprecedented in Bill's experience—Marty might now be focusing on how to cover his tracks.

"Just to be clear," he said. "Marty Capaldi has not called you. And neither has Victor Bishop."

She shook her head. "Not a peep."

"I think you're fine. And I recommend you stay in the area, but it wouldn't hurt to check into a hotel off the mountain for a few days. Don't tell anyone where you're going. We have your contact information if we need you."

Rachel swallowed hard and bit her lower lip with her front teeth in a way he found enormously attractive. She gave him a quick nod and said, "I'll be gone in fifteen minutes."

TWENTY-SIX

Back at his condo, Bill texted Cindy Quintrell to see if she wanted to join him for dinner. He offered to cook this time, a personal chili recipe, but she didn't reply. She must be busy working. On a whim, he spent ten minutes shopping online for a sparkling water maker. After skimming reviews, he bought one for a little less than two hundred dollars. It was late in the day to track down Marty Capaldi for an interview, and he felt a bit tired, so he sat on his balcony with a glass of water.

Not a single cloud marred the powder blue sky. His ridge's shadow had begun its slow climb up the hill on the valley's other side. A large bird soared above the gorge. Bill got out his binoculars, but the bird was too far away for him to make out distinguishing characteristics.

Bill leaned over his balcony, cast his gaze down to the lawn, and spotted the neighborhood groundhog. The creature stood erect and calmly surveyed his domain. Not a busy animal, this one. He seemed content to observe the world's nature, as might a philosopher or a lifelong academic. Then Bill recalled he had yet to come up with a name for his new furry friend. Hmm. This required careful consideration. Such a task could take weeks. But with a flash of inspiration, Bill knew the answer.

Mr. Chips.

Yes, nothing else would do.

Bill gave the groundhog a wave. "Hello! Hello, Mr. Chips."

The groundhog turned his head, and for a moment, Bill believed he had made a connection with the animal, but then a noisy family with a yard game rounded the building's corner, and Mr. Chips hurried into his burrow.

Bill sipped his water and regarded the mountains to the north. Fifty miles away, the team had begun searching the AT for Andre Lewis. He wondered if they had knocked off for the day. That question prompted him to send Alex Sharp a text. Did Alex want to swap notes on the investigation? Alex asked if he could come to visit Bill in thirty minutes. Sure.

Bill washed his face, tidied up the main living area, and poured some pretzels into a bowl.

"Want a beer?" he said when he opened the door for Alex a short while later.

"Yeah. It's close enough to quitting time."

Bill carried the pretzels out to the balcony and placed the bowl on the drinks table.

Alex took a seat and savored the view. "Darn, this is nice. What price did I get you for this place? Two thirty?"

"Two thirty-five."

"It was a good price. Just wait. I'll bet you could get three hundred in a few years."

"That's great, but I have no plans to sell. Wintergreen agrees with me, except for all the police work."

Alex chuckled. "Oh, bull. You love it."

The chief said that the search team had covered twenty

miles but not found Andre Lewis. They would expand the search area by another twenty miles the next day.

"They'll find him tomorrow," said Alex, "and we'll get this whole thing buttoned up."

"Don't be so sure. I know they'll find Andre, but I doubt he's our driver."

"Hmpf." Alex screwed his lips into a bunch. "You're still holding to that line of thinking. Some might call you stubborn."

"Run the timeline numbers with me, Alex. Assume Andre *was* the driver. After accidentally running over Lou Thorpe, he had to freak out, right? At least for a few minutes. Then he got out his phone and used his GPS to come up with a plan. He drove down the mountain, back up to the parkway, and then over to the picnic area. The planning and driving had to take at least twenty-five minutes. Now he got crazy lucky by finding the boulder to hide the Pilot behind. He painstakingly arranged leaves to hide the Pilot tracks in the dark. That had to take him another twenty minutes. Then he hiked back to the campsite, which took another thirty minutes. Add it up, and I get an hour and twenty minutes, easily, and in the dead of night. The girl at the campsite said Andre had returned by three thirty-seven."

"I'll admit it seems improbable, but the math *does* work. The medical examiner said the time of death was two to five a.m. If the accident happened on the front end of that window, there's enough time."

"Then there's the issue of the key. How did Lewis get a key?"

Alex bit into a pretzel and turned back to the view. "That's easy." After chomping a few times, Alex swallowed. "Whoever got the spare key from Turner was keeping it on the vehicle seat or the workbench for convenience." Alex studied the remainder of his pretzel as if trying to decide whether to talk or eat. "Andre's fingerprints were on the passenger door. That's compelling evidence, right?"

"Yes, it is. But I don't believe we have the full story yet."

The chief asked Bill what he'd learned that afternoon, and Bill related the interviews he'd conducted and the monetary motive for Marty Capaldi.

"How much?" said Alex.

"Over a half million."

Alex whistled. "All right. Talk to Marty and talk to Victor Bishop. But go easy, right? Like we discussed. If Andre Lewis *is* our driver, I don't want to anger a bunch of people for no reason."

Bill reassured Alex that he would be nice.

They sat in the shade of the balcony and enjoyed the view. Before leaving, Alex said, "You might want to go see Kim Wiley at Café Devine first."

"Okay. Why?"

Alex drained his beer. "Kim is a clearinghouse for Wintergreen personal news. Very little goes on up here that Kim doesn't hear about sooner or later."

TWENTY-SEVEN

When Bill's alarm went off at five-forty the next morning, he was already awake, lying in bed, mulling things over.

Why hadn't Cindy returned his text? Was everything okay? Maybe she had reconsidered him as a romantic prospect and found him lacking. It wouldn't be the first time a woman had arrived at that conclusion.

Bill's mind turned to the hit-and-run investigation, and he played a game he called *Get in the Victim's Head*. When Lou Thorpe walked down Wintergreen Drive that morning, as he had so many times, did he worry that he might have overextended his credit at the Bank of Capaldi? Did he wonder, perhaps, whether his years of infidelity had finally pushed Jeanne to her breaking point? Before the Honda even approached, did the hairs on Lou Thorpe's neck stand up, warning him that the good life had run its course? Or did he whistle, oblivious to his pending doom?

Was it an accident or premeditated?

Ten minutes later, Bill drove his car up the far side of Devils Knob Loop and took a right on Cedar Drive. The sun had risen and now cast its light through the forest at a sharp angle. He parked next to a marker for the Old Appalachian Trail and got out of his car.

A tall thin man wearing jeans, a long-sleeved T-shirt, and a gillie hat hiked toward Bill on the road. This did not surprise Bill, for on his early morning exercise routes, he often came across other walkers, elderly for the most part, those for whom sleeping in was easier said than done. The man strode at a good clip, his arms and legs swinging energetically, as if he had little time to waste. At a distance of twenty feet, Bill realized he had met the man at the memorial service for Lou Thorpe. He was one of the trio of friends who had approached Bill after the service. Quieter than the other two, he had stood a little to the side and watched Victor Bishop pressure Bill about the thru-hiker scenario. What was the guy's name?

"Hey," the man said with an easy smile, "I know you. We met at Lou's memorial service. You're helping with the investigation. But I've forgotten your name."

"Bill O'Shea."

"Cyrus Hunt."

The two men shook hands.

Cyrus had wrinkles on his neck and wisps of hair growing from his ears, but his handshake was firm, and his blue eyes were bright and sharp. He had bushy gray eyebrows that matched his well-trimmed mustache. Hunt lived in a cabin farther down Cedar Lane and said he often hiked on the OAT for exercise. He guessed from where Bill had parked that Bill planned to take the OAT as well and suggested they go together.

Ferns and tall weeds encroached on the path, brushing against Bill's jeans, and he surmised that section of the OAT was seldom used. Initially, the trail sloped gently downward, but it soon grew steeper. Loose rocks littered the ground, forcing Bill to carefully watch where he stepped.

Cyrus was either an introvert or as focused on the path as Bill, for he offered little conversation. For his part, Bill wasn't exactly sure how to approach Cyrus. As Cyrus was a golfing partner of the other men, Bill wanted to ask him whether Lou had recently argued with Capaldi or Bishop, but he had promised Alex he'd tread lightly. Bill had no reason to believe Cyrus knew of Rachel Dunn or that whole situation, and he didn't want to be the gossip source that broke the story on the mountain.

"I gather you and the other two guys golfed with Lou Thorpe regularly," said Bill.

"Yep." Cyrus pulled a small branch out of the path and turned to make sure it didn't smack Bill in the face. "We had a foursome, but we haven't played since Lou died. I don't think the other guys are up for it yet. They knew Lou a lot better than me."

Cyrus paused, for they had come to a section of the path that required them to scramble down a narrow crevice in a rock wall. At the bottom of the wall, Bill turned to examine the section he had traversed, at least a twenty-foot drop. He breathed hard from the exertion.

Unfazed, Cyrus continued down the path and picked up where he'd left off. "And we need another golfer to round out the foursome." He stopped, turned to Bill, and said, "Hey, I don't suppose you golf."

"No, I've always wanted to but never got around to it."

Cyrus turned again and kept going. "Never too late to start. The course up here is gorgeous and plays to an old man's game. The fairways are narrow but not too long."

"I'll give it some thought," said Bill. It was all he could

manage to say because the downhill slope had grown even steeper, and he had to plan every step to keep from tripping.

For his part, Cyrus might have been ambling down a flat road. His arms hung loosely at his sides. He wore dirty hiking shoes, and Bill consoled himself with the thought that Cyrus knew the trail because he had hiked it many times.

Mercifully, they soon came to a level section, and Bill noticed a sign marking an intersection with another trail. Yellow lettering indicated that the new path led to Hemlock Drive. It was the other end of the route he'd seen at Jeanne Thorpe's cul-de-sac.

Pointing at the sign, he said, "So that leads up to a street?"

"Yeah, it's a connector. In fact, Lou Thorpe's house is at the end of that street." Cyrus laughed. "I got the bright idea of taking the path to their house for a dinner party once. But after three glasses of wine, I wisely chose to return home via the streets."

Cyrus had not mentioned a wife or a partner, and Bill guessed he lived alone. He spoke in a neutral accent Bill could not place.

"Where are you from, Cyrus?"

"All over." Cyrus continued hiking. "Cliché army brat, that's me. My father dragged us all around the US: Fort Campbell, Fort Riley, Fort Sill, and Camp Mackall. I joined up in sixty-five, did my bit in Vietnam, and stayed in for twenty years. After that, I moved to Tampa and got into the home building business."

Apparently, Cyrus had done well enough in home construction to retire comfortably in his early sixties. He had played a lot of golf and sailed his yacht but eventually grew tired of the hot summers. When a friend had raved about

Wintergreen the previous year, he came up for a visit and decided to buy a place.

Cyrus wrapped up his life's summary, and Bill figured he had to ask at least one question pertinent to the investigation.

"Did you hear we located the vehicle that ran into Mr. Thorpe?" he asked.

"Yep. I saw the email yesterday—a gold Honda. Did you find the driver?"

Cyrus slowed his pace to navigate a sharp switchback. Bill grabbed a small tree for extra support.

"Not yet," Bill said. "The vehicle belongs to a man named Joel Turner."

Cyrus turned to Bill with his eyebrows scrunched. "Joel Turner? I know that name. Yeah. He played golf with my foursome but developed some kind of dementia and had to drop out. That's how I got in—they needed a fourth."

"That's interesting," said Bill, although he already had that information. "As it turns out, I've learned that all three of your golfing buddies had access to the car."

Cyrus pulled his shoulders back, and his eyes narrowed. "You're not serious."

Bill nodded. Cyrus kept his eyes steady, but his mind had to be racing as he sorted through the implications of Bill's revelation.

"It's fortuitous that we met today," said Bill. "I would have reached out to you soon."

"Reached out to me? Why?"

The two men stood four feet apart. The muscles in Cyrus Hunt's arms and chest grew tense.

"Well," said Bill, "since you spend a lot of time with the others, I wanted to ask whether you noticed anything odd going on between them recently."

"Odd? What do you mean by odd?"

"Arguments. Any sort of conflict between Lou Thorpe and one of the others."

Cyrus's eyes grew wider as he comprehended Bill's meaning. "Oh, I see." He cleared his throat. Wind rustled leaves in the treetops.

Bill counted to five in his head and then said, "You saw something, didn't you?"

"Maybe."

The old soldier didn't want to betray his buddies, but he had no choice. This was a police investigation.

"All right, then," said Bill. "Tell me."

"It happened a couple of weeks back. We were on the fairway of seventeen. I was riding with Marty; Victor and Lou were in the other carts."

Cyrus paused to take a deep breath. A vein stood out on his neck.

"Victor and Lou had been engaged in a serious conversation for much of the round, which was unusual. Our chatter is generally light, jokes and smack-talk, that sort of thing. Then, out of nowhere, Victor yelled at Lou. Something along the lines of, 'You don't have to do that.' Something like that. Lou answered in a quieter voice, and Victor yelled again. His voice echoed among the trees in the forest. Marty and I were embarrassed, and we drove ahead to give them space. In fact, we played eighteen without them. But they must have worked it out, because we saw them after the round, and Victor had cooled off."

"What day was this?" said Bill.

Cyrus rubbed the back of his neck. "Let's see. I guess it was Monday. Yeah. It must have been Monday the week before last."

"Do you know what issue Victor was referring to?"

Cyrus shook his head. "I figured it was between them.

You know, those guys used to work together. All three of them. Maybe it had something to do with that. They discuss industry stuff once in a while. I can't follow it half the time because I don't know anything about coal."

"Okay. Thank you."

Cyrus stared at his feet. "I feel like I've put Victor in a bad spot. I can't imagine he would do anything violent. He's generally a great guy, you know?"

"Forget it. Probably doesn't mean a thing. We're still gathering information."

They hiked in silence for ten minutes. Bill guessed that Cyrus was churning the conversation in his head. He had to know he'd given Bill the seed of a potential motive for Victor Bishop. Indeed. Another bit of information. Bill felt good about the investigation now; they were progressing on multiple fronts, and one way or another, the driver's days of anonymity would soon come to an end.

The trail reached a low point, inclined at a gentle slope for a few hundred yards, and then came to an overlook. It was the same spot Bill had reached when he hiked in from the other direction a few days earlier. The sky was crystal clear. Far below them in the small valley, a pickup drove on the two-lane highway. The great Shenandoah Valley opened up on the right.

Though Bill remained a safe distance from the cliff's edge, Cyrus clearly did not share his fear of heights, and he walked right to the precipice. Bill could not tell for sure from that angle, but it appeared Cyrus's toes extended beyond the edge into open air. A chill crossed Bill's shoulders, and his chest grew heavy. Bill recalled the sheer drop of a hundred feet or more, but Cyrus paid no mind to the danger. He stared in the direction of faraway mountains, as if thoughts consumed his mind.

Bill inched forward until he was close to Cyrus; then he reached to grab the other man's arm. "Could you come back from the edge a few feet?" he said. "You're making me nervous."

Initially startled by Bill's touch, Cyrus backed up two steps and grinned. "Sure. Didn't mean to frighten you."

"Sorry," said Bill. "I'm not a fan of heights. I'm fine back here, but at the edge, my hands begin to sweat."

"No problem," Cyrus said. "Heights never bothered me. I spent some time in helicopters in Vietnam, and I always enjoyed it. Not the violence. I hated that part. But flying, jeez, that was awesome."

Cyrus's eyes returned to the small valley before them, and Bill noticed a large bird floating high on the wind.

"Like that vulture out there," said Cyrus, pointing. "Wouldn't it be great to spread your wings and soar? Alone. Totally independent. Higher than everyone else."

"Yeah, I guess. Although most days, I'm pretty happy on the ground."

TWENTY-EIGHT

After a short break at the overlook, the two men parted ways. Cyrus Hunt would hike farther on the OAT, but Bill needed to begin his formal workday. He returned to his condo to clean up and grab some breakfast, and then he drove to the station to meet with Krista Jackson.

Krista stared at her computer monitor with her fingers flying over the keys. Not wishing to disturb her mid-task, Bill paused and stood ten feet away. She sat straight, her uniform crisp, her ginger hair falling down her back. She finished typing, and her eyes scanned the screen to review her words. Bill cleared his throat.

"Oh, hey, Bill. Morning. How's it going?"

They exchanged pleasantries, and Bill said he had stopped by to see if her internet research had turned up anything. Krista replied that she had spent a few hours on the task the previous day and was typing up her notes. Bill grabbed an unoccupied chair and rolled it next to Krista's so they could chat.

Krista said, "As you mentioned yesterday, the men have all retired, so there wasn't a heck of a lot to find." She reviewed the positions the three men had held—Capaldi and Bishop had worked as executives for Appalachian Energy, a company primarily focused on coal and headquartered in Huntington, West Virginia. Lou Thorpe had acted as a lobbyist for the industry. Bishop maintained active status as an attorney and was a trustee for a charitable foundation in DC. Capaldi served on the board of directors for a Texas wind turbine company. She had found little mention of Thorpe in recent years.

Krista's notes were well organized, and she reported her findings articulately and in a clear, crisp voice. She elaborated points if the extra content added value to her overall observations. Her professional demeanor differed markedly from the carefree persona she had adopted when telling the funny story about her dogs.

"I also did a search on Lou Thorpe's lobbying firm," she said, "and found one thing of interest because it may also involve Victor Bishop." She pulled an article up on the screen. "According to this lobbyist watchdog website, the FBI is investigating a potential bribery-for-influence scheme involving the coal industry. Apparently, a whistleblower has accused Thorpe's firm of facilitating conversations between coal companies and federal agency officials responsible for regulation enforcement. The scheme purportedly goes back a dozen years and has involved the general counsels of several coal concerns."

"Let me see that," said Bill.

Bill rolled his chair closer to the screen, and Krista moved to give him space. She sat with her legs together and her hands in her lap. The two of them were close enough that he could sense her bodily presence. He detected a light flowery fragrance. A bottle of lotion rested on her desk next to the monitor. It must be that. Bill read the article but learned nothing other than what Krista had reported. Bribing federal officials could result in serious criminal charges. What was the statute of limitations for such a crime? Had Lou Thorpe or Victor Bishop been drawn into the FBI's investigation?

"That's a great catch," he said. "Nice work."

"Do you think it's relevant to the hit-and-run?"

"I'll definitely ask Victor Bishop about it."

Krista said Mitch called in to report the search team had started at dawn. He was confident they'd find Andre Lewis that day.

Bill's eyes drifted back to the framed photos of Krista's boys in their football uniforms.

"Any more stories from the home front?" he said. "How are David and Goliath getting along?"

"They've made peace, but I have other big news. My youngest, Trevor, has a girlfriend."

"Do tell."

"Yeah, he's a player in the making. A natural-born salesman. This last spring, he talked his grandma into letting him drive her car in the driveway. Then he promptly ran over her azaleas. Now he wants an increased allowance to take his girlfriend to the movies." Krista shook her head. "My four-teen-year-old? The polar opposite. Painfully shy. He has a crush on a cashier at the grocery store, but he can barely answer if she asks whether he wants a receipt."

Bill chuckled and said, "Brings back memories."

Krista touched the picture of her youngest son in his uniform. "Hey, they'll begin practicing in a few weeks. Maybe you'd like to come to a scrimmage game."

Boy, that sounded fun. He could almost smell the freshly mown grass. Parents shouting encouragement to their kids. At sunset, spotlights illuminating the green field.

"Yeah, I'd like that," he said.

"Great. They'll have their first scrimmage in about a month. We usually go for hamburgers after. You could tag along for that if you like."

Why not? His calendar was wide open.

"Sounds like fun."

Krista's eyes smiled, and then she asked if he had anything else for her to do on the investigation. He told her to stay tuned.

Then he grabbed a cup of coffee and considered his next steps. For sure, he needed to talk with Marty Capaldi and Victor Bishop. But first, he wanted to stop by the golf course and learn a little more about Lou Thorpe's foursome.

TWENTY-NINE

While eating a bowl of cereal earlier that morning, Bill had realized he missed a key point Cyrus Hunt made on their impromptu hike. Cyrus had said he witnessed Lou Thorpe and Victor Bishop arguing on the golf course on a Monday. This statement conflicted with the information he'd gotten from Rachel Dunn. Rachel said Victor Bishop came to visit her every Monday. One of them was mistaken. Unless . . .

The tennis courts, golf course pro shop, and resort clubhouse were all located directly across Blue Ridge Drive from Bill's condo building. After parking in the lot next to the clubhouse, Bill walked toward the pro shop. Tall hardwood trees bordered the lush green fairways, and puffy white clouds dotted the blue sky. The eighteenth green was nestled in the shade of tall branches in clear view of the clubhouse patio. Startled by Bill's approach, a gray squirrel scampered across the walk and up the trunk of an oak tree.

The pro shop was unoccupied, but the register was on, and Bill concluded the attendant had stepped away. While waiting, he perused the display of golf shoes. Picking up the game would require an upfront investment in clothing, clubs, and other equipment. It would also involve ongoing expenses for green fees. Lessons too, Bill gathered, if he wanted to be any good at the game. He'd have to weigh the benefits of golf versus other hobbies he could pursue with his disposable income.

A young man in a tan polo shirt entered the room from a back hallway and strode behind the counter. Bill introduced himself, said he was investigating the hit-and-run, and asked about Lou Thorpe's golfing habits.

The attendant's name was Zach. He stood a few inches under six feet tall, had short brown hair, a clean-shaven face, and big ears that stuck out from his head. At the mention of Lou Thorpe, Zach's eyes tightened.

"It's an awful thing that happened. I'm going to miss seeing Mr. Thorpe because he was here almost every day, even days when he didn't play. I think he liked hanging around the course and the clubhouse."

"I understand he played in a regular foursome."

"He played a lot and with a lot of different people. But you're right; he had a regular foursome. They played every Monday, Wednesday, and Friday, even if it rained. It took a big storm to keep those guys off the course."

Bill asked who played in the foursome, and Zach confirmed the names Bill already had.

"What time did they play?"

"They teed off at nine fifty-five. They'd grab a sandwich at the turn and finish up at two thirty or so depending on the speed of play."

Huh. Rachel Dunn had clearly stated that the men came to see her in the middle of the day on Monday, Wednesday, and Friday.

"Did you happen to see them when they made their turn to the back nine?" Bill asked.

Zach shook his head. "No. I don't know for sure that they ate, to tell you the truth. I guessed that part. Most golfers grab a sandwich unless they stop for a longer lunch. I know they didn't do that. They would have come by here to get to the clubhouse."

"Anything odd about the foursome?" asked Bill. "Maybe one of the guys not showing up now and then?"

"Not really. I would have noticed that. We don't have many regular foursomes during the week—a lot more traffic on the weekend. Oh, one thing different with those guys, they always wanted three carts. Said it made the round go faster."

Bill reflected on the casual shoes they'd found in the back of the Honda Pilot. Then he asked Zach for a map of the golf course.

Bill drove down Blue Ridge Drive a short way, turned left on Fawn Ridge Drive, and took that to the Turner house. He idled the car on the road and stared at the garage where Turner had kept his Pilot. Through the trees behind the garage, Bill could make out one of the golf course fairways. Fifty yards ahead on the street, white stripes marked a golf cart crossing. He eased his car to the crossing, parked, and hiked to the next tee. It was the sixth hole.

Then he returned to his car, drove back to Turner's garage, and parked. Tall trees behind and to the left of the garage cast it in constant shade. The concrete pavement at the front of the house provided ample space for guest parking. On the garage's right side, the builder had poured a lane of concrete wide enough for a small trailer. When standing in that lane, the garage building blocked Bill's view of the road. In back of the garage, a pile of neatly stacked firewood covered with a tarp leaned against the wall. Next to the wood were several upside-down terracotta flowerpots.

Bill walked into the garage and turned on the overhead fluorescent lights. The men had used Turner's Pilot to visit Rachel Dunn. They might have shared a key and kept it hidden in or around the garage to avoid having to pass it back and forth between them. A bored Andre Lewis out for a stroll might have searched the garage of a dark home for something to eat or drink. Perhaps the men had left the spare key in the open, on the car seat or the workbench. If so, Andre might have found the key and taken the Pilot for a ride. But getting to that outcome required a combination of assumptions that Bill continued to find improbable.

At that moment, standing in the Turners' garage, Bill's cell phone rang. He jerked at the noise and then pulled the phone from his pocket. It was a northern Virginia area code.

"Hello," he said.

"Is this Bill O'Shea?" asked a man with a deep voice.

"Yes."

"It's Marty Capaldi. Alex gave me your number. I need to speak with you as soon as possible."

THIRTY

Marty Capaldi asked to meet at a pavilion next to the community pool on Timber Camp Drive. It was less than a mile down from the clubhouse, and Bill agreed to meet Capaldi in ten minutes. The pavilion had concrete flooring, screened windows all the way around, and a dozen picnic tables. Wintergreen property owners could reserve the space for casual events.

When Bill arrived, Marty Capaldi was already seated at a corner picnic table. He clipped the end of a cigar and proceeded to light it. They were alone.

The sound of playing children carried from the pool a hundred feet away. Capaldi stood to shake Bill's hand, then lifted his cigar.

"Do you mind?" he said.

"Not at all. I enjoy the smell."

"Ahh! It's a bad habit, but I limit myself to two a week." Capaldi raised his eyebrows. "Sometimes I cheat."

The two men sat across the table from each other.

Marty Capaldi was a big man, tall, broad shoulders slightly hunched now, with thinning gray hair. Bill tried to imagine a younger version of the man and decided Marty had once been handsome. His hands trembled slightly, an age-related condition, Bill guessed. Bill examined Capaldi's hands more carefully and realized they looked familiar. They were big hands with long, strong fingers. Any wide receiver would love to have those hands. Suddenly, Bill realized why Marty Capaldi had asked to meet immediately.

Marty's eyes moved around a lot. He picked at lint on his short-sleeved cotton shirt, then flicked his cigar as if to rid it of ash that didn't yet exist.

"I mentioned this to Alex. He was unsure of how to proceed and strongly recommended that I talk to you."

"Okay. How can I help?"

"Andre Lewis is my son."

Bill rubbed his hands together under the table and considered the implications of Marty's confession. By his own admission, Andre Lewis had camped near Wintergreen and left his campsite for several hours during the night. But he'd lied to Bill and Mitch when he said he'd hiked up to the overlook and fallen asleep.

Marty brushed a bit of leaf from the picnic table. "Andre and I don't see each other often. His mother and I don't speak at all—we only ever saw each other a few times." Marty's mouth turned down. "Barbara doesn't want to have anything to do with Andre. My other kids, Andre's step-siblings, are two decades older than him."

"So you met Andre that night," said Bill.

Marty dipped his head. "Yeah. He had texted that he was coming through, and I wanted to see him. To give him some money and to talk. We don't get that many chances. I've helped with money along the way, child support, college, given his mother some extra a few times when they needed it. But I haven't been much of a father otherwise."

The smoke from Marty's neglected cigar drifted off and dissipated. He stared into space, wrestling with his past actions. "I couldn't acknowledge Andre publicly. Not then. That sort of thing was seriously frowned upon at Appalachian, and my career had reached a critical juncture. If the board had known, I never would have gotten the COO position. That was the pinnacle of my career. It meant everything."

Bill wondered if Andre's biracial status had influenced Marty's decisions. He recalled the anger Andre had expressed toward his unnamed father at the police station in Waynesboro. But Andre had not said he'd met his father, only that they had talked. Why? Had he honored his father's wishes to keep their connection a secret? Or had he sought to cover up a much greater sin?

"I'm not here to judge you," said Bill. "But I do need to know what you did with Andre that night."

Marty sniffed and gave Bill a nod. "I met him on foot at the little parking lot near the AT. Our house is not far from there. From the parking lot, we walked to Turner's house to get the Honda. Barbara didn't know Andre was here, and I didn't want to take our car because she might have heard the garage door and woken up."

"Where did you go?"

"I had brought a six-pack. We drove up to the Devils Knob Overlook and had a few beers. We had fun. Just talking. We debated his next career move a bit. Not too much."

Bill scratched his cheek and recalled that Officer Hill had noticed a parked SUV at the Devils Knob Overlook that night. That was consistent with Capaldi's story.

"What then?" said Bill.

"Nothing. We drove back to Turner's place, returned to the parking lot, and said goodbye."

"Are you sure? Are you sure you didn't ride down Wintergreen Drive and run into Lou Thorpe?"

"No!"

"If it was an accident, you should go ahead and tell me now so we can get this sorted. You might not even do time."

Capaldi's eyes locked on Bill. "That did not happen. We left the car at Turner's like I told you."

"It's a tough sell," said Bill. "By your own admission, you were in the car on the same night."

"I didn't do it."

"And you have a motive too."

"Motive?" Capaldi's head snapped back. "What motive? That's preposterous."

In an attempt to convey confidence, Bill lifted his chin and straightened his shoulders. "We've learned that Lou Thorpe owed you a lot of money."

"Who told you that?"

"Never mind how we know. We know."

Capaldi snarled his disdain and cast his hand to the side as if half a million dollars was nothing.

"Also," said Bill, "your loan to Lou was secured with a million-dollar insurance policy."

Marty took time to casually relight his cigar. "Yes, I insisted Lou take out the policy to secure the loan."

"When the insurance company pays, you'll get your money. You knew Lou would never repay you otherwise."

Scowling, Capaldi said, "It's ludicrous to assert that I would kill a friend over half a million. I've known Lou for thirty years, for Chrissake."

"Most people wouldn't see it that way. Five hundred and fifty thousand dollars is a heck of a lot of money to most people. It's a heck of a lot of money to me."

Annoyed, Capaldi sucked on his cigar. Over at the pool, a young child shrieked, and then water splashed.

Capaldi had not denied the facts of his motive, only the relevance. How much was a guy like Capaldi worth? Five million? Ten million? More? Whatever. It was time to shift the conversation. Bill wasn't done yet, not even close.

"Why haven't you come to the police sooner?" asked Bill.

Capaldi opened his mouth to speak, then closed it again. His eyes darted away from Bill. "I only saw the email with the Honda Pilot yesterday."

"Why didn't you call Alex then? You waited a whole day."

Marty ran a hand through his thinning hair and then rushed his words. "I didn't know what to think. Andre and I had been in the car. I thought perhaps it was a different Honda, so I stopped by the Turner house to check."

"And you found the garage empty."

Marty's eyes grew wild with fear. "But we left the car in the garage. I swear it."

"Which means someone else came and got the car. And you know who that was? Andre. After you left him at the parking lot, he came back to the garage and took the car out for his own ride. He ran into Lou Thorpe."

"No. Andre didn't do that. He wouldn't do that." Marty's head shook back and forth mechanically as if he wanted to convince Bill even though he had lingering doubts.

"How would you know what your son would do? By your own admission, you haven't spent much time together."

"I believe him. When I read the email, I had the same thought as you. Maybe Andre came back and got the car. So I called him. He was hiking on the AT. I said to him, 'Andre, if you did this, if you accidentally killed a man, we've got to go the police.' Andre swore. He swore on his mother's soul."

Marty rubbed his chest as if in pain. "Andre doesn't give two hoots about me. Why should he? But he worships his mother. He would never . . . I believe him."

Bill studied the old man's face: droopy bags under sad, worried eyes; age spots; and wrinkled skin. Marty believed what his son had told him. But should Bill? He tried to imagine Andre's frame of mind. Andre was nearly halfway through a long trek undertaken to prove he could achieve a seemingly impossible objective. He took a break from this great adventure to visit a father he barely knew. They shared a few beers. They debated his future. Andre got some money, and they parted ways. But instead of returning to his tent, he decided to double back and steal a car for a joy ride? Why would he do that? He was tired as hell from the hiking and the beer. A sleeping bag with his name on it was minutes away. No way he'd risk his quest to drive an SUV around at night. Or maybe the hiking had bored him senseless. Perhaps the old man had pissed him off. Maybe he wanted to travel at speed for a change.

The table's surface vibrated under Bill's elbows, and he realized Marty was bouncing his knee. Jittery about something.

"If you didn't hit Thorpe with the Honda," Bill said, "and Andre didn't hit Thorpe with the Honda, then who did?"

"I don't know." Marty chewed his lip.

"But you can guess."

"I happen to know that Victor Bishop had access to the Pilot."

"How do you know this?"

"Joel Turner gave Victor a spare key to watch over the Pilot while he was gone. Victor let me use the SUV. Barbara and I only have one car up here, and sometimes it's nice to have access to a second vehicle. Victor and I keep the key under a flower pot around the back of the garage."

Apparently, Marty believed he could avoid disclosing that he and his buddies had used the Pilot to visit Rachel Dunn. Never mind. Bill could wait to get to that part.

"Okay," said Bill. "Did Mr. Bishop have a reason to want Lou Thorpe dead? Maybe Thorpe owed him money as well."

Marty puffed on his cigar then shook his head. "It's not about money—not that I know of. But Victor does benefit from Lou's death in another way."

Bill leaned forward. "I'm listening."

"Back when Victor and I worked for Appalachian Energy, Lou Thorpe was our lobbyist in Washington. All the coal interests worked with Lou. We followed regulatory developments closely because the slightest tweak in the wording could drive millions of dollars in cost. Lou knew everyone in town. That was his business, and he was good at it; he hosted events that were fun for bored bureaucrats."

Marty checked over both shoulders as if concerned about eavesdroppers. Only the trees and birds could hear them, but Marty lowered his voice anyway. "Apparently, at some point, Lou and Victor and others organized some sort of pay-for-influence scheme." Marty put his hands up. "I didn't know anything about it, but now a whistleblower has come forward, and an investigation is underway."

Marty paused to examine Bill's face as if to make sure he was following along.

"I'm with you," said Bill.

With a big nod, Marty said, "For years after he retired, Victor worked part-time for Appalachian, mostly on the regulatory side, stuff that would be in the scope of this investigation. I know Victor is very concerned. He and Lou had a fierce argument in the middle of the golf course. And here's the thing." Marty jabbed a finger at the tabletop. "Lou was supposed to give his deposition *this week*."

Marty's head hung lower. "I've known Victor Bishop a long time. It's hard to fathom that he could commit murder, but he has definitely benefited from Lou's death. Lou would have known the ins and outs of such a scheme. The investigators always want to get to the corporate sponsors; they would have cut a deal with Lou to testify against executives."

Bill brought his hands together and touched them to his lips. In his mind, he compared the strength of Marty's motive for wanting Lou dead—money—against Victor Bishop's motive—avoiding disgrace and possible jail time. He found Bishop's motive more compelling. But was it reasonable to believe that Marty and Victor had both used the Pilot for secretive purposes on the same night? The timing was feasible, but on its face, it seemed improbable.

"Tell me about Rachel Dunn," said Bill.

Marty pulled his head back and widened his eyes, but he recovered quickly. "Sounds like you know of her already."

"I know bits and pieces. Give me your version."

After a deep breath and a pause to collect his thoughts, Marty gave an overview of his relationship with Rachel Dunn. They had met in DC more than twenty years earlier when she worked as a high-priced escort on the government and diplomatic scene. At some point, Lou's charm and money convinced Rachel to become his mistress, and she quit working as an escort. When Lou retired, he didn't have the same financial resources, and he had devised a new arrangement—Lou paid for Rachel's housing in Wintergreen plus an allowance, and Rachel met once a week on a friendly basis with Lou, Marty, and Victor.

"What do you mean by a friendly basis?" said Bill.

"Do we have to go into those details?"

"Please keep it PG, but yes."

Marty rubbed the back of his head and gave Bill a hard smile. He might have concluded, correctly, that sharing everything he knew was the best way to reduce Bill's suspicions.

"When I was younger, and Rachel still worked as an escort, I slept with her a few times. She was hard to resist. But at my age, the act of sex is a lot trickier than it used to be." Marty studied the wrinkles on the back of his hand. "Anyway, Rachel is still quite a peach, and she's up for anything. Last summer, I wanted to give it a go and managed to get through the exercise a few times without embarrassing myself, but this year . . ." He shook his head. "I'd just as soon sit on a balcony, drink a glass of wine, and flirt with a beautiful woman. Sometimes she gives me a neck massage, and it feels good. That's all there is to it these days. Hard to even call it cheating."

At that point, Bill could not resist interjecting, so he said, "A lot of people would still call it cheating."

Marty got all huffy, twisted his mouth into a sour expression, and then said, "Hey, I'm not proud of this."

"I don't imagine you should be."

Flustered, Marty threw his cigar to the floor and stomped on it. "My marriage is not perfect, far from it. But I'm not the only guilty one. Barbara's had an affair or two of her own. She told me as much when—" But then he cut himself off as if he knew he'd gone too far.

Bill said, "When what?"

Marty's anger disappeared as quickly as it had come. He leaned forward, folded his arms on the table, and sighed. "When she learned about Andre. A long time ago."

They had spent enough time on Marty's life, and Bill

chastised himself for letting the conversation veer in the wrong direction.

"How did you work the scheme to use Turner's Pilot to visit Rachel?" he asked.

Marty wiped a hand across his face and sat upright again. "That was Victor's brainchild. When Lou first came up with the proposal for us to share Rachel's time, Victor got all excited. It was two years ago come September, and I remember the conversation clearly. We drank beer on the club's patio after a round. I don't believe Victor had ever done anything like that, but he was certainly willing to give it a try. The Turners had already gone for the winter, and Victor had a key to their Honda."

What a nice crew, enjoying a beer on a sunny day while they plotted their infidelity.

Marty started to get into it, proud of how well the scheme had worked. "We'd take three carts out and play the first five holes. Then whoever's turn it was to see Rachel would cut out and park his cart on the side of Turner's garage. Grab the key from under the flowerpot and be off. After the visit, we would return the Pilot and use the cart to catch up with the other three on sixteen or seventeen. The course is rarely busy during the week, so it was easy to scoot around anybody else."

Bill had to admit the men had devised a slick scheme. Only a truly suspicious wife would think to verify that her husband had played a full round of golf.

"Yep," said Marty, "it worked well for the most part. But every third or fourth week, Lou would forget to put the key back under the flowerpot, and he'd have to drive over to Turner's place after the round."

"What about Cyrus Hunt? Was he in on it?"

"No." Marty shook his head emphatically. "When we

started visiting Rachel, we were only a threesome because Turner didn't return last year. But playing with only two seemed conspicuous, and then Cyrus moved here and was looking for a foursome."

"What did Cyrus say when one of you cut out on the sixth hole every day? That must have seemed odd."

Marty shrugged. "Cyrus is a savvy guy. We gave him some bullcrap about sharing a consulting gig with a coal industry consortium."

"Did he know about the car? Did he ever visit Rachel?"

"No. I think Cyrus knew what was going on, but he never pried. And he never wanted in on it. Cyrus is a loner. I don't know for sure, but he might be gay. He was in the military back when homosexuality was unwelcome."

"Did anyone else have access to the key?"

"Not that I know of. But you should ask Victor that question."

Marty stood to stretch his back. He moseyed to the edge of the pavilion and gazed at the children swimming. Perhaps he remembered taking his own kids to the neighborhood swimming pool. Maybe he regretted never taking Andre. Now, he worried about Andre, which of course, was why he had called Bill in the first place.

"There's a team of law enforcement officers searching for Andre on the Appalachian Trail," said Bill.

Marty came back to the table. He grabbed the side of it and said with a great deal of confidence, "They won't find him."

Bill had missed something in the conversation: despite their tenuous relationship, Marty loved his son. What would Bill have done if one of his sons was on the Appalachian Trail under similar circumstances? Nothing, initially, because he could never have imagined either of his sons stealing a car.

But once he had seen the Honda Pilot in the blast email, he would have immediately sought to protect his son.

"You have Andre stashed somewhere," said Bill. "Not up here because of the tension with Barbara. You put him in a hotel. I would guess Harrisonburg."

"Charlottesville," said Marty. "A two-star place that will attract little attention. I told him to turn off his phone because I know they'll trace it."

"What's the name of the hotel?"

Marty pressed his lips tightly.

This was not good. As a police detective, Bill would have threatened Marty with arrest until he gave up his son's location. Then he would have notified colleagues to go question the young man. But Bill was no longer a policeman. His name badge said *Advisor*. And sending officers to Andre's hotel carried its own set of risks. Andre might see them coming. He might run. Someone could make a poor decision ending in catastrophe. These sorts of things happened all too frequently.

"Marty, you're obstructing an investigation," he said. "That's not good."

The old man appeared unmoved. Perhaps he had already considered those implications.

"Listen," said Bill, "the safest place for your son is at the sheriff's office in Lovingston." He pointed east in the direction of Charlottesville. "The longer Andre stays out there, the greater the risk. Now here's what I'll do. It'll take you an hour to drive there and less than that to get back to Lovingston. Do that immediately and call me when it's done. If I don't hear from you in two and a half hours, I'll call it in. By nightfall, a dozen officers will be showing Andre's picture to every hotel clerk in Charlottesville."

"He'll need a lawyer."

"Do that later. Get him into custody. Tell him not to say anything if you're worried about that."

Marty Capaldi frowned as he considered his options. Upon making a decision, he stood tall. "I'll leave immediately."

"There's one other thing," said Bill. "I need to talk to your wife alone. The thing with Rachel is going to come out. I'll give you until tomorrow to sort that with your wife."

Capaldi nodded. "Fair enough. I made the bed, so . . ." He stepped toward the door, then paused and turned. "One thing you should know about Barbara—she drinks a lot. She's what some would call a functioning alcoholic. You should try to get her in the morning."

After Capaldi left, Bill remained in the pavilion. It was a peaceful place to think, an outdoor room within earshot of playing children. How many families had held reunions or birthday parties here? They were cheerful, noisy events, where children played games of tag and kick the can, and parents ate fried chicken and drank sodas and remained faithful to one another until the day they died. People still held events like that, didn't they? Surely they did in a beautiful place like Wintergreen. Yeah. He had stumbled upon an unhappy crew. That's all it was.

Several hit-and-run scenarios involved Marty and Andre. First scenario: Marty had visited with Andre, said goodbye at the parking lot, and then retrieved the Honda to kill Thorpe. Afterward, he'd driven the Honda to the picnic area, hidden it in a spot he had picked out previously, and hiked back to Wintergreen on the AT. But Marty was in his late seventies. His hands trembled. Could he have managed such a hike in the dark?

Second scenario: After the father and son visit, Andre had returned to the garage to take the Honda out for his own ride.

Bored of hiking and perhaps feeling a bit rebellious after meeting with Marty, why the hell not? What could go wrong? But then he'd gotten distracted, playing with the radio settings perhaps, and accidentally killed Thorpe. Then what? He had used his GPS to figure out the picnic area was close to the AT, hidden the Pilot behind the boulder, and returned to his campsite to sleep fitfully. The next day, on the edge of freaking out, he had hitchhiked into Waynesboro and gotten drunk at a Buffalo Wild Wings. Bill rubbed his chin. That one still didn't make sense.

Third scenario: The father and son special. Despite Marty's earlier assertions, the drag of supporting Andre combined with the loan to Thorpe had put a strain on his retirement plan. So Marty had convinced his son that he needed to get rid of Thorpe to shore up his finances. For Marty to continue underwriting Andre's adventure and lend money to Andre's mother on occasion, Marty would need help. Then what? Marty ran over Thorpe, had Andre drop him off at his own home, and then Andre had driven the Honda to the picnic area. Bill scrunched his nose. He found the third scenario even less likely than the second.

Maybe someone else did it after all. Victor Bishop?

Perhaps. But before chasing down Bishop, Bill would stop by Café Devine for another cup of coffee, and with some luck, a bit of gossip.

THIRTY-ONE

Bill opened the door to Café Devine, and the bell hanging on the doorknob announced his arrival. Not that Kim Wiley needed the notice, for the shop was empty of customers, and she was standing right behind the counter playing with her phone. Although it was difficult for him to comprehend, her voluminous auburn hair was even frizzier than when they'd first met. Perhaps it had something to do with the humidity.

"Hello, Bill," she said as if they were now old friends, "seen any more bears?"

Bill's neck and ears grew warmer, and he covered his eyes with a hand. "How did you know about that?"

Kim's eyes rose to the ceiling. "I have my sources."

Hmm. Mrs. Spooner, no doubt. What a scoop. Big City Cop has Pastries Stolen by Local Bear.

"No, no more bears."

"Nothing to be ashamed of," said Kim. "Last year Frieda Chang left a full bag of dog food in the trunk of her convertible. Oh. My. Gosh. You talk about a mess. The bear ripped open the soft top and tore up the back seats to get to that dog food. Now *that* was dumb."

Bill chuckled. "Seriously. Dog food?"

Kim gave him a monster nod. "Uh-huh. Twenty pounds of turkey-flavored Doggie Dinner. And it gets better. Frieda has a poodle named Curly. Well, Curly noticed the bear was ripping up the car, and he started barking at the bear from the window. I guess Curly has figured out how to jump on the bed to spy on folks coming and going. Anyway, Curly was barking and barking. Frieda walked onto the front porch and started yelling at the bear. The bear didn't pay her any mind because she was gobbling Doggie Dinner with her fat butt sticking out the top of the car. Frieda didn't know what to do, so she called the police and demanded that they come get the bear."

Bill's shoulders shook. He could scarcely catch his breath.

"Of course, the police told her there was nothing to do. No one on God's earth could move the bear until she got her fill."

In contrast, Bill's encounter with Ms. Betsy seemed harmless. Cute, almost. Yeah, a cute story he could share with others.

"You hear all sorts of stories here at Café Devine, don't you, Kim?"

She lifted her heels and grinned. "I try to keep up. What can I get you, Bill?"

He ordered a decaf latte and an orange scone. While Kim prepared his coffee, he meandered over to the wine rack to check on the Châteauneuf-du-Pape. Whoops. Only two bottles left. Someone had scooped up the forty-dollar one, leaving only the more expensive vineyards. Maybe he should grab a bottle. Would that impress Cindy? She had still not returned his text, and he had a bad feeling about it.

Kim placed his latte and scone on the counter and rang him up.

"Hey, Kim," he said, "you know I'm helping Alex with the hit-and-run investigation, right?"

"Sure. Did you guys solve the case yet? I saw that you found the car. Lindsey Turner used to drive that Pilot over here on Fridays after tennis. She and the other three ladies would grab a glass of wine and sit on the patio." Kim leaned across the counter and lowered her voice even though no one else was in the room. "Jeanne Thorpe is in that group, you know, her and Barbara and Marilyn."

Kim had a habit of talking fast, and Bill paused to analyze what she'd said. "No, we're still working on the investigation. Would that be Barbara Capaldi by any chance?"

"Yep. One and the same. And I'll tell you something about Barbara—that woman can drink a glass of wine. The other ladies will sip theirs and make them last a full hour, but not Barbara. She'll have a second glass, and before the end of the hour, she's ready for a third. Not that she orders a third, I'm not saying that, but she almost always picks up a bottle on the way out."

Hmm. Kim's reference to Barbara's wine consumption was consistent with Marty's description of her as a functioning alcoholic.

"The fourth woman, Marilyn, what's her last name?" he asked.

"Marilyn Bishop. The four couples used to socialize together a lot, with the men doing the golf thing and the women playing tennis. But the Turners stopped coming to Wintergreen. I hear he's sick."

Bill sipped his latte and munched on the scone. He lifted his eyebrows. "Whoa. This scone is excellent."

"Thank you. A friend of mine in Waynesboro bakes them for me. She makes everything in the display case."

Bill glanced at the door to make sure no one was about to enter, then glanced over Kim's shoulder to the kitchen. "Where's your nephew?"

"Nathan's not in yet."

Adopting a serious expression, Bill lowered his voice, "I need to ask you a confidential question. Do you know of any tensions between Lou and anyone in his circle of friends?"

Kim leaned forward. "You mean between Lou and the other men?"

"Not necessarily. The men or the women. Anything at all."

"Well, I don't think so." Kim cupped an elbow with a hand. She must have remembered something because her eyes widened, but then she began to straighten the ballpoint pens in the holder next to the register. "Nothing recent, anyway."

"Doesn't have to be recent. If you know something, tell me. I'll know if it's important."

Kim chewed the side of her lip and stared at Bill. Then she reached under the counter and pulled out a sign that read *Back in Fifteen Minutes*. She quick-stepped around the counter to hang the sign on the door and then led Bill to a table for two at one side of the café.

She sat with both arms on the table. All the humor had left her face. "I like to gossip. You've surely noticed that by now, but some secrets are too dangerous to share."

"Okay."

"This happened a long time ago, at least twenty years because it was soon after I took over the café. Anyway, Barbara Capaldi came in and ordered sandwiches for two, said she was going to have lunch at the gazebo up behind us here." Kim paused to point through the wall toward the little park behind the café.

Bill had visited the park earlier and knew of the gazebo.

"I figured Barbara was going to meet Marty for lunch, and I told her the food would be ready in ten minutes. She said she would carry some other things up and return for the sandwiches. Well, traffic was light that day, so when I had the sandwiches fixed, I decided to carry them to the gazebo to save Barbara the trip."

At this point, Kim paused and blinked her eyes several times for dramatic effect.

"I'm with you," said Bill. "What happened then?"

"No one else was at the park. I got to the top of the stairs, and uh . . ." Kim stared into space as if reliving the scene. "Under the gazebo, Barbara Capaldi was kissing a man. It wasn't just kissing either. I mean, his hands were all over her. Her hands were all over him too. I'm telling you, Bill. It was as close as they could get to making a dirty movie with their clothes on."

"That's a sweet story, Kim. I guess Marty and Barbara got a little carried away."

"Here's the punch line. The man was not Marty. Barbara was all tangled up that day with none other than your victim, Lou Thorpe."

"Lou Thorpe? Are you sure?"

Kim gave Bill a nod. "As sure as sure can be."

"What did you do?" Bill asked.

"I got out of there, pronto. They were too busy with each other to notice me. Barbara came down for the sandwiches later with her hair freshly brushed and lipstick reapplied."

"Who else did you tell?"

Kim crossed her heart and said, "No one else. I swear. I've kept that secret for twenty years. People get downright upset when it comes to cheating. Folks have been killed for less. Like I said, I don't spread that kind of gossip."

"Did you ever hear a rumor from someone else that Barbara and Lou were a thing?"

"Nope. Not a peep."

Hmm. Marty Capaldi had said that when Barbara first learned of Andre's existence, she had struck back at Marty by revealing she'd had her own affair. That might have occurred around the same time that Kim witnessed Barbara and Lou at the gazebo.

Jeez. Lou Thorpe got around.

"Thanks, Kim. That might prove helpful. I'll keep it to myself."

Kim had no other helpful gossip and soon got up to reopen the café, leaving Bill to plot his next move. Alex had shared Victor Bishop's contact information, and Bill called Victor's cell number. Bishop was golfing down in the Rockfish Valley, and they arranged to meet after his round.

Next, Bill checked his phone for text messages. He had still not heard from Cindy and now worried she was sending a signal he was too dense to understand. Fearing that further delay would exacerbate the problem, he resolved to meet her face to face.

THIRTY-TWO

Standing at the door to Cindy's condo, Bill recognized his heart rate had accelerated more than justified by the steps from the parking lot. He inhaled deeply and pressed the bell.

At first, nothing, and then he sensed movement from inside her unit. Footsteps approached, and the door opened.

Barefoot and wearing jeans and a faded concert tour T-shirt, Cindy stood in the entryway holding the heavy door. Her hair was pulled back, but a lock had come loose and dangled over her forehead. Her other hand appeared to be damp as if she'd been working in the kitchen. When she realized it was Bill, vertical creases formed on her forehead.

"Hey, Cindy. What's up?"

"Not much, Bill. How are you?" Her voice was as flat as a desert road.

"Did I miss something?"

"Don't think so. Seems to me you're catching everything coming your way." Cindy's eyes were hard, and she breathed hotly through her nose.

Holy jalapeño. What on earth had possessed her? He

believed for a moment that Cindy was not well. And then he recalled their brief and tense conversation in the parking lot the previous day.

"Does this have something to do with Krista Jackson?" he said.

"I don't know. Are you doing something with Krista?" Cindy stood her ground in the doorway, making it clear he was not invited to come inside.

"You can't be serious."

Cindy turned her hand flippantly to the side to indicate that if Bill knew everything, he needn't bother her with questions.

"Why would a young woman like Krista have an interest in me?" he said. "I'm just a retired cop."

Cindy tilted her head. "Let's see. Why would she? She's a single mother pushing forty with two growing boys and an empty bed. In Nelson County, like everywhere else, a good man is hard to find. Now here you come. You're single, reliable, and handsome. Plus, you're financially independent. This is not thermodynamics."

Bill had never considered himself a handsome man, but his wife had called him that occasionally over the years. "My handsome devil," she would say at the oddest times, when he came inside wearing a dirty T-shirt from working in the yard, or back in the days when he was a patrol officer in uniform. He had considered her words a term of endearment, not an actual opinion. His nose was too big, and although he'd always been strong, he'd never had that chiseled look some cops got from working out all the time.

"Let's be real," he said. "I'm more than twenty years older than Krista. I'll be eighty before she hits sixty."

"Krista's not thinking that far ahead. She thinks about the bills she's got to pay every month. She thinks that winter will come soon, and the nights will be cold. Oh, and wouldn't it be nice to have a man sit beside her at the football games?"

Wait a minute. Football games? What put that notion in Cindy's head? Had someone from the police station told Cindy that he and Krista had discussed her boys' football activities? Lord Almighty. The spies were everywhere.

"Now, Cindy," he said, "nothing is going on here. Krista and I are working on the investigation. We're . . . we're like co-workers. Actually, she's sort of working for me right now. That's all there is to it."

"Oh," Cindy said with sarcasm creeping into her voice. "She's working underneath you. Nothing to it, I see." But a moment later, her expression changed. Her shoulders sagged, and her eyes softened. "I'm sorry for twisting your words. That was uncalled for, but I'm sure you've learned by now that word travels fast on the mountain. You'll never guess what a friend told me today."

A sinking feeling entered Bill's chest, the feeling he got right before learning he had clumsily stepped into a mess.

"What?" he said.

"She told me Krista Jackson is dating a new guy, an ex-cop from Columbia, South Carolina."

"That's crazy talk."

"Specifics were provided. Apparently, the ex-cop is attending a scrimmage game with Krista and her boys, and afterward, the whole crew is going out to dinner."

Oh, boy.

What now? He couldn't lie to her. Lying weakened the foundation of any relationship. Not that he had much of a relationship with Cindy, if any at all. The realization left a hollow feeling in Bill's chest.

"Um," he said, "that part's true, but it's not like we're dating or anything."

Cindy sighed. "I have no claim on you, Bill. None whatsoever. I just want to know where I stand. If you want to see Krista, that's fine. We can still be friends, but we won't make out on my couch again."

"But—"

"I'm not trying to put you on the spot. Not at all. Take your time, think it over, and let me know where you come out."

Cindy had held the door open all this time with her eyes locked on Bill. Now she closed it, and a few seconds later, the bolt lock clicked.

Doggone it. Life isn't fair. How could he see that coming?

He considered knocking on her door to see if she would talk this through further. Truthfully, he had only the best of intentions toward Cindy, but judging by the tension in her voice, more discussion would help little at this point. No, Bill needed to act, and he needed to act fast.

THIRTY-THREE

"Hey, Krista, you have a minute?" said Bill.

He stood near her cubicle in the police station. After the unnerving conversation with Cindy, Bill had stopped by his condo for a late lunch. Over a sandwich, he had planned his next move.

Krista swiveled in her office chair and smiled. "Sure thing. Anytime." She crossed her legs and put her hands on her knee in a cute way.

"I need your advice on a personal matter."

She raised her eyebrows, and her eyes twinkled. "Well, let's get personal."

"Good. Good." Bill rolled a chair next to Krista and sat. "So, here's the thing. Do you know Cindy Quintrell?"

Krista pushed her lips out, perhaps wondering where Bill was headed. "Yes," she said slowly. "Everyone knows Cindy. She's lived in Wintergreen for years, and she has a catering business."

"Yes. That's right. Cindy happens to live in the condo building next to mine."

Krista bit the inside of her cheek. "Hmm. Is that so?"

"Uh-huh. Anyway, she and I met each other recently, and we've been hanging out together a bit."

With her smile long gone, Krista sank farther in the chair.

"Here's where I need your advice," said Bill. "The next time I meet Cindy, I want to bring something special to show I'm interested in becoming more than friends. What would make the best impression? Flowers or wine?"

Bill remained skeptical that Krista had an interest in him, but obviously, Cindy believed otherwise. He had designed this question to make his intentions clear to Krista without embarrassing anyone. A flicker of disappointment entered Krista's eyes, but then it was gone, and in the next moment, her expression changed to that of a helpful friend.

"Flowers," she said. "You can't go wrong with flowers. She can buy all the wine she needs on her own, but flowers from a man are always special."

"Oh, good. That's great advice. Thank you."

Krista sighed, uncrossed her legs, and made to turn back to her monitor. "Anything else?"

Bill had planned for this part of the conversation as well. "Yes, there is. That bit of information you uncovered on the pay-for-influence scheme is proving to be helpful. It could be pivotal to sorting this whole thing out."

"Really?" Krista's eyes brightened instantly. She put her hands on her thighs and leaned forward.

"Definitely," said Bill. "Let's try to build on that success. Keep mining the internet to see if you discover anything else. Broaden the net to include everyone in that close circle of friends—the golfing buddies and their wives. Oh, and bring Andre Lewis into the scope of your search."

"Andre Lewis? The thru-hiker?"

Bill explained the father-son connection between Marty and Andre. They discussed various ways she could approach the assignment, and then Bill went to give Alex Sharp a briefing on his conversation with Marty.

With each revelation—Marty being Andre's father, the pay-for-influence scheme, the men using their golf outing as a cover-up for side visits to Rachel Dunn—the shock on Alex's face grew more pronounced. Finally, he buried his face in his hands.

"We're like a reality show," he said. "Wintergreen Wonderland. What's next? A camera crew?"

Bill shrugged, then said, "Who knows? I'm heading down to Stoney Creek to meet Victor Bishop. I'll see what he has to say."

"All right. No word from Mitch on Andre Lewis yet. I thought they'd find him by now."

Bill left soon after that. He didn't tell Alex he had warned Marty Capaldi to bring Andre in, and he didn't relate the makeout session Kim had witnessed between Lou Thorpe and Barbara Capaldi. Throughout his career, Bill had never told his boss every little detail. Why start now?

THIRTY-FOUR

Bill drove down to the Rockfish Valley and took State Route 151 another three miles to Nellysford. The larger Wintergreen community included a residential area in the valley called Stoney Creek. Stoney Creek had its own golf course with wider fairways and slightly longer distances than the mountain course.

As the elevation declined from the mountaintop to the valley, the temperature rose, and when Bill stepped out of his air-conditioned Mazda, he was assaulted by a wave of hot, sticky air. Even so, the blue haze of the neighboring mountains and the deep green of the fairways made for a bucolic setting. Small wonder that some people spent many hours trying to knock a ball into a hole.

Around the back of the clubhouse, Bill asked an attendant where he might find Bishop and was directed to the practice tee. Once there, he watched the small septuagenarian hit golf balls straight and far consistently. Noticing Bill, Bishop asked if he could give him a few more minutes. No problem.

Victor Bishop finished, grabbed his bag, and walked spritely to where Bill waited. It occurred to Bill that Bishop would have little trouble hiking several miles on a dark mountain trail.

"You're hitting the ball hard," said Bill.

"It's an infuriating game." Bishop reached for Bill's hand. "The better you get, the better you want to be. Only a few hundred people on the planet can play the game extremely well, but millions of others want to reach that level." Bishop pointed to the clubhouse. "Let's get something to drink."

Within a minute of entering the clubhouse lounge, Bill went from warm to chilled. The room was not large, with six round tables and a long bar on one side. A flat-screen mounted on the wall showed a baseball game in progress. They sat at a table, and the lone waitress took their orders. Bishop drank a draft beer in a tall glass. Bill had a fountain soda.

Bishop said, "I gather from Alex you guys have a team searching for the thru-hiker."

"That's right. I'm sure he'll be in custody soon."

A smile of superiority crept onto Victor Bishop's face. "Would have been a lot easier if you had never let him go."

Upon first meeting Bishop after the memorial service, Bill had found him a hard guy to like, but Bill needed the man's cooperation, so he let the dig slide. "You're right. I can see that now."

Bishop awarded his own cleverness with a pull on his beer. "Well, hindsight is everything. How can I help?"

Victor Bishop colored his hair to a dark brown with gray at the temples. The coloring knocked years off his age, but casual inspection revealed many wrinkles around his eyes and on his neck and hands. His arms were marred by dry skin.

"We're working through several hypothetical scenarios for the hit-and-run. You can help us with some of the context." Bill had brought his manila folder along and now shared the Honda Pilot photo with Bishop. "Did you see the email we sent out revealing the vehicle that struck Lou Thorpe?"

"No, I didn't." Victor frowned at the photo, and then his eyes darted to Bill. "Wait. This is the vehicle?"

"Yes."

Bishop continued to study the photo, and his face clouded with worry. "But I know this car, or at least, I know a car that looks like this. Joel Turner drives a Honda Pilot this color. I watch over it for him. I have a key."

"It's the same vehicle," said Bill in a matter-of-fact tone.

"It is?" said Bishop, by all appearances genuinely shocked.

Was he lying? Bill had learned over the years that attorneys were often quite good at hiding their true motives.

"Yes," said Bill. "We found it stashed in the Humpback Rocks Picnic Area. Would you know anything about that?"

"Me? No. Why would I? I haven't seen the car in a month."

"Is that so? I understood that you drove it at least once a week. On Fridays."

Bishop's face grew pale as he began to realize that Bill knew quite a lot. "Fridays?"

"Yes, on Fridays, you visited Rachel Dunn. You have a lot of explaining to do, Mr. Bishop, and not only to me. Why don't we start with the visits to Rachel? What did you have going on with her, and how did Lou Thorpe fit into that equation?"

Bishop pushed his beer away, as if he no longer had a taste for it.

Bill watched Bishop assess the situation. Bishop didn't know how much Bill already knew. He ought to stick to the truth, but he tried lying anyway.

"Lou introduced me to Rachel."

"Uh-huh."

"We're just friends."

Now it was Bill's turn to smile. "Mr. Bishop, we both know that's not true. You can forget about concealing your afternoon delights with Ms. Dunn. Your wife's going to hear of it, so you might as well go ahead and tell me. It'll give you some practice."

Bishop put his elbows on the table and pressed his palms against his forehead. His back rose and fell as he took several deep breaths. When he sat straight again, his eyes seemed tired, but his mouth was firm with resolve.

"I've never done anything like this, not in forty-five years of marriage." He poked the table with his finger for emphasis. "Not once."

Bill gave Bishop a sympathetic nod.

"But Marilyn won't care about that," said Bishop. "She'll drag me through hell. And I didn't even have sex with the woman. It was just a good time, just some fun. Our marriage, like others, I'm sure, has grown stale with age. We go through the motions, mostly because we can't think of anything else to do. We're too old, damn it, to try anything new. Those are the facts."

Bill pondered Bishop's words for only an instant before deciding he disagreed completely. In the early years of adult life, humans were too ignorant to know what to do. They wasted their time chasing other people, not realizing they were answering an instinctive call to procreate. In the middle years of life, humans spent all of their time working to support and raise the children they had created. Not until they retired—assuming they had the economic freedom to do so— did humans finally have both the knowledge and the time to try new things. In the past week alone, Bill had begun to fathom how much he didn't know. He knew of concrete and buildings and the motives of bad people, but he knew nothing of the natural world. And now he had time to learn all about it.

Bishop rambled on about his oh-so-platonic affair with Rachel Dunn.

"I tried to have sex with her once." He cringed. "It was a disaster. But the afternoons on her balcony were quite pleasant. We'd have lunch and a drink, and Rachel would give me a neck massage. She'd run her fingers through my hair as if she enjoyed it. Oh, to sit there with a beautiful woman, to talk, to laugh, and to remember, it's hard to describe. The view of the mountains and the valley on a sunny day was extraordinary. Despite the cost, and in the end, I suspect it may cost me a lot, it might have been worth it."

"Tell me about the Honda," said Bill. "How did the three of you share the Honda to visit Rachel Dunn?"

Bishop explained the logistical scheme Bill had already discussed with Marty Capaldi.

"What about Cyrus Hunt?" said Bill. "Did he ever use the car?"

"No, I think he actually bought the consulting story. Cyrus is a good guy. He's not that curious, you know, he stays in his lane."

"Did anyone else know where you kept the spare key?"

Bishop bit his lip and glanced away. "I don't believe so. Marilyn asked to borrow the Pilot once when our second car was in the shop. I drove her to the garage and then had to go around back to get the key. She asked about it, and I told her I loaned the Honda to Lou once in a while and that we kept the key hidden behind the garage."

"Anyone else?"

"No."

Okay. It seemed as if Marty Capaldi and Victor Bishop were the only persons with easy access to the car. Although Bill should also get Marilyn's side of the story. With his Honda access questions answered, Bill could now turn to motive.

"Word on the mountain has it that you and Lou have had some tense moments recently," said Bill.

For a moment, Bishop tried his innocent expression again. "Tense moments?"

"Arguments. You want to tell me about it?"

Bishop drummed his fingers on the table. He breathed loudly through his nose. "You're talking about this BS whistleblower investigation."

"I'm not talking about it. I want *you* to talk about it."

After tweaking his nose several times, Bishop said, "Everybody loves to hate coal. Ever notice that? All the environmental wannabes—bad, bad coal. We should do wind and solar, right? Well, twenty-five percent of US electricity still comes from coal. Who wants to give up their lights and heat? Their computers and their televisions? No one."

"Get to the bribery-for-influence investigation. Lou was scheduled to give a deposition this week, right? That must have hurt given you'd channeled so much money to him over the years."

Bishop rocked his knee so hard under the table his head bobbled. His eyes burned with anger for the dead.

Bill watched the retired corporate attorney struggle with his emotion. Bishop's logical mind knew he should remain quiet, but everyone has a limit.

"Yeah," said Bishop, "it hurt. All those years and Lou still couldn't keep his mouth shut. Covering up his backside and leaving me out in the cold."

"It felt good to run him down," said Bill. "Didn't it? Keep that mouth shut."

"I didn't do it."

"You had the motive and the means. Come on. Admit it. You'll feel better about yourself."

"I was at home in bed all night. I didn't even know the Honda was involved until now."

"Maybe. Maybe not. I'll have to talk to your wife to verify your alibi. Admit it now, and we can skip that part. We might even leave out the Rachel Dunn mess."

Victor Bishop solemnly shook his head. "I'm innocent. Go ahead and talk to Marilyn. She can fry me if she wants, but it's better than going to prison for something I didn't do."

THIRTY-FIVE

After he met with Victor Bishop, Bill stopped at the IGA grocery store in Nellysford to buy ingredients for his chili recipe: ground turkey, Italian ground sausage, diced tomatoes, cannellini beans, tomato sauce, garlic, onions, and chili powder.

On his way up to Wintergreen, Bill called Cyrus Hunt to see if he could stop by with a quick follow-up question. No problem. Cyrus lived in a small cabin on Cedar Drive not far from the Old Appalachian Trail. They sat on his back deck and drank iced tea. A crow cawed in the trees behind the cabin. Two squirrels chased each other around Cyrus's lawn and up the trunk of a maple tree.

"This morning, I asked if you had noticed anything unusual going on between Lou and the others," said Bill. "Why didn't you mention that they took turns cutting out of the foursome? That would seem to fit the definition of unusual."

Cyrus wiggled his bushy eyebrows and said, "No, you asked about recent conflicts between Lou and the others, and I described the argument I witnessed. The guys took turns doing their consulting gig on every round we ever played. That's not a recent change."

"Don't tell me you bought that consulting ruse? In the middle of a golf round? Come on."

Cyrus paused to elaborately sip his tea, and then he said in all innocence, "You mean they were doing something else?"

Bill frowned to communicate his disbelief in Cyrus's feigned ignorance. He said, "Let's cut the BS."

"All right," said Cyrus. "The thought crossed my mind that my buddies were engaged in some other activity, but they never volunteered details, and I didn't ask. It's not my place to speculate about what they were doing on their time."

"Fair enough. But I'm curious. Would you be shocked if I told you they were skipping out on golf to secretly meet with a woman?"

Cyrus rubbed his chin. "Shocked? No. Disappointed? Yes."

Bill handed Cyrus the photo of the SUV. "This morning, we discussed the vehicle that struck Lou Thorpe. You said you'd seen the email with this image."

"Yes. That's right."

"Have you seen a Honda Pilot this color driving around Wintergreen?"

"No. Not that I recall."

Satisfied with Hunt's answers, Bill made to leave. Cyrus then asked Bill if he cared to stay for a beer and an early dinner. The man lived alone, obviously, but Cyrus didn't come across as lonely. Bill had perishable groceries waiting in his car, so he suggested they try it another night. After comparing schedules, they tentatively agreed on Friday, and Bill left.

THE MOUNTAIN VIEW MURDER

Upon returning to his condo, Bill stashed his groceries and promptly marched to Cindy's condo building. His mouth was dry, and he could scarcely catch his breath. Standing at her door, he squeezed his hands together but then realized that made him appear nervous, so he consciously let his arms fall to his sides. Footsteps approached, and Cindy opened the door wearing the same clothes as earlier, jeans and an old T-shirt. She heaved a sigh.

Bill said, "I didn't need a lot of time to think about it."

Cindy lifted a hand toward him. "Bill, I came on a little strong earlier."

"No problem. Here's where I stand. I'm not romantically interested in Krista, but I am interested in you."

A smile began to form on Cindy's lips.

He held his hands out. "I joke around when I talk with people, both men and women. I like joking around and will continue to do so, maybe even with Krista. I also like watching kids play football. It reminds me of when my boys were that age. Maybe sometime you and I could go watch Krista's boys play."

She lifted her face, and her eyes sparkled. "Yes, I'd like that." Then she opened the door wider and gestured inside. "Do you want to come in? The place is a bit of a mess, but I could pour some wine."

"No, thanks. I'm making a chili recipe I've perfected over many years. It's hearty and tasty and will be ready in an hour. Want to try some?"

Cindy stepped forward, and the door closed behind her. She reached to touch Bill's face and then kissed him. "It's a date."

Cindy brought a six-pack of a local brewery's IPA. They sat across from each other at the dining table and ate chili with salad and cornbread. Cindy sat with her back to the sliding doors. Behind her, the ridge across the valley sloped down to the left. The setting sun turned the bright day softer. It was a stunning view, but Bill had a tough time tearing his eyes away from the beauty before him.

"This is excellent," she said.

"It's the sausage. Italian sausage makes everything taste better. I could eat it for dessert."

"Can I have the recipe? I'm putting together a casual menu. Some clients want options for simpler occasions, kids' birthday parties, events like that, and I don't have a great answer."

"Sure. It's even better after it simmers for a few hours."

Cindy spread peach preserves on her cornbread. "Mmm, that's good."

After doing the dishes, they walked onto his balcony to enjoy a second beer. Bill leaned over the railing to search for Mr. Chips, but the neighborhood groundhog was either inside his burrow or off foraging.

"Look." Cindy pointed. "A rabbit."

The rabbit hopped cautiously from his hiding place in the hillside brush to nibble on the lawn's lush grass. He ate in a deliberate way. First, he pulled grass into his mouth, and then he raised his head to chew, all the while keeping a watchful eye on his surroundings.

A shadow crossed the grass, and Bill glanced up in time to see a large bird coast to a neat landing on the roof of Cindy's condo building. The tail of the bird was a reddish-brown. A red-tailed hawk. Bill congratulated himself because he recognized the raptor from studying his *Birds of Virginia Field Guide*. The hawk eyed the ground.

Cindy, who had also seen the bird, now grabbed Bill's forearm. "Oh, no! The rabbit."

Bill handed Cindy his beer. The hawk tilted its head down and toward the rabbit. Adrenaline surged through Bill's body, and he leaned far over the balcony. Clapping his hands loudly, he yelled, "Hey. Hey. Hey. Hey. Hey!"

The hawk swooped. The rabbit dropped his food and turned toward the brush.

Fear shot through Bill, fear that he would witness nature's cruelty first hand.

Hop. Hop. Hop.

The rabbit scampered into the brush, and the hawk's talons closed on empty air. Frustrated and angry, the hawk made two quick turns and soared over the valley in search of other prey.

Cindy turned toward him. "Saints alive, Bill. You're a hero!" With beers in both hands, she threw her arms around his neck and kissed him. He pulled her to him and felt very much alive.

THIRTY-SIX

"The search is over, Bill," Mitch said when he called the next morning at seven o'clock. "Andre Lewis turned himself in for questioning."

"Oh."

Of course, Bill knew this already because Marty Capaldi had texted him after delivering Andre to the sheriff's office in Lovingston. Standing in his kitchen, Bill considered whether he should share that information with Mitch. Better not.

"Apparently," said Mitch, "Andre's father is Marty Capaldi, but I guess you already knew that."

"Yeah. Marty told me."

"Andre maintains he had nothing to do with Thorpe's death. He has a lawyer now, but he's agreed to stick around for a week. He's staying with the Capaldis."

Interesting. Bill wondered how Barbara Capaldi had reacted to that development. He made a mental note to find out. He had exchanged texts with the two wives the previous night—Barbara Capaldi and Marilyn Bishop—and he had appointments with both of them later that day.

"What's the next move?" said Mitch.

Bill invited Mitch to join the interviews, and Mitch offered to drive.

∽

Marilyn Bishop greeted them at the door of a large mountain home on Laurel Springs Drive not far from the little parking lot near the Appalachian Trail. A trim, energetic woman, Marilyn wore black leggings and a long wool sweater. She had sharp facial features, brown eyes, and white hair styled in a short cut. Bill guessed her age at early seventies, similar to that of her husband.

She invited them into a large kitchen and poured them coffee from a chrome pot with a spout. Comfortably seated at the breakfast table for four, Marilyn opened the conversation by saying, "Victor is not here, so we can speak frankly."

"Okay," said Bill, perfectly willing to let Marilyn lead the way. "Good."

"He has revealed to me the absurd arrangement he had with Ms. Dunn. He's a moron." Clearly agitated but not out of control, Marilyn Bishop glared at Bill and Mitch in turn.

It felt as if he were a student about to receive a lecture from a stern teacher.

Then her eyes drifted to the kitchen, and she became distracted by another matter. "Damn," she said, "I forgot the muffins." She hopped up, scurried to the kitchen counter, and returned with a plate of mini-muffins and several napkins.

Bill and Mitch murmured quick thank yous.

"Seriously," she said, "what sort of man in his mid-seventies carries on like that with a woman half his age? What did he think he was going to do? Have glorious sex with her? Experience physical pleasure hitherto unknown to man? What a moron."

Bill could not help himself. In his head, he divided the approximate age of Rachel Dunn by that of Victor Bishop. Rachel was more than half his age, more like two-thirds.

Mitch, God bless him, popped a muffin into his mouth and munched on it.

Marilyn stared at Bill with anger smoldering beneath the surface of her face. The fingernails of her right hand dug into her left palm. She snarled and said, "I still haven't decided what to do with him. Should I divorce him?" Her eyes roamed through the kitchen and then over to the well-appointed living room and the magnificent windows overlooking the forest behind the house. "There's more than enough money for two. This place is paid for, as is the home in Fairfax, which is worth a small fortune on its own." She pointed at Bill. "I could do that. I could take Victor to divorce court and walk away with enough money to move someplace warm. Then I could find a young man to take care of me." Marilyn capped her fury with a question. "How would he feel about that?"

Confident that she had asked the question rhetorically, Bill kept his own counsel. Mitch sat still with his eyes bulging.

After taking several deep breaths, Marilyn grew calmer. "I'm sorry for dragging you through our domestic mess. You guys are here to do a job, trying to figure out who killed Lou Thorpe."

"Yes, that's right," said Bill.

"Lou Thorpe," she said with disdain. "There's another jerk. I blame Lou for arranging the sordid meetings with Ms. Dunn. Victor would never have had the gumption to do something like that on his own. Anyway, I said I'd stop going on about that. How can I help you?"

"Your husband told me he was with you the entire night that Lou Thorpe was killed. Can you verify that for us?"

Marilyn leaned back and bounced an index finger against her mouth. "You have Victor down as a suspect? Why? Oh, that's right, the pay-for-influence investigation. Sorry for not keeping up. I'm clearly not all there today." She paused to smile. "You guys are clever. Victor has clearly benefited from Lou's death. Me too, for that matter. Lou's deposition could have transformed that preliminary probe into a full-blown criminal investigation." Then she scrunched her nose. "But Victor couldn't do something like that. He lacks the constitutional fortitude to run a man down with an SUV. That's not his style. He's more likely to talk a man to death."

"Be that as it may," said Bill, "can you verify that Victor was with you all night?"

"No, I can't."

Mitch, who had not moved for several minutes, now sat straight.

"I can tell you that Victor and I got in bed together at our usual time, around eleven o'clock, and that he was here when I got up around six thirty. But as to the intervening hours, I cannot be certain." Marilyn casually leaned across the table to take a mini muffin and a napkin. "I sleep like death. Honestly, when my head hits the pillow, I'm out, and I don't move until I wake up. I don't even go to the bathroom. Victor could throw a party in the living room, and I wouldn't know."

Marilyn's frank comments concerning her sleeping habits did nothing to help Victor, which was unusual. Many wives would have assured Bill that their husband had lain beside them all night. No question. He got in bed with me, and he didn't move until the morning. What kind of wife had Wanda been? Put in a similar situation, would Wanda have verified Bill's alibi with confidence? Bill wasn't sure.

Marilyn finished her muffin and wiped her mouth with the napkin. "I can't verify Victor's alibi, but I'll stand by my earlier statement that Victor didn't do it. He couldn't. He doesn't have it in him. But I could have done it. No problem."

Whoa. Here was something Bill didn't see every day.

After reaching for yet another mini muffin, Marilyn said, "Victor sleeps soundly too. I could have slipped out for hours, and he would never have known."

She bit into the second muffin and chewed slowly, making Bill and Mitch wait.

"Lou Thorpe was killed with Joel Turner's Honda Pilot, right?" she said.

"Yes, that's correct."

"Victor had a spare key to the Pilot. He told me once that he kept it hidden behind Turner's garage. How hard would that be to find? Easy. Tucked behind a log or hidden under a stone. How many places can you hide a key along one wall?"

She eyed Mitch and Bill as if to assure herself they were listening. She needn't have bothered.

"Everyone knew Lou's exercise routine. He bragged about it all the time."

Marilyn spoke casually, and Bill could see her in his mind. First, she rose from the bed she shared with Victor and dressed quickly in dark clothes. She easily found the key under the flowerpot. After parking somewhere that afforded her a clear view, Marilyn waited for Lou Thorpe to pass. Then she ruthlessly knocked him across the ditch.

"What would you have done with the car?" he asked.

"Ditched it," she said without hesitation. "Someplace hard to find but also close enough that I could walk back here with ease. Probably out on the parkway somewhere."

Mitch's mouth dropped. Bill's body tingled all over. His

mouth was dry, but he could not tear his eyes away from Marilyn to reach for the coffee.

"Here's the best part," she said. "I hated Lou Thorpe."

"Why?" Bill managed to say. "Why did you hate him?"

Marilyn filled her lungs with air and pulled her shoulders back. "Because he was a monster." She clenched her fists. "Jeanne Thorpe and I are good friends. We've played tennis together for many years, and she always wears long sleeves. Here on the mountain, it gets cool in the shade, even in the summertime, and tall trees surround most of the courts. But on one of our rare warm days—must have been mid-eighties—we played on a sunny court. Jeanne was wearing a sweater, and she must have grown unbearably hot, for she took it off. And then I saw them."

Bill leaned forward. "Saw what?"

"Bruises. Jeanne had bruises on her arms." Marilyn touched her arms above the elbows to indicate the location of the bruises. "They were dark blue and black, deep bruises, and I asked her about them. She tried to laugh them off. 'Oh, that's nothing. It's kind of embarrassing. It's Lou. When we're in bed and having, you know, an intimate moment, he gets very passionate.'" Marilyn's shoulders sagged, and she continued. "That's not passion, that's abuse, and I told Jeanne as much. She wouldn't listen to any of that. 'No. No. It's not,' she said. But I knew better. Lou had given her those bruises intentionally."

"When did this happen?" said Bill.

Marilyn pushed her lips out. "Not long ago. Two weeks, I guess, maybe three."

"So, not long before the hit-and-run?"

"Right, just a few days earlier. I remember thinking when I heard the news that I was glad Lou was dead." Marilyn's eyes were dark brown, almost black, and a fire of rage burned deep within them. "I hated him."

"Did you kill him?" said Bill. "Did you take the SUV like you said, run Thorpe over, and ditch the car up on the parkway? Did you?"

She studied her hands and then slowly lifted her head. "Sadly, no. I wish I had killed him. If I had thought of it, I might have, but I didn't."

"You sure?" said Bill. So caught up was he in Marilyn's story that he half expected her to confess at that moment. A glance at Mitch told Bill the patrolman felt the same way.

But Marilyn shook her head, by all appearances disappointed to admit that she had *not* murdered Lou Thorpe.

THIRTY-SEVEN

When they had returned to the squad car, Mitch said, "What do you make of all that?"

"I'm still processing it."

They had an hour and a half to wait until the meeting with Barbara Capaldi. Bill observed the Bishops' house. The forest behind the house was thick with hardwoods, and the hill sloped downward gently. "How far is it from here to the Appalachian Trail in a straight line?"

Mitch frowned. "Not sure. Less than a quarter of a mile."

"Let's go to the little dirt parking lot and take a walk."

Once again, Mitch led the way. Two hundred yards from the parking lot, he turned right on the AT. Bill watched the big man move, his arms relaxed at his sides, his legs climbing the first hill with little effort. Mitch's head swiveled from side to side, and his eyes devoured the terrain.

"How was the search?" said Bill.

Mitch took a few steps before answering. "As it turns out, with Andre stashed in a hotel, the search was like fishing in a swimming pool. Even the world's best angler couldn't catch a fish. Still, I can't complain. First time I ever got paid for hiking."

They reached a slight turn in the trail, and Mitch stopped and pointed in the direction of Wintergreen. "We've been moving parallel to Laurel Springs Drive. I'd guess we're a few hundred yards from the road now, but the trail angles away from it up here. You want to keep going?"

"Yes."

Bill began discussing the investigation, bringing Mitch up to speed and using the exercise to organize his own thoughts. He went through the list of suspects: Lou Thorpe's wife, his mistress, his buddies, and their wives. Oh, and also Andre Lewis. Once he had gotten through the list and shared his latest thinking on motives and access to the Honda, Bill asked Mitch for his top candidate.

"I still like the thru-hiker theory," said Mitch. "Of course, I've got fifty bucks on the line for that outcome."

"How's that?" said Bill.

Mitch pulled up short. "What? You don't remember the bet? Don't pull the senior card on me."

In truth, Bill had completely forgotten the wager he'd made with Mitch and Krista. "No, I'm not trying to welch on the bet. Run the terms by me again."

The big man put a giant hand out with his fingers spread. "Krista and I each bet you five dollars that a thru-hiker drove the SUV into Lou Thorpe. And the best part is you gave us ten to one odds." Then Mitch chuckled. "Of course, at the time we didn't know Andre's prints were on the Honda. Tell you what. If you want a chance to cut your losses, I'll take twenty-five right now."

Bill believed that Mitch genuinely intended to cut him a break, but Bill still didn't see Andre as the driver, so he declined the offer.

They walked farther, and Mitch stopped again. On the right, the land rose gently for fifty yards and then leveled off.

"If we climb to the top of this hill, we might see the Bishops' house. Wait. Look at that." Mitch jogged ahead on the trail a hundred feet and stopped.

Bill hurried to catch up, mindful of the rocks on the path.

"There's a trail up and over the hill. It's faint, and I didn't see it when we passed here a few days ago. People must use it as a shortcut."

Even with Mitch pointing at the so-called trail, it was difficult for Bill to distinguish it from the surrounding brush. That section of the forest floor was covered with dead leaves and the occasional fern or sapling. With concentration, Bill discerned that the leaves were flattened on a narrow path that ran up and over the hill.

"Let's follow it," he said.

They had only hiked a few minutes when Mitch halted. He waited for Bill to catch up, then pointed farther up the hill. Bill blinked a few times and then made out the wooden siding and roof of a house.

"That's the neighbor's place," said Mitch. "The Bishops' house is to the left. See it?"

"Yeah."

Which they both knew meant that Victor or Marilyn Bishop could have easily hidden the Honda in the picnic area, hiked a mile on the AT, and then taken the shortcut to their home.

Back at the squad car, Mitch nodded at Bill and said, "All right, so tell me. Who do you think did it?"

Bill signaled his ignorance with a big shrug. "It's like I've got an itch I can't reach to scratch. Can't help feeling I'm missing something." He rubbed the back of his neck. "I always have to remind myself that it's harder to spot a lie of omission than a lie of commission." Bill checked his phone for the time. "But ask me after we've talked to Barbara Capaldi. That could change everything."

⁓

He had planned to meet Barbara at the tennis center after her scheduled lesson, but on the way there, Bill received a text from her asking to meet at the Devils Grill lounge instead.

"Ah, there you are," she said when Bill and Mitch entered the lounge area. She stood at the bar and accepted a glass of white wine from a man in a white shirt. Barbara asked the men if they cared for something. Mitch passed. Bill asked for a Diet Coke. She thanked the bartender and asked that he put the drinks on her tab. It appeared they had done this many times. It was five minutes after eleven o'clock in the morning.

"Let's sit on the patio," she said. "It's glorious outside."

An apt description, for the late morning sun brightened the eighteenth fairway. An early foursome of two couples stood on the green to finish their putts. A woman sank a long one and thrust her arms in the air. Off to the right, several men practiced shots from the driving range. There were ten tables on the patio, most of them empty. An elderly couple drank coffee at a table out of earshot.

As had been his first impression days earlier, Bill found Barbara to be an attractive woman in her seventies, with stylish gray hair and a figure she must have worked hard to maintain. She wore a white tennis skirt and a pink top with a navy sweater tied around her neck. She sipped her wine. It must have been her third or fourth healthy sip, for the glass was at least a third empty.

"I won't apologize for drinking this early," she said. "I expect this to be an unpleasant conversation, what with us having to go through Marty's history with Andre. Oh, and then we have the Rachel Dunn thing as well. Delightful." She took another sip.

"Are you aware that your husband met with Andre the night Lou Thorpe was killed?" asked Bill.

"I am now," she said, making a face. "Andre is staying with us, if you can believe that. Not that I blame Andre. He seems like a nice kid, far as I can tell. It's not his fault that Marty chose to cheat on me. But I never felt the obligation, or had the right, to play Andre's mom. He has his own mother."

Bill said, "Can you verify what time your husband returned to your home after he met with Andre that night?"

"No." She answered immediately. "When I go to bed, I sleep like a rock until I wake up, which is usually between four and five o'clock. After I wake up, that's it for me. I can't sleep anymore, so I get up to make coffee and read. That morning, I got up around four thirty. Marty was asleep in our bed, but I don't know what time he came in."

So no alibi for Marty Capaldi. But what about Barbara? Kim Wiley had seen Lou Thorpe and Barbara Capaldi engaged in a vigorous make-out session twenty years earlier. What was Barbara's recent history with Thorpe? And there was the issue of money as well. How should Bill broach these issues with Barbara? He couldn't think of a diplomatic approach.

"I don't mean to pry into your personal life, Mrs. Capaldi, but I'm afraid I have to. This is a homicide investigation."

"What have we got to lose at this point?" she said. She waved off any concern of his as if she couldn't give a damn.

"Did you have an affair with Lou Thorpe?" he asked.

She blinked several times and tilted her head. "An affair? With Lou?"

"This might have been many years ago. I have to ask."

Barbara Capaldi's face sagged. She appeared to age before Bill's eyes, and her hand shook as she reached for the wine glass. "How on earth did you learn that?"

Bill pressed his lips together tightly.

Barbara took a pained breath and closed her eyes. "Jeanne doesn't know. Please don't tell her."

"I won't tell anyone I don't have to," he said. "You have my word."

She grabbed the wine glass and swallowed half of what remained. A waitress stopped by to see if they needed anything, and Barbara pointed at her drink.

"Marty and I bought our place up here more than twenty years ago," she said. "Our marriage was not in a good place because I had recently learned about Andre. Marty believed this would give us a needed change, a new beginning. Our children were in college then, and I didn't want to get a divorce, so I went along with it. Tennis. Wineries. Maybe it could work."

Barbara frowned at the recollection, and she smoothed a wrinkle on the tablecloth. "Marty swore he would be faithful for the rest of our lives, but I had my doubts. He was spending a lot of time in Washington, perhaps more than necessary. Then I met Lou." She winced, as if she found her memories distressing. "Lou was something to behold in those days—like an honest to God celebrity or something. And he made it clear that he wanted me—he was upfront about it. Not shy. Not ashamed. He wanted me, pure and simple."

She rubbed her hands together gently. "Well, that sort of attention is hard to ignore, and I was still steamed over Andre, so we got right to it." She nervously touched her hair.

"What was I thinking? Sneaking around. In retrospect, it seems absurd. It only lasted a couple of months. During that time, I met Jeanne through tennis." Barbara shuddered. "When I realized what a nice person Jeanne was, I felt horrible and immediately broke things off with Lou."

Barbara finished the wine and glanced over her shoulder as if impatient for the waitress to return. Her chest rose and fell, and her voice began to falter. "I always w-worried that Jeanne would find out, that Lou might tell her, but he never did. For many years, things were pleasant between all of us. We were normal retired couples living the good life. And then one day, Jeanne told me about Rachel Dunn."

"Wait a second," said Bill.

Mitch sat straight in his chair.

"Jeanne knew her husband was seeing Rachel Dunn?" asked Bill.

"Oh, yes. Rachel was Lou's mistress for years back in Washington. Jeanne knew of the arrangement because a friend of a friend had warned her. She thought the affair was over, but then one day, she saw Rachel Dunn at the Market up here, and she knew Lou was still seeing her."

"When did that happen?" said Bill.

The waitress stopped by to deliver Barbara's wine, and Barbara paused to take a healthy sip. Her eyebrows furrowed as she searched her mind for an answer. "Sometime early last year. It must have been April, soon after we came up for the season."

"Did you know that Marty was seeing Rachel?"

"Not at first. But one day not long ago, Lou told me all about it. I was sitting at that table over there having a drink and minding my own business." She pointed at the corner of the patio nearest the eighteenth green. "Then Lou stopped by and said he wanted to tell me a funny story. He gave me the whole Rachel set up: how they used the golf outings as cover for the weekly visits and the convenience of having access to Turner's Honda. He even told me where they hid the key."

Barbara Capaldi made no pretense of hiding anything from Bill and Mitch, let it all come out, and Bill concluded that she was a woman living on the edge of doom.

Her eyes widened. "Lou made the most preposterous proposal. He said he wanted us to rekindle our affair." She wrinkled her nose. "At my age? Seventy-four? I didn't even answer, just shooed him away with my hand."

Until that point, Barbara had maintained much of her composure, but now she appeared to shrink. Her shoulders rounded, and her eyes grew weary. "Life can be such a disappointment," she said. "Dreams become disillusionment. When Marty and I married, we were in love. We had modest hopes. A nice house. A healthy, happy family. But now, I don't know what we have."

Bill cleared his throat, and Barbara startled.

She had a clutch purse and fumbled with it to find a tissue. After wiping her nose, she said, "I'm sorry to go to pieces on you."

"No," said Bill, "I'm the one who should apologize for ruining your morning. As you said, it's a glorious day."

Barbara gave the two men a hesitant smile. "Yes, it is."

Once back in the squad car, Mitch turned in his seat to face Bill. "If both Barbara Capaldi and Jeanne Thorpe knew about Rachel Dunn, does that make both of them suspects as well?"

"Hypothetically, yes," said Bill. "Although according to Jeanne, she didn't know about the Honda Pilot."

Mitch nodded. "Right."

"We've got a lot of moving parts. Let's go back to the station and see if we can get Alex and Krista. We'll put everything up on the whiteboard."

They called the station for sandwich orders and stopped by the Market to get food. Then the four of them holed up in the conference room to review everything they had so far. They were there for three hours. Mitch drew a diagram on the whiteboard with Lou Thorpe in the center. Over the course of the conversation, they added each suspect as a box to the outside with a line to Thorpe. In neat handwriting, Mitch wrote a few words under each box describing motive and ability to access the Honda.

It was a fine diagram, but it didn't change their fundamental problem: they had many plausible suspects but no proof—rock-solid jury proof—to link one of the suspects to the crime. For that matter, some other person may have found a way to take the vehicle and run over Thorpe, either intentionally or accidentally.

Bill had done most of the talking with help from Krista and Mitch along the way. Alex had studied the whiteboard from a corner of the room. He listened with great interest and asked frequent questions, but as the inconclusiveness of their findings became more apparent, he crossed his arms and frowned.

When the diagram was complete, Alex asked, "Any update on the shoeprint?"

Mitch shook his head. "I think we're done. We still have one unidentified bystander and no way of finding him. The shoeprint is either his or the driver's."

Soon after, the meeting broke up, but Alex asked Bill to stick around.

Alex lifted his hands in a sign of frustration. "Are we going to solve this thing?"

"Possibly not." Bill tilted his head toward the whiteboard. "In all likelihood, the driver is up there. But we can't prove who committed the crime. Short of a confession, which seems unlikely at this point, this case is headed for the unsolved pile."

"No more tricks in the bag?"

"Not really. I've got Krista following up on a couple of long shots, but I don't hold out much hope."

Alex slapped his thigh. "That sucks. It's going to hurt Wintergreen for sure. The doubt will hang around like a storm that never leaves."

With nothing else to go over, Alex soon left, but Bill stayed to stare at the whiteboard for another twenty minutes. In his mind, he replayed the conversations he'd had with each suspect, cross-referencing what they had said about each other, aligning facts and timelines. After all that, Bill came to the same conclusion that he had arrived at twice before: Jeanne Thorpe had the best motive. But her face had shown no recognition when Bill first shared with her the Honda photo. He couldn't get over that point, which is why he had asked Krista to search the Internet for old connections. Unfortunately, despite crawling through online attics far and wide, her search had found nothing new.

Oh, well. Such was the job. And frankly, he wasn't even employed. He would flip this thing in the cold case folder without blinking. Alex could worry about storms all he wanted; Bill saw nothing but clear skies. Cindy had asked him over for dinner, and he was beginning to grow hungry again.

On his way out, Krista grabbed him at the door.

"You still here?" he said. "I thought you'd left after the meeting."

"Never mind that. I found something."

Krista's excitement showed in the speed with which she returned to her cubicle. Bill's pulse quickened as he followed her.

She slid into her webbed chair and signaled for Bill to hurry it up. When he had rolled up another chair, she pointed at her monitor.

"I found this website that specializes in cataloging high school yearbooks. They go way back, but some years are missing. I don't know how they source the old yearbooks' material—it seems like the pages are scanned. Anyway, it took me a while to locate Jeanne Thorpe's high school—the Ashmont Bobcats. Her senior and sophomore years are missing, but here is her junior high school photo. 1963. Get a load of that hairstyle. Cute, huh?"

"Very."

"Anyway, I went through all the junior boys' photos. Nothing. Same thing with the senior class." Krista moved her cursor on the screen and clicked back several pages in the yearbook. "Then I searched through the sophomores." She pointed at a photo and name on the screen.

"Holy headshot," said Bill. "Look at that."

THIRTY-EIGHT

Four hours later, Bill lay on his back in Cindy Quintrell's bed and stared at the ceiling. Cindy lay on her side next to him with her hand on his bare chest.

Yes, he thought, *I am perhaps the luckiest man in the world.*

From the moment he entered her condo that evening, she had gone out of her way to touch him. When he was slicing carrots for the stir fry she planned, she had come close to him, put her hand on his side, and reached around to snatch a piece from the cutting board. She had acted similarly throughout the dinner preparation, the actual dining, and the cleanup. They sat on the balcony with wine after dinner and observed the evening. The horizon turned dark purple as the sun set behind them. At one point, Cindy stood to take Bill by the hand and said, "Come with me."

Now, lying next to him, after all the excitement, she said, "What are you thinking about?"

He turned to kiss her. "You. How lucky I am."

"Hmm." She reached to hold his hand. "I thought maybe you were pondering the investigation."

"No chance. Not now."

"Well, I'm asking. Tell me—will you guys solve the case?"

"You're going to make me talk about this now?"

She nodded her head vigorously. "Yes, dummy. In case you didn't know, homicides are kind of a big deal here in Wintergreen. We don't get them every day."

Duh. Try to keep up, Bill.

He turned to lie on his back again. After Krista found the link, they had met with Alex again and gone through the logic. Although the new information led them to a greater degree of certainty, they still lacked evidence to prove the crime. A ploy had come to Bill almost immediately, a trick they could play that had a slight chance of success. But he had not shared his idea with Alex.

"What should I do?" Bill asked Cindy. "When the victim was more evil than any of the suspects? Evil enough, I would say, to deserve calamity." He looked to her for wisdom. "Should I even try to solve the crime?"

She pulled away from him as if surprised by his question. "That's not your decision to make."

"Why not? I have no obligation. I'm not a policeman anymore."

She pursed her lips. "True. But neither are you judge, jury, or executioner. More than that, if you walk away now, it'll worry you forever. You're still a detective—it's not in your nature to let a murderer go free."

Bill wasn't sure about that, but he would go to great lengths to avoid arguing with Cindy in her bed. Anyway, it was a long shot at best.

"Okay," he said. "But I'm going to need your help."

THIRTY-NINE

At five o'clock the next afternoon, a small group invited by Alex Sharp assembled in a meeting room for twenty at the Mountain Inn. Jeanne Thorpe was there as well as her husband's golfing buddies—Marty Capaldi, Victor Bishop, and Cyrus Hunt—plus Barbara Capaldi and Marilyn Bishop. Andre Lewis also came, the youngest invitee by decades. One or more of those in attendance may have been surprised to see Cindy Quintrell had come to the meeting, but if so, they didn't mention it. Alex stood at the front of the room before a simple podium. Most of the group sat facing Alex in red cushioned meeting chairs. Bill sat on the left in a chair angled so he could observe the other attendees. Mitch—who had a short line to deliver—sat on the opposite side of the room from Bill.

Rachel Dunn was not invited because Bill didn't consider her a likely suspect, and her presence would have created an unwanted distraction. A flat-screen monitor was mounted on the wall behind Alex. A small black box with a tiny red light glowing on its side had been fastened with a special clamp to the monitor's top. An observant person familiar with such matters might have recognized the box as a miniature surveillance camera. Earlier, Krista had plugged the black box's power cord into a wall outlet behind the monitor. She now sat in the next meeting room to mind the video software program.

"Thank you all for coming," said Alex. "Sorry for the short notice, but I know everyone here cared deeply for Lou Thorpe." Alex paused to recognize Jeanne's presence with a nod. "And I know from your questions that you are keenly interested in our progress on the investigation."

Alex took his time going through the steps the team had taken. Bill had coached him to drag it out to lull the audience into complacency. Reading from notes, Alex recounted their efforts, the initial and exhaustive house-to-house search for the vehicle, the roadblock they had erected at the community entrance, and the forensics. He acknowledged that many in the room had been interviewed, and with a glance to Andre Lewis, mentioned the two-day search of the Appalachian Trail.

Bill watched the faces of the audience. Barbara Capaldi's eyelids grew droopy. Victor Bishop yawned.

"The team has worked tirelessly, days and nights," said Alex. He fidgeted with his notes, unsure of his place. Then he turned a page to read the backside and frowned. "But, uh, recently, we have discovered an exciting piece of new evidence." Alex examined the next page and scratched his temple.

Marty Capaldi straightened in his chair, and Andre Lewis lifted his head.

"And," Alex said with much hesitation, "ah, we have every reason to believe this evidence will lead us to the driver."

Alex lifted his papers, glanced at the podium, and then

leaned over to stare at the floor. This was the crucial part of the performance. The silence dragged on, and the audience began to fidget.

Finally, Victor Bishop could stand it no longer, and he cried out, "Confound it, Alex, what is the new evidence?"

Bill's eyes moved from face to face.

Alex appeared utterly confused.

Then Mitch leaned forward in his chair and said, "You mean the shoeprint. Right, Chief?"

"What shoeprint?" asked Cindy.

Bill's attention was drawn to Jeanne Thorpe. Her shoulders tensed, and she began fingering her necklace.

By appearances, Alex located his place in the papers and said, "Yes, new analysis of evidence from the crime scene will undoubtedly lead to a quick resolution."

"What about this shoeprint?" said Marty. "What's the deal?"

Jeanne Thorpe's chest heaved.

Alex drew himself to his full height and said, "That's all I'm prepared to share at this time." He glared at Mitch. "Frankly, I hadn't planned to discuss the shoeprint at all. That was a premature disclosure."

Mitch shrank in his chair.

Alex ad-libbed awhile, thanking everyone for their patience and cooperation during the interview process. Then the meeting broke up. As soon as the invited guests had left, the five of them—including Cindy—huddled around Krista's laptop to review the video several times. Upon hearing of the shoeprint, most of the audience displayed mild curiosity, a tilt of the head, a raised eyebrow. Except for Jeanne Thorpe.

"Great job, Alex," said Bill. "You should get an Oscar nomination." He checked his phone for the time. "Let's get some food. It's going to be a long night."

FORTY

"What time is it?" said Cindy, perhaps a quarter of an hour after the last time she'd asked.

"Twelve fifteen," said Bill.

They sat in Bill's Mazda, parked in the Nature Foundation lot across Wintergreen Drive from the fitness center.

Mitch and Bill had gone over the plan several times and agreed: Mitch had to act as their scout. Mitch had parked his personal vehicle three hundred yards from the target's house and then hiked through the forest to sit in the dark with a pair of binoculars around his neck. He had been there for three hours.

The plan hinged on one particular attribute of the mountain community: freestanding homes had no trash pickup service. Condominium and townhome associations had their own dumpsters, but single-family homeowners on this side of Wintergreen all brought their trash to a lone compactor in the fitness center lot.

Krista sat in her car in the Westwood community lot on the far side of Devils Knob Loop. Her job was to report the target's progress en route. Alex was in a squad car with

Officer Hill at the Mountain Inn. They would follow the target's car if he drove past the fitness center and continued down the mountain.

"What if he doesn't show?" said Cindy. "What if he tosses them in the woods?"

"Then we're done," said Bill. "Let's discuss something else."

"The theater group will begin rehearsals for *Mary Poppins* next week. We get to listen in free from our balconies."

"When do you want to see the show?"

"I think we should go twice. You miss a lot the first time you see a musical."

Bill could not remember the last time he had attended a musical theater performance, perhaps in high school. Did it make sense to see the same show twice? Hey, whatever she wanted.

Next to Bill on the console, the handset crackled, and Mitch whispered, "Porch light came on."

Bill's pulse jumped. Cindy jerked in the seat, and he touched her arm.

"The door is open," said Mitch. "He's down the stairs and walking fast. He's at his car."

"Come on," said Bill. They held hands and hurried across Wintergreen Drive to the spot in the trees where they had arranged a blanket on the ground earlier. Cindy lay on the blanket and double-checked her camera. Bill turned the volume down on the handset and held it to his ear, waiting for Krista's report. They had a clear line of sight across the lot to the trash compactor. The streetlight cast an eerie glow over that section of the lot.

"Target is passing by on Devils Knob," said Krista. "He's turning on Wintergreen. Moving at a good clip."

Bill turned off the handset, pulled a flashlight from his back pocket, and lay down next to Cindy. "Any second now."

A Subaru Forrester pulled into the lot. Cindy's camera clicked several times, and Bill's ears prickled at the sound. Could the target hear the camera from this distance? They were a good fifty yards. No way. Not with the engine running.

The target pulled the Subaru a few feet past the compactor and stopped. He got out, opened the hatch, and stood in the glow of the streetlight. Cindy's camera clicked, and the target turned in their direction. He paused, unhurried, and Cindy took another photo. Then the man grabbed a small sack from the cargo hold, tossed it in the compactor, and returned to his vehicle.

After the Subaru left the lot, Bill counted to ten and tapped Cindy on the shoulder. "Let's go."

With his heart thumping, he ran ahead, his hands tingling with anticipation.

"Wait, Bill," she called. "Wait for me."

He slid the compactor door across, and Cindy took five shots of the contents. If it proved necessary, they could later compare these photos with the ones she had taken earlier in the night.

"Okay," she said.

"Did you see it?"

"Yeah. You can reach it."

Bill aimed the flashlight's beam into the compactor. There. A white kitchen trash bag. He retrieved the bag and held it aloft. Illuminated by the streetlight was the distinct outline of two running shoes.

FORTY-ONE

Five hours later, the sound of Bill's cell phone woke him from a dead sleep. He shook his head several times. It was Mitch.

"EMS got a call," Mitch said. From the background noise, Bill gathered Mitch was in a moving car.

After finding the shoes in the trash compactor, the team had debated the next step awhile. Alex decided to wait for the morning to call Nelson County, and Bill had concurred with that decision. Fresh minds made fewer mistakes.

"What is it?" Bill asked Mitch.

"Not sure yet. They said a female—prescription med overdose. Possible suicide. The address is 172 Hemlock Drive."

"That's Jeanne Thorpe's home."

"Yep."

"I'll meet you there."

Mitch had to drive up from Waynesboro. He must have flown or already been halfway there when he called Bill, for the two of them arrived at Jeanne's Thorpe home at the same time. An ambulance and a Chevy Silverado rescue vehicle were already parked in the driveway. From behind the mountains to the east, the sun brightened the early morning sky to a soft blue. As Bill and Mitch hustled toward the residence, the ambulance pulled out. A rescue volunteer walked back into the house, and they followed him.

Mitch knew the man, and after quick introductions, the volunteer filled them in. By appearances, Jeanne Thorpe had consumed a bottleful of pain medication.

"She's groggy now, but Mara—the paramedic—said she'll be all right."

They stood in the middle of the living room. A blanket lay half on the sectional and half on the floor. The volunteer picked up a notebook from a side table. Bill glanced in the kitchen and a darkened hallway but saw no one else.

"Who called it in?" he asked.

"Her guardian angel," said the volunteer. "The guy saved her life, probably. He got here just in time."

"Where is he?" said Mitch.

The volunteer shook his head. "Search me. He hung around at first, but then I turned around, and he was gone. I think he went out the back way." The volunteer looked through the windows toward the deck.

"This guardian angel have a name?" said Bill.

"Yeah, I wrote it down." The volunteer consulted his notebook. "Bill O'Shea. Vistas Condos."

"Hell's bells," said Bill.

Outside, the wind had picked up. The sound of leaves rustling climbed the mountain from the north.

They jumped in the squad car, and the tires screeched as Mitch pulled a wicked Y-turn in the cul-de-sac. Mitch barreled up the mountain a half mile and turned right on Cedar Drive. Then they marched up to the cabin with Mitch in the lead. The front door was halfway open, and Mitch reached for his handgun.

"What are you doing?" said Bill. "Put that away."

"The situation calls for it."

"No." Bill's voice grew louder. "Put it away or sit in the car. You go in like that, and someone is liable to get shot. I don't think he's dangerous."

"He killed a man," said Mitch. But with great reluctance, he holstered his gun.

Bill brushed past Mitch, climbed the steps to the front porch, and peered inside. No one was in the main room. He knocked on the door and called out, "Mr. Hunt? We need to speak with you."

"Come in, Bill," said Cyrus Hunt. "I'm in the kitchen."

A doorway opened into the kitchen. Bill leaned his head forward to inspect the room. Cyrus sat at a dinette table for four with his left hand on a cup of coffee and his right hand in his lap. He wore a long-sleeved olive shirt and appeared perfectly at ease.

"There's hot coffee in the carafe," he said. "Pour yourself a cup."

Adrenaline coursed through Bill. He took a deep, slow breath and reminded himself to stay calm.

"Thanks, Cyrus," he said. "I'll do that. What about you, Mitch?"

"No, thanks. I'm good." Mitch stood rock still and stared at Hunt as if he'd like to take care of business right away.

"Sorry to give you guys such a chase," said Hunt.

Bill chuckled. "Yeah, you could call it that."

"I figured it was up when you staged that shoeprint reveal and kept watching Jeanne. How did you put the two of us together?"

Bill strolled to the table, took a seat, and sipped his

coffee. He lifted the cup toward Cyrus. "Thanks. Good coffee. It was the time frames. They were too convenient. Rachel Dunn moved to Wintergreen as Lou's mistress last spring, and then Jeanne spotted her in the Market. Soon after that, you showed up and took the empty slot in the foursome."

Cyrus nodded.

Bill continued. "And you told me your father was once stationed at Camp Mackall. I've been to Camp Mackall—Eastern Carolina—a place where the local women sound exactly like Jeanne. We found an old yearbook. My guess is you two have been friends all these years. She got upset when she saw Rachel Dunn and called you. You came running."

"Darn internet," said Cyrus. "No one has secrets anymore."

"Capaldi and Bishop said you didn't know anything about the Honda," said Bill. "I figure you sorted that easily since the house is only sixty yards from the course."

Cyrus shrugged.

Why did he keep his right hand in his lap? thought Bill.

"How did you know where to find the key?" Bill asked.

"Easy," said Cyrus. "Lou kept forgetting to put it under the flowerpot, and then he'd talk about it with the other two. Still, I was surprised to find the garage empty that night. Nearly shot my plan to hell. But I hid in the bushes awhile, and then Marty came back with the kid."

Mitch approached the table, not happy. "What were you thinking? You love birds would wait a year and then fly away together?"

Cyrus ignored him. Instead, he turned to Bill. "Lou cheated on Jeanne for forty years and still insisted on sleeping with her. A guy like that doesn't deserve to live."

"Why now?" said Bill. "You've been here for most of two summers. Why wait so long?"

Cyrus crinkled his nose like he smelled something rotten. "For some reason, Lou started hurting her. She had bruises on her arms. I believe he did that because Jeanne had grown happier. On days when he was at the course, I would hike up the back trails to her house, and we'd visit. She began to smile more and laugh at silly jokes. I think Lou picked up on it and wanted to cause her pain."

"You two were lovers?" said Bill, trying to sort out one last piece of the puzzle.

"No, our relationship was never sexual. We were friends; that's all. But when a friend calls for help, you're supposed to come. Right? It didn't take me long to realize that Lou would never change, and Jeanne would never leave him."

"She didn't help you?"

"No. Jeanne didn't know anything about the hit-and-run, but afterward, she guessed I had done it. I denied it, but she kept working me over. Then after that ploy you pulled with the shoeprint, well, she was certain you were on to me then. I left here at midnight to go toss the shoes. She had settled down, and I believed we were in good shape, but later, I became nervous and called her. No answer. I got to her place at four thirty. Thank goodness."

"You knew we were at the compactor, didn't you?"

"No. I thought you might be. If you were, it meant the game was up anyway. I never intended for anyone else to take the blame. I had hoped the investigation would wind down and go cold."

"So Jeanne took the suicide option to shift the blame from you," said Bill. "I bet she even left a note."

Cyrus raised his eyebrows. "If she did, *you'll* never find it."

Mitch took two steps closer. "This has been a crazy party, but now it's time to go, Mr. Hunt."

Cyrus squinted in the direction of Mitch's nameplate. "Officer Gentry, is it? What's your first name, son?"

Mitch snarled at being called son but answered the question anyway.

Finally, Cyrus pulled a pistol from his lap. He placed his hand on the table with his finger outside the trigger guard. "I don't want to shoot anybody, Mitch. But this nine-millimeter is loaded, and the safety's off."

"You're not going to pull the trigger," said Mitch.

With a stampeding heart, Bill raised his hand to caution Mitch. "Take care. We don't make bets we can't afford to lose."

Cyrus stood and motioned with the pistol that Mitch should sit. "Keep your hands on the table. Thank you."

"Where the heck are you going?" said Bill. "There's only one road off the mountain."

Cyrus snickered. "I'm not driving. After I tossed the shoes last night, I worked on a contingency plan, but I need twenty minutes to finish. Can you give me that much, Bill? One vet to another?"

Bill shook his head but said, "Sure."

Without another word, Cyrus strode to the back door and left the cabin.

Mitch waited five seconds and then ran to the window overlooking the back deck. Bill got there a moment later. A twenty-foot strip of land had been cleared around the deck. Beyond that, dense hardwood trees covered the gently downward sloping mountain.

"You see him?" said Bill.

"No."

Mitch reached for his gun again. "I don't care what you said. I'm not waiting twenty minutes."

"Let's think it through. Where could he go? Wait. The OAT is a little ways up the street, right?"

"Yeah," said Mitch. "Cyrus could make that easily. From the trail, it'd be a slog through the woods to the parkway, but he could manage it. Or, he could take the OAT back out to Laurel Springs and hijack a car. I can catch him if I leave now."

"No," said Bill. "He might shoot you if he hears you coming. He won't shoot me because he knows I'm unarmed. You drive down to the other end of the OAT and come back up that way. Call it in from the car, and the office can summon the park rangers. We'll box him in."

Mitch's jaws clenched. "All right. You're going to give him the twenty minutes, aren't you?"

Bill bobbled his head. "Maybe five minutes."

Mitch left, and Bill studied his phone. Twenty minutes? Five minutes? He compromised on ten minutes. Then cut it to nine. Then eight. At seven and a half minutes, he stepped through the back door and peered into the forest. Oh, to heck with it.

He trudged through the ferns and saplings, wanting to go faster but worried about tripping over an unseen rock. After a hundred yards, he could no longer see Hunt's cabin behind him. The downward slope leveled out, and every direction began to look the same—tall trees, brush, and the occasional boulder. Where was the darn path? He should have reached it by now.

Wind whipped the treetops far above him. Bill stopped and turned in a circle. Wait. Was he headed in the right direction? From which way had he come? Calm down. Facing downhill, the path had to be on the right, but the terrain had nearly leveled out. He got on his knees to examine the plain of the earth more carefully. That way. That way was up, no doubt. Feeling better, he continued on his way for another twenty paces and stumbled onto the path. He paused to take three long breaths and then jogged down the OAT.

He had hiked the trail with Hunt only a few days earlier, but it didn't seem familiar. Could he be on the wrong path? No, there was no other trail in this area. This had to be correct. Then he came to the rock crevice he had to navigate to get down. Yes, he remembered that part. At the bottom of the wall, he began jogging again. Mitch had likely parked his car by now and was headed back this way. They would reach each other before long. Who would find Cyrus first? Bill passed the switchbacks. The slope leveled out again, and he increased his pace, careful to watch for rocks. He noticed the cutoff to Hemlock Drive but didn't stop. It made no sense for Hunt to go that way. He reached a part of the trail that seemed familiar. Bits of bright sky showed through the trees. In a few minutes, he would come to the overlook.

Then Bill heard the unmistakable sound of a gunshot from close range.

Jumping June bugs!

With two big steps he hid behind a tree, but then his legs began to shake. The trunk was slightly narrower than Bill's width, and he turned sideways.

Another shot fired, and Bill's whole body twitched. Bits of something peppered the ground on the other side of the tree. He glanced around the tree but saw nothing.

"Cyrus?" he called. "What the heck are you doing?"

The pistol fired, and again bits of something rained on the ground.

"I can't believe we're having a gunfight," said Bill.

"We're not," called Cyrus. "You don't have a gun."

"Mitch does."

Cyrus chuckled. "Nah. You sent him around to come up the other way. He'll be here in fifteen minutes or so."

Bill realized the sounds he'd heard were pieces of bark from above him landing on the ground. Cyrus was aiming high on purpose.

"You cut me short on the twenty minutes, Bill. I need that time. Give me ten more minutes."

"What the heck for? What are you doing?"

"Promise? Ten minutes?"

Bill's lungs heaved. He'd gladly give Cyrus an hour if Mitch weren't coming up the other way. If Cyrus took a potshot at Mitch, Mitch would undoubtedly shoot back.

"All right," said Bill. "Ten minutes. But you have to promise me you won't shoot Mitch."

"I can do that. You have my word."

Bill leaned to catch his breath and rub his hands on his pants.

Running feet pounded the earth farther down the trail. Bill peered from behind the tree, and Cyrus disappeared around a curve.

What in the world was he doing?

Okay. Bill would give him a bit more time, but not ten minutes.

FORTY-TWO

Bill tried to reach Mitch, but his phone had no cell service.

He gave it six minutes and then slogged down the trail a short distance before reaching a section he recognized. The forest brightened, and he neared the cliff. The overlook was just ahead, and a breeze came from the valley.

The swath of green leaves between Bill and the cliff waved with the wind. He blinked several times and stopped. Bright red and yellow fragments peaked through the leaves. The muscles in his stomach and legs grew tense. He stepped slowly toward the cliff with his eyes on the bits of red and yellow. Some sort of material flapped in the breeze like a flag. Bill drew closer. A human form scurried around the red and yellow fabric. Cyrus.

Bill reached the overlook. Cyrus hurried to snap a piece of fabric onto an alloy tube. A hip-high boulder stood less than three paces from Bill. Apparently, Cyrus had placed his pistol on the boulder to free his hands for the work.

"You can't keep track of time, can you?" said Cyrus. "That wasn't ten minutes." He continued to move with haste, assembling something that resembled a giant kite. Cyrus glanced at the gun. "If you want to shoot me, now's your chance."

A pair of tree loppers with wooden handles was propped against a tree. It dawned on Bill what Cyrus had in mind. He had trimmed branches and saplings from the immediate area to maximize the cleared section of the overlook. But the span from the nearest trees to the edge could not exceed thirty feet. Surely, the hang glider Cyrus worked feverishly to assemble required a greater area for take off.

Bill approached the cliff and stopped five feet from the precipice. He leaned forward and recalled the sheer drop of the face, at least a hundred feet. Before him, the mountain sloped gently down to the small valley. A narrow strip of cleared land lay several miles in the distance and two thousand feet lower in elevation. The two-lane road to Waynesboro weaved through the forest and the fields. From that distance, a large red barn resembled a toy. The wind from the valley ruffled Bill's hair. It was an otherwise gorgeous day.

"I assume you've done this many times," said Bill.

"A few," Cyrus smirked. "But never from up here. The place I used had a much gentler slope."

Cyrus had finished assembling the kite, which stood seven feet tall and had a thirty-foot wingspan. Wires ran from the nose and wings to a triangle of tubes under the kite's center. From the positioning of the harness, Bill guessed that the pilot would control the kite from within the triangle. The wind brought the kite to life, and it appeared restless. Cyrus had anchored the glider by arranging bagged weights over the bottom tube.

"But you are an expert, right?" said Bill.

"I took a course a month ago. I don't believe the

instructor would call me an expert, but she did say I was a quick study."

Bill glanced at the trees below. "You'll surely die."

"That is a possibility," said Cyrus frankly. "But it's not the plan." He strode to where the loppers lay, picked up a helmet, and showed it to Bill. "Safety first."

Cyrus began to strap himself into the harness.

A block of cement formed in Bill's stomach. The back of his neck tingled.

"You don't have to do this," he said.

Cyrus tightened a strap and turned to Bill. "It was premeditated," he said, his voice serious for once. "We both know I wouldn't outlive the sentence." His eyes turned to the sky. "I'd rather go this way. And there's a good chance I'll escape."

He smiled and kicked away the weights, and the kite grew unruly. It tilted to one side, and Cyrus struggled to maintain control. "Help me out, Bill. Grab hold of the wing on the end and keep it level."

Bill ran to the kite and did as instructed. The wind was strong in the kite, and Bill felt queasy all over. He willed his legs to stay steady.

Cyrus's chest heaved, and his eyes burned with excitement. "Yeah, that's good. Now, we'll wait a minute for the wind to lull so I can take off easily."

Instead of lulling, the wind picked up. It sounded its anger as it rushed through the trees behind them.

"I have a question," said Cyrus, serious again. "Do you believe in hell?"

Bill's mouth opened. Perhaps only moments from death, did Cyrus fear what lay beyond? What answer did he want to hear?

"No," said Bill. "I don't believe in hell."

"Me neither. Which is a shame. Because of all the men I've known, Lou Thorpe was angling the hardest to go there."

The wind began to lull, and Bill eyed the valley. His heart pounded, and he licked his lips.

"I'm counting down from three," said Cyrus. "Let go on one. Three. Two."

Bill closed his eyes.

"One!"

Bill unclasped his hand and heard Cyrus take three steps on the rock.

"Yo," said Cyrus, and then only the wind reached Bill's ears.

He opened his eyes and saw blue sky and the mountain on the other side of the valley, but no kite.

Cyrus crashed!

He ran toward the cliff's edge and stopped two feet short to look down.

And Cyrus and the kite soared.

He must have dipped initially and then caught the wind. The glider easily cleared the treetops and then gained elevation. Cyrus found an updraft and circled higher and higher. Bill crouched and crab-walked to where he could dangle his legs over the edge. Cyrus climbed higher still. Bill feared Cyrus had been seduced by the sun and would suffer the fate of Icarus. But then Cyrus pulled out of the circle and floated across the mountain's face a thousand feet in the air. He took a wide turn and came back across the mountain toward the Shenandoah. Then he turned toward the small valley and flew across to the other side, several miles from Bill, a bright speck of color against the hazy green of the mountain. Cyrus had realized his dream. He was a broad-winged bird carving elegant curves in the sky. Soaring. Soaring. Bill imagined for a moment that Cyrus might fly until he disappeared on the horizon, but then he came back across the valley and halfway up Bill's side again.

Now Cyrus began to lose elevation, and Bill willed him to stop screwing around and land the darn thing. Apparently, that's what Cyrus had in mind, for he turned back toward the valley and flew down the mountain. But he was losing elevation too fast, and Bill feared he would crash. Please. Please. Let there be another updraft. Cyrus turned again and angled toward the valley, scarcely a hundred feet above the trees but drawing closer to the field beside the red barn. Could he make it? Did he have enough clearance? His kite seemed to bounce on the wind. It must be gusty down there. Yes. Yes. He could make it, but it was going to be close. Bill stretched his neck as if by raising his eyes a few inches, he could better see whether Cyrus made it to the field. The trees at the edge cut an uneven line. Were there openings in the trees? Cyrus's kite drifted lower, nearly in the trees now, and Bill imagined him lifting his legs to avoid the highest branches.

Then the kite disappeared.

Bill held his breath and lifted his head even higher. Wouldn't he have seen the kite land if Cyrus had made it to the field? Had Cyrus crashed?

"Hey, what's going on?" said Mitch, from behind Bill. "Where is he?"

Mitch appeared winded, as if he'd been running through the forest. Bill pointed toward the valley, afraid that his voice might crack.

"Cyrus jumped?" Mitch ran to the edge. "From this height, he's dead for sure."

"No. He put together a hang glider, and . . . and he flew down." The words sounded strange to Bill's ears, as if he had joked. He half expected Mitch to laugh.

Mitch gave Bill an incredulous stare. "He flew a hang glider? Sheesh. What nerves."

"I don't know if he made it. He was at the edge of the field, but he might have crashed in the woods."

"Let's go," said Mitch. "We have to call it in, then go find him."

Bill shook his head. "Not me. I signed up to help with the investigation, not to catch a fugitive. That's a young cop's game."

"Come on," said Mitch, impatient. "You love this stuff."

"Do me a favor, Mitch. That's Cyrus's pistol on the boulder. Take it with you."

After Mitch left, Bill sat on the cliff's edge for twenty minutes, hoping to see Cyrus loping through the field next to the red barn. But it was a long way off. A line of trees ran across the field to the road. Bill could barely distinguish cars driving on the two-lane highway, let alone a single man. Still, he kept his eyes on the line of trees, and a few times, he thought he saw movement.

FORTY-THREE

Later that day, Mitch reported that they had located the hang glider crashed in the trees near the field but not found Cyrus. Mitch and several officers from the sheriff's department had interviewed folks in the area, but no one reported seeing an unfamiliar man in an olive shirt, injured or otherwise. Over the next two days, a search of the surrounding forest was conducted without success.

The day after the search ended, Bill received a text from Alex asking him to stop at the station. He strolled by Krista's cubicle and noticed Mitch and her sitting there, so Bill wheeled up a chair. The two of them wore their dark uniforms and hints of amusement on their faces.

Mitch exchanged a knowing glance with Krista, then turned back to Bill. "You hear the news?"

"What news?" said Bill.

Krista laughed.

"Well," said Mitch, "some dude finally heard the Cyrus story on the television this morning and called Nelson County. Apparently, the guy picked up a hitchhiker wearing a Vietnam service cap near Sherando and drove him all the way to West Virginia for two hundred dollars in cash. He dropped him off at a local storage facility."

"No way," said Bill.

Krista's shoulders shook with mirth.

"It gets better," said Mitch. "Cyrus had a bank account in Waynesboro, and he's been withdrawing chunks of cash every other week for six months. Almost two hundred thousand dollars."

At that point, Krista nodded hugely. "Uh-huh. You know, Bill, if I had a used pickup, no kids, and two hundred thousand in cash, I could disappear for a long time."

An image flashed in Bill's mind. Somewhere in the Canadian Rockies, a Ford F150 with a shell was parked next to a campsite. Cyrus sat in a canvas chair with a pitched tent in the background and contemplated an open fire.

"That's one for the record books," said Bill. In the background, he heard Alex's voice, and he stood to leave. "Catch you later, guys."

"Aren't you forgetting something?" said Mitch, his eyes twinkling with mischief.

Bill scratched the back of his head. "Like what?"

Krista said, "Like you owe us a hundred bucks, that's what."

"A hundred dollars?"

Mitch pointed at him. "You said you wouldn't welch on the bet."

"The thru-hiker bet?" Bill scowled. "But Andre Lewis didn't do it. You guys owe me ten bucks."

Mitch rubbed his hands with glee. "In Krista's usual thorough manner, she took a close look at the Ashmont Bobcats yearbook and found the *I've Got a Dream* page. Wouldn't you know it? Cyrus's dream in 1963 was to hike the AT from end to end."

A sinking feeling entered Bill's chest.

"Of course," said Krista, "a lot of people dream of hiking the AT. That alone is insufficient proof. But I checked the Appalachian Trail Conservancy records. In 1965, Cyrus Hunt was one of only five thru-hikers to complete the full twenty-two hundred miles."

Mitch held his hand out. "It's tough to lose, I know."

They had him on a technicality—the bet had not stipulated a specific timeframe for when the driver had hiked the AT. Bill reached for his wallet.

"This is between us, right?" said Bill. "I don't want everyone on the mountain giving me a hard time about this silly bet."

"Oh, no," said Krista solemnly. "We won't tell a soul."

Mitch snorted.

Krista smirked. "Maybe just one or two of the guys in the office."

Rather than taking endless abuse, Bill skedaddled over to Alex's office and knocked on the doorjamb. "Hey, Chief."

Alex jumped up and hurried to close the door behind Bill. "Thanks for coming in, Bill. Sit down. How's it going?"

"I'm feeling suddenly poorer."

Alex shot him a quizzical look but then smiled. "Oh, right. The bet. Don't worry. I can help with that."

"How so?" said Bill.

"As it happens, I've received a bit of bad news today. You know Emily Powell?"

Bill frowned. Emily Powell. The name sounded familiar. Oh, yeah. The deputy chief who was out on maternity leave.

"Sure, I met Emily the first day I stopped in."

Alex raised his hands in desperation. "Emily had planned to return to work after six weeks, but now that she and her husband have experienced life with three kids, they've reconsidered. Bottom line: she's not coming back."

Whoa. Bill struggled to resist laughing. Alex was close to panicking. Sitting in an acting chief's role with no experience and no deputy put him in a bad way.

Alex beseeched Bill. "Buddy, help me out here. Take the deputy chief role. You know you can do it, and it'll boost your cash flow."

"Shoot. I'm honored, but I'm also retired, and my growing list of hobbies will keep me far too busy to take on a full-time job."

Alex tried to sweeten the pot. "You could even have the chief's role. I know I could sell the directors on it."

"I'm definitely not doing that." Alex's shoulders slumped, and Bill felt compelled to modify his refusal. "But I'm only a phone call away. If you get in a bind, call me."

Alex screwed his lips into a bunch. "Yeah, sure, next time a dead body shows up—"

Bill thrust his hands forward. "Don't even say that."

FORTY-FOUR

After driving to Waynesboro on an errand, Bill returned to Wintergreen and stopped at Café Devine, where Kim Wiley gave him a hard time about losing the bet. Jeez. News sure traveled fast in the thin air.

Cindy had invited him to come over at five o'clock for drinks and dinner. The sparkling water maker he'd purchased had arrived at his door, and he spent the intervening time trying it out. Nice. Quite refreshing with ice and a twist of lime.

With his hair neatly brushed and wearing a clean shirt and jeans, Bill stood at Cindy's door with flowers and a bottle of wine. When she opened the door and saw the flowers, the delight on her face was proof that he should drive to Waynesboro more often. Then she noticed the wine.

"Châteauneuf-du-Pape!" she said. "Oh my word, we must open it at once."

Cindy placed the flowers on the counter and fussed with the arrangement while Bill opened the bottle. They sat outside to enjoy the view. He had checked his phone earlier and learned that the temperature in Columbia had reached ninety-five that day, but on the mountain, it was a delightful seventy-five degrees. The sun behind them cast a glow onto the hillside across the valley. The American goldfinches—Ricky Bobby and Cal—rode their rollercoaster pattern between the condos and the forest.

Suddenly, from the depths of the gorge came a boisterous sound—a chorus of singers belting out *Let's Go Fly a Kite.*

"Hallelujah!" said Cindy. "They've begun practicing for the musical. We get to listen for free for the next three weeks. Isn't that grand?"

"Uh, sure."

She giggled and reached to touch his cheek. "It's all right. You don't have to listen every night. We can't tomorrow anyway because we have to work the Russells' dinner party." Her forehead wrinkled with doubt. "You still up for it?"

When an assistant had quit working for Cindy to take a job in Charlottesville, Bill volunteered to help with preparation and serving. It was a great way to meet other residents, and he would get to spend more time with Cindy.

"Yep," he said. "I bought a new pair of black khakis and two white shirts. I'm ready to go."

She caressed the back of his arm. "You'll look so handsome. I'm going to have to keep my eye on you. Some of these women are fierce competitors."

Knowing she made the comment in jest, Bill bobbed his eyebrows and said, "They say a little competition sharpens a person's skills."

Cindy gave him a playful shove, but then she frowned, and her eyes darted to the sliding door. "Shoot. I forgot the appetizers. Be right back."

She hustled into the kitchen, and Bill strolled to the railing and gazed at the distant mountains. Leaning over, his eyes searched for Mr. Chips. The groundhog stood next to his burrow with his head raised as if to examine the building's upper floors. Bill lifted his glass.

"Here's to Wintergreen. I've found a new home."

To Bill's amazement, Mr. Chips gave him a quick salute, although the groundhog might have merely intended to scratch his head.

ALSO BY PATRICK KELLY

Thank you for reading *The Mountain View Murder*. I hope you enjoyed meeting Bill O'Shea and his new friends. Join my Readers Club and read a **FREE** forty-page Bill O'Shea novella.

The Curse of Crabtree Falls

In 1851, Jedediah Bundt, the son of a poor Nelson County farmer, fell in love with Henrietta Youngfellow, the daughter of the richest landowner in that part of Virginia. Henrietta loved Jedediah in return, but in those days, the classes never mixed, and her father arranged for her to marry a wealthy merchant in Richmond. At the news that Henrietta was now wed and his love gone forever, Jedediah hiked to the top of Virginia's tallest waterfall and leaped to his death. Thus began the curse of Crabtree Falls.

One hundred and seventy years later, Bill O'Shea, a retired police detective from Columbia, SC, moves to the bucolic mountain resort of Wintergreen to begin a new life. When a friend invites Bill to hike the falls, he readily accepts because he is eager to learn about the area. But then he hears the story of the curse. Not given to superstition, Bill feels compelled to investigate the mysterious waterfall that has doomed lovers since 1851.

Clean read: no graphic violence, sex, or strong language.

Join my readers club and get a free ebook version of this Bill O'Shea novella. Not available anywhere else.

www.patrickkellystories.com/newsletter-signup

If you like thrillers, you'll love *The Joe Robbins Thriller Series*. Joe is an Austin-based amateur boxer turned amateur detective who searches for a hidden killer in a high-tech startup, battles a drug cartel, and tracks a serial killer in this four-book series.

Learn about *The Entrepreneurs: Joe Robbins Book One* at Amazon. You can read it free on Kindle Unlimited.

ABOUT WINTERGREEN

Several years ago, we bought a condo in Wintergreen, Virginia, to escape the hot Texas summers. Not by coincidence, our condo is in the same location as the one owned by Bill O'Shea. Outside our balcony, an American Goldfinch sports his bright summer colors as he flies on his rollercoaster. We call him Ricky Bobby. The groundhog named Mr. Chips is a fictional character. Black bear sightings and stories are common.

There are many wonderful hiking trails in and around Wintergreen. The Appalachian Trail was re-routed modestly when Wintergreen was developed in the nineteen eighties. A part of the old section remains and is called the OAT. As in the story, the Appalachian Trail and the Blue Ridge Parkway both pass close by the Wintergreen property.

Most of the places and establishments mentioned in the story are real; however, the characters and events are all fictitious. The Wintergreen Police Department does a fine job of protecting the community. The police procedures depicted in the novel are from my imagination and undoubtedly an inaccurate portrayal of how a real police department would go about its business. As a writer, my interest lies primarily with the mystery and the interaction of the characters.

As always, my wife Susie tried to help me write a better book. She is the love of my life.

ACKNOWLEDGMENTS

Thank you to Lori at Great Escapes Book Tours for working tirelessly to support the cozy genre and for hosting a fantastic book tour.

Sleepy Fox Studios designed the book cover. Liz Perry of Per Se Editing edited the manuscript.

Many Wintergreen residents were kind enough to read an early draft and give me feedback, including Emily Ferguson, Valerie Calhoun, Diana Hickert-Hill, Katie Moran, Kristins Gembara, Linda Ehinger, Debby Missal, Mary Beth Cowardin, David Stewart White, Susan Wood, and Denise Berry. Thank you to the many people who work hard to make Wintergreen a wonderful resort community.

Praise for *The Joe Robbins Series*

Joe may be a good CFO, but he's an even better detective and carries the mystery like a seasoned professional." —**Kirkus Reviews**

"Fast-paced and engaging, particularly the ever-changing cat-and-mouse games at the story's peak"—**Forward Clarion Review**

"I just love that Joe Robbins, the hero, is a CFO."—**Patricia Little, CFO, The Hershey Company**

"Patrick Kelly is the Austin version of John Grisham, but with more of a business grounding." —**Brett Hurt, Founder of Bazaarvoice and Coremetrics**

"Joe Robbins is a freelance CFO who's not afraid to kiss ass and take names."—**Mark Miller, CFO, Active Network**

FIVE STAR AMAZON REVIEWS!!!

"A fast-paced murder mystery/thriller with twists and turns through the Austin high-tech scene."

"Patrick Kelly clearly knows the world of finance and the city of Austin and uses this knowledge to write a taut and very entertaining book."

"Joe Robbins feels almost like an old friend by this point in the series."

KEEP IN TOUCH

If you enjoyed meeting Bill O'Shea and his friends at Wintergreen, lend me your email address, and I'll keep you posted on their next adventure.

www.patrickkellystories.com/newsletter-signup

Follow me on Goodreads to read my latest writing updates:

www.goodreads.com/patrickkelly

I often put photos I like on Facebook and Instagram.

Instagram: pkellystories

Facebook: patrickkellywriter